ALSO BY SIERRA SPENCER

Standalone Novels

Developing Feelings

Troped

Eastern Standard

Bad for Business Series

Model Behavior

Grove Meadow Witches

Something's Witchy

SOMETHING'S WITCHY

SIERRA SPENCER

To Parker, it's you in every lifetime

There's a little witch in all of us.

— ALICE HOFFMAN, AUTHOR OF
PRACTICAL MAGIC

A NOTE FROM SIERRA

Dear reader,

Thank you for picking up this book. It's a little different from anything I've written before.

Before you read, I wanted to let you know a few things. This book has depictions of anxiety, violent or graphic interactions that may make some individuals uncomfortable, and on-page sexual activities. There are also mentions of the deaths of loved ones.

I would love for you to meet these characters, but not at the expense of your well-being.

With love,

Sierra Spencer

PLAYLIST

willow - lonely witch version | Taylor Swift
all the good girls go to hell | Billie Eilish
Season Of The Witch | Lana Del Rey
Rhiannon | Fleetwood Mac
Is This Real? | lisahall
Crystal | Stevie Nicks
ivy | Taylor Swift
Liability | Lorde
Nightmare | Halsey
that way | Tate McRae
So Criminal | The Maine
Power Over Me | Dermot Kennedy
I Put A Spell On You | Annie Lennox
Start a War | Klergy & Valerie Broussard

Scan this code in the Spotify app for the full playlist!

CHARMINGLY FAMILIAR

Tucked away in the secluded town of Grove Meadow is a coffee shop with a painting that is unlike any other. *Charmingly Familiar* has no known artist, and it can not be dated. Sometimes, when you're not looking...it changes.

The painting is simple until it isn't. Its landscape always remains the same: a park with a tree sitting to the right of a small body of water. A long, thick branch extends midway between the water and the tree's stalk. The end of the branch is warped, almost curling around itself, and depending on the season, it is coated in leaves with five-pointed ends.

In the Winter, the tree is bare, and the painting grows colder somehow. The air around it feels heavier, and those who linger too close swear they can see their breath fogging in front of them, even though the shop itself remains warm.

In the Spring, flowers bloom along the grass, and in the Summer...the painting radiates a warmth that is difficult to describe to someone else. It's not a comforting feeling, like the sun on your face, but rather a sense that if you were to touch the painting, you might suffer a burn. The kind of heat that feels unnatural, as though the warmth is alive, waiting for a touch to sear itself into your skin.

And now, in the Fall, the leaves of the tree are a mixture of reds and oranges. A smattering of them surrounds the ground at the base of the trunk. The colors are so vibrant that it's almost as if the painting pulls in the changing season itself, reflecting the world outside with such accuracy that, if you didn't know better, you might believe it had been freshly painted.

The seasonal changes are slow, but it is not the most peculiar thing about the painting. Sometimes a black cat that looks alarmingly like the one people see perched in the window of the coffee shop appears to walk along the water's edge. Occasionally, the cat in the painting naps in the grass covered by the shade of the tree. But most commonly, the cat is seen swatting at the tree branch above its head. *Wait. No, not the branch...* a python is wrapped around the branch in a way that could be described as leisurely if it were a human. It appears so content that it allows a section of its dark body to droop over the branch just out of the cat's reach.

The python's presence is one of the painting's most debated features. Some say it wasn't always there, that it appeared one day out of nowhere, and no one can agree when exactly it showed up. At first, it was hardly noticeable, camouflaged among the deep greens and browns of the tree. But over time, as people observed the painting more closely, they began to see it—coiled, relaxed, watching.

People who see the painting get a feeling that something has changed, but they can't put their finger on it. The sense of unease is subtle at first, like the tickle of a forgotten memory trying to surface. There's a familiarity to the scene, but it's just off enough to set people on edge. As if they've been there before. As if they've seen that exact cat, swatted at that same branch, only in another life, another time.

And yet, no one talks about the painting for long. Something about it feels too personal, too strange. Even those who frequent the shop and glance at it daily tend to brush off its oddities, convincing themselves that it's just their imagination. After all, how could a painting—no matter how strange—truly change on its own?

But some suspect there's more to *Charmingly Familiar* than just brushstrokes on canvas. They believe it's not merely a painting but a window—something alive, shifting in ways that reflect more than just the seasons. For those who pay close attention, the subtle changes in its details are said to hold secrets, perhaps glimpses of what's hidden beneath the surface of the town itself. They say if you watch long enough, the painting will reveal things Grove Meadow may not be ready to face.

If you have time, stop by. Take a seat near the painting and watch it for a while. You might catch a flicker of movement out of the corner of your eye or notice something that wasn't there before. And as you leave, you might find yourself thinking, *how charmingly familiar.* But be careful—once you've seen it, it has a way of staying with you, like a half-remembered dream that lingers just beyond your reach.

CAROLINA

The clock reads 3:03 a.m. when I jolt upright and find myself clutching my throat. Its bright, neon-red numbers taunt me in the otherwise dark room. Breathing is no longer an unconscious process. I'm forcing myself to gulp down breaths that don't quite reach my lungs. It's painful to go through the motions, but eventually, air finds its way down my windpipe.

The panic begins to subside, but the lingering sense of dread remains. It always does. I've learned to live with it.

I know when I hold my hands out in front of me, I won't find any trace of the flames on my skin, but I can't help it. The flames from my dream felt so real that I needed to see them to be sure. The heat, the crackling sound, the smell of burning flesh—my burning flesh—it all stays with me like a ghost that refuses to leave.

Blinking my eyes to make them adjust to the darkness, a wave of my hand creates an orb of light to illuminate the area around me. No burns coat my skin, and no heat lingers in the air, but I'm there again when I close my eyes.

I see the torch's flame catch at the base of the pyre, but I can't make out the face of the catalyst. Ropes tear at my wrists as I try to loosen their hold on me. Tendrils of fire lick up my legs, and I whisper an incantation to dull the pain, but I don't finish because screaming begins from beside me. My head whips to the side, but I can't see his face. He's a shroud in the smoke that consumes my vision.

Burning. I'm burning.

It's all I can think to myself as the screaming becomes more desperate and the heat seeps into my skin. While visceral, I know the pain belongs to a version of me that no longer exists. I *know* that I'm safe at home in my bed, but it's the pain that wrenches me from the vision, nonetheless.

The pain is always what brings me back—back to the present, back to a life that, no matter how much time passes, feels borrowed.

My eyes spring open and refocus on the dimly lit room. My hands grip my sheets for purchase. The softness of the sheets juxtaposes the memory of the ropes biting.

Another forced breath in, I exhale slowly through my mouth. I wiggle my toes, and the tips of them rub against the velvet comforter I put on my bed every autumn. It's then that I realize there's a chill biting at my shoulders. Our home has always been drafty, and I'm thankful for it now. The cold is a welcome reminder that I'm here, in this body, in this life—not burning, not dying.

I wipe away the sweat that has collected at the back of my neck and roll my shoulders. The tension in my upper back loosens but doesn't disappear. It's always there in the background of my mind and body.

When I was little, I was plagued with nightmares so vivid I was afraid to close my eyes.

As I grew older, I learned that the nightmares were real and not just figments of an overactive imagination, but I became better at telling apart visions of my past lives from the lives of strangers that also consumed my dreams.

When others' memories or futures found me in my sleep, it was more like I was an observer. I couldn't feel their emotions or what was happening to them, no matter how severe the dream was. If I could feel flames on my skin, water filling my lungs, or a rope taut around my neck, I knew the dream was about me—or, more accurately, a me that once was.

From another time when witches were burned at the stake or hung for their gifts. A time when being different meant a death sentence. But even now, in a world that claims to be more accepting, I know better than to reveal too much. The past has taught me that.

The distinction between a gift and a curse in my world is a blurred line with breaks along its path for the two to bleed into each other.

Magic isn't good or bad. It just *is*. What we choose to do with it, how we wield it—that's what defines us. But history has a way of painting witches in shades of black and red—evil, dangerous. And I've seen firsthand what fear of the unknown can do.

I'm still sitting upright in my bed when my eyes dart to the corner of my room, where I meet Luna's gaze from her perch in front of my window. The sky is cloudless, and the moon hangs high against the dark backdrop.

A waning gibbous. A bad omen.

Luna's stare is unwavering, as if she knows what I saw. Her eyes are wise, and sometimes, it feels like she knows the future just as well as she knows the past. It's as if she shares in my suffering, watching over me, protecting me when I can't protect myself.

"Go back to sleep. It was just a dream." It's been my mantra for years, but my voice comes out weaker than I intend, and whether I'm trying to convince her or myself is uncertain to even me.

Swinging my legs over the edge of the bed, the second my toes touch the cold wooden floor, I feel more grounded in this reality. Pulling my robe off the post at the end of my bed, I wrap it around myself and secure it with a satin sash at my waist. I don't put on my house shoes; I want to feel the floor under my feet.

My steps are light as I make my way to the stairs so I don't wake Camila down the hall.

I grew up in this place. I know every creaky floorboard and warped plank that would threaten to trip me in the dead of night. In the darkness of the hallway, I don't even have to reach out to find the railing of the staircase because I know exactly how many steps it is from my room.

Camila and I live in the apartment above our coffee shop, *Cup & Cauldron.* When our grandparents immigrated here from Mexico, they bought the building and opened the first-floor storefront as an apothecary. When they passed away a few years ago, they left the property to Camila and me.

As I get to the upper landing, I realize my intentions not to wake Camila were fruitless because I can see the glow emanating from the kitchen light downstairs.

Using the moments walking down the stairs to pull myself together, I mentally recite tokens from our childhood to keep me from reliving the past life from my vision.

A Castillo witch does not let past lives interfere with the present. A Castillo witch hangs sage and lavender above her bed to soothe restless spirits. A Castillo witch always–

"Silas woke me up," Camila says, pushing a mug of what I can only presume to be tea with some sort of sleep aid to lull me into a dreamless sleep. She's always been better at potions than me, so I know once I drink it, sleep will find me not long after.

The soft, earthy smell of chamomile mixed with a hint of lavender reaches my nose, and for a moment, I feel the tension in my body release just from the scent alone.

Despite the time, Camila's brown eyes are bright, almost a shade of bronze, unlike my muddy ones. Her lashes are dark against her tanned skin as she blinks slowly. Their delayed movement is the only sign she'd recently woken. Her dark hair cascades over her shoulder in loose waves that don't show any sign of the frizz I have to manage daily. Even in an old cut-off T-shirt and sweatpants, she's flawless.

It's not just her beauty, though. It's her kindness, her grace, the way she moves through the world as if nothing could touch her. She's everything I'm not—pure, good, untouched by the darkness that clings to me like a second skin.

"Go back to sleep. It was just a dream," I tell her, taking the mug from the table and savoring the warmth it emanates in my hands.

Our eyes meet, and she holds my stare for a beat too long before standing and brushing past me, her feet silent against the usually whiny floorboards. Her fingertips brush my arm, and I know she's checking for injuries, just like I did when I woke. But Camila's touch is different.

Camila's a healer. A slight touch of her hands mends shallow cuts and bruises before they form. She can sense pain and decay. Pressing her palm against someone—sometimes *something*—for a prolonged period of time can heal even the deepest of wounds.

When she doesn't find anything that her powers can heal, she drops her hand from my skin. The desire to comfort her is overpowering, but there's nothing I can tell her. I'll always have these dreams. I'll always be *this*.

"I had a dream too, Lina," she says on the staircase, drawing my attention back to her.

I swallow, trying to ignore the prickling feeling that runs down my spine. "About a fire?"

The idea that my power might be growing and I've accidentally sent her my *nightvision* is horrifying. I wouldn't wish them on anyone, especially not my sister. But her response both quells my fears and ignites new ones.

"About a darkness so endless, I could only pray for a fire." Her voice is tired, and her usually sunshiney face looks worn. This is not the first time she's dreamed this recently; I could tell from the gravity of her words.

My lips seal in a firm line as I take them in. "Then we should prepare for whatever's coming. Go into the city tomorrow to see Esme and stock up on supplies. I'll open the shop in the morning."

Camila dips her head in a nod. It's unlike her to be so solemn, let alone to agree with me. I know it's because of her dream, but I stop myself from questioning what she may have seen in her darkness. I know better than to force a witch to relive her nightmares; I have spent an eternity running from my own.

Still, a part of me aches to know. What did she see in that darkness? What's waiting for us on the other side of it? And why do I get the sinking feeling that no amount of preparation will be enough?

As I watch her ascend the stairs, her figure casting long shadows against the walls, I feel an overwhelming sense of dread settle deep in my bones. It's as if the house itself knows something we don't and is bracing for whatever storm is brewing. Camila doesn't turn back, but I can feel her energy still lingering, a soft pulse of concern that echoes my own fears.

I clutch the mug tighter, my knuckles whitening. It's always been the two of us—against everything, against everyone. But now, I wonder if, even together, we'll be enough. Whatever's coming, it's bigger than anything we've faced. And this time, I'm not sure we'll make it through unscathed.

2

CAROLINA

When I was a witchling, I used to "cast spells" in our family's magic room. To the outside world, the room was a doorway into the pantry of the apothecary (now coffee shop), but to a *Castillo*, it was our most sacred of places. A place where you could be completely yourself.

On the floor in front of the worn, red couch, I'd write scribbles of verse I thought would grant me invisibility...or, at the very least, get Cami to stop stealing my clothes. The stanzas were harmless and, more often than not, didn't work. Magic without careful intent and desire is not magic at all.

The first spell that *did* work gave Suzie Carmichael, a girl who bullied Camila in middle school, a terrible acne problem.

Blemish here, blemish there
On skin so soft and fair
Only kindness can repair

When I cast it, the candlelight that burned the parchment

with the spell inscribed flickered black, and my magic felt tight around my bones.

I knew then it had worked. I never cast another spell like it again, but I remember the uneasy feeling of it—the tightness and the darkness that washed over me when I saw Suzie the following day with raised bumps scattered over her chin and jaw.

Dark magic, magic crafted with harm, retribution, or punishment in mind, steals something from the witch when used—bits of their goodness, pieces of clarity, and, in the worst cases, their sanity.

Dark magic steals, but it also leaves behind its traces.

It's the memory of those traces I feel when I wake the next morning, having forced myself back to sleep after drinking the entire mug of Camila's tea.

I try to ignore the dread in the pit of my stomach as I flip the shop's hanging door sign to *OPEN*.

It would do us no good to feed into the panic when we were already preparing for whatever was causing it. Camila had left just after sunrise to go into the city and stock up on our harder-to-get herbs from a horticulturist, Esme.

We've known Esme and her family since we were small. Her mother worked in my grandparents' shop. *Abuela* said she could sense a weak Wiccan line in them, and they became part of our family. Most beings with dormant witchcraft in their lineage could use inactive magic. While Esme and her mother couldn't cast or wield an active power, they could brew potions and make weak charms.

Esme had once asked Camila and me what our magic felt like, which was the first time I had considered how different we were from our friend. Camila and I described the hum beneath our skin when our magic woke and the feeling of strength in our bodies even when it wasn't active. When we trained or overused our magic, our bones ached, and we could sleep for days without waking.

Magic was a muscle for us but not for Esme. She didn't feel the presence of power in her veins like we did, but she was quite apt at potions. Perhaps that was her specialty.

Growing up, Esme would help us practice our incantations, and we'd help her identify various plants and mix elixirs. She moved to the city a few years ago to start a botanical shop. Now, when we need to restock our witch's cabinet, one of us drives into the city.

With the omens Camila and I have been noticing around town, I would have gone with her to see Esme, but it would have left the town vulnerable to whatever was coming (or might already be here). Not that the town wanted our protection. They preferred to blame every suspicious event on us.

Our ancestral history with Grove Meadow is not long but undoubtedly tumultuous. Our mother's family emigrated from Mexico when she had started her witch training. She fell in love with a mortal, much to our grandparents' dismay, but not just any mortal. Our mother, a Castillo, married our father, a Mason, making Camila and I descendants of a Grove Meadow founding family.

To say there was a lot of...uproar about their union would very much be an understatement. But we were a family of witches, so...the gossip and isolation? It was second nature.

For a long time, I wondered why my father would willingly accept that fate, becoming a black sheep in his family and town. *Love* is the answer I got back then from my parents, but I couldn't imagine loving anyone so much that you might be willing to change everything about your life to be with them. To have kids with them. To be part of a magical family when there wasn't a drop of Wiccan blood in your line.

Camila thought it was *romantic*. Giving up all you've

known for someone else. To love someone irrevocably and so overwhelmingly that you would do anything to be with them.

To me...it seemed like a prison sentence, and Grove Meadow was prison enough.

No matter how many times I tried to leave this town, I always found my way back here. Sometimes, I wouldn't even remember it happening. Falling asleep in a bed somewhere on the West Coast and waking up here. On a cross-country road trip, only to end up on a highway that led right back home. *Talk about Route 666*. Most horrifyingly, boarding a plane to Italy and emergency landing in a field outside Grove Meadow.

I'd finally stopped trying to escape it when our grandparents got sick about 5 years ago, moving back into the apartment.

On the other hand, Camila had never left. She loved the town that avoided her like the plague.

What's worse, Camila truly believed one day, this town would love her back, and I'd given up arguing with her about it a long while ago.

Despite my disdain for the town, I knew my family had good reason to come here. I just didn't have to romanticize it like she was so inclined to.

Before Grove Meadow, my mother and grandparents lived in Veracruz, Mexico. The witch trials had been over for centuries, but witches remained in hiding, practicing their magic discreetly. The people of Veracruz were still wary of witchcraft and unexplained occurrences, and they grew more cautious with every passing year. It was no longer safe for them to live there.

Many witches moved to new places after the trials had ended. Typically, they chose to relocate to larger cities where they'd be unlikely to be detected based on sheer population density, but not our family. No, our family moved here. To

Grove Meadow. A town with less than 5000 people back then and not many more than that now.

Our grandparents, both magical, opened the apothecary to provide homeopathic options to the town. It was risky, but *abuelo* said it called to him.

A Castillo witch trusts their intuition above all else.

Abuelo's intuition had spoken to him; that was all he and *abuela* needed to know.

It was magic that brought us here, and it's magic that forces us to stay.

Like my *abuelo*, my intuitions were strong. I was used to my dreams and the prickling of suspicion that lingered in the crevices of my mind, but Camila's dream had me more on edge than usual.

If *she* was seeing darkness, then there was undoubtedly something amiss. I was pretty sure all she dreamed about were rainbows, puppies, and being Mrs. Glen Powell.

Gathering a small bundle of sage and tying it with twine, I hang it beside the other bundle in the window. We needed all the clarity we could get.

The bell above the door clangs as Dr. Darrien Hendrix comes in for his daily coffee and tea. One of each.

Dr. Hendrix runs the private practice in town and is one of the founding families. He's also one of the few townspeople who regularly comes into the shop. My grandparents got along well with him when they were alive, and Camila and I maintain a good business relationship with him.

"Dr. Hendrix, good morning," I say with a smile, walking behind the counter to ring him up. "One coffee and one medicine ball?" I ask, already pulling the to-go cups from beside me.

His wrinkled smile is kind but tired. The dark circles under his eyes tell me he didn't sleep well, but Camila opened the shop yesterday, so I'm not sure if this is a new development.

"Better make it two medicine balls. There's some sort of cold going around town, but I haven't figured out what it is yet. Better safe than sorry," he says, pulling out his wallet.

If the town knew Dr. Hendrix was supplying his patients with a cure-all potion, they'd probably have him hung in the town square...or worse, have his medical license pulled, if you asked him.

I nod. "Of course. I'm going to give you a sleeping draught for tonight. Mix half the vial with tea, and you should get some sound shut-eye."

He gives me a grateful smile. "Thanks.

With a "thank you," his coffee, and a few vials of potions, Dr. Hendrix leaves the shop. I return to my daily cleaning routine, but something tugs at my chest.

I pause in my wiping down tables, glancing at the door. Silas slinks between my legs, accompanied by a soft meow and perked ears.

A warning.

Someone is coming.

3
CAROLINA

I sense him before he walks into *Cup & Cauldron* that afternoon. Maybe we all felt him the moment he stepped foot into Grove Meadow if he was the cause of the energy shift and omens we'd been experiencing. Silas and Luna had been on edge for the past week, and last night's dream hadn't been a one-off. Sleep hadn't found me easily since the weather had shifted, and I hadn't gotten through a night without waking up in a cold sweat at least once. Frost and fog had prematurely coated the town, which usually didn't happen until mid-December.

Something was brewing in town, and it wasn't coming from the shop.

The bell on top of the door jingles as he enters. If he were the source of this unease, I would expect the air to suffocate me in response to his presence, but instead, it feels charged. My gaze flicks up to the painting across the cafe—a simple landscape with a mid-autumn tree and a patchy area of grass. I narrow my eyes at it before redirecting my attention to the visitor.

I've never seen him before, but I feel like I have. I'm sure I haven't come across him in town because he stands out. His clothing borders on professional, but he's trying to appear casual. He's wearing a dress shirt and tie, but the jeans he's paired them with are worn. The coat he has over the shirt is new. I can tell because he doesn't seem comfortable in it. It's bulky but slightly too fitted on him. A mistake lots of people make when they are new to the cold of the East Coast. His clothes are notable, but it's really him that makes them so.

Those eyes.

Eyes so blue, they look like pools of cerulean.

A current of magic flows to my fingertips, and I curl my fingers into a fist on the counter to stifle it.

"Welcome in." I paste a smile on my face and shove away the discomfort that bubbles in my stomach. My magic doesn't seem to share the same uncertainty.

Like calls to like. It's a whisper in my mind. But he's not a warlock; Silas would have signaled me, so I'm not sure what it's trying to tell me. *Like calls to like*, it whispers again.

Magic, while mostly silent, is a living thing. It grows and matures with the witch it's chosen. On rare occasions, it voices opinions...or, in this case, nonsensical thoughts about strange men.

The man isn't looking at me. His gaze darts around the shop, lingering on the paintings and then on the menus above my head. A corner of his mouth turns up ever so slightly.

"You've really got a theme going on here." His voice is deep, gravelly in a way that makes me want to brush against him like Silas might. "The paintings are...interesting."

He looks at me then, his head inclined to the wall I had just fixated on. *Had he noticed that?*

But he isn't wrong. *Cup & Cauldron* is not as vibrant as the kitschy shops in town, with its dark green walls and black accents. Camila hates it, but she got to pick the paintings, and I hate those just as much.

"Renaissance Gothic fit the theme," I say with a shrug. "It's a beautiful collection of pieces that reflect the darkness of exploration and the duality of man." I recite the words Camila has said a million times when someone comments on the artwork. Except she says it much less sardonically than I do.

He blinks, coming closer to the counter. "I don't know what that means." *That made two of us.*

"Me either. Someone much more…" *Pretentious.* "…into art than I am bought them, and that's what she tells people."

He lets out a snort, and his hands slide into the pockets of his coat. "That wouldn't have been one of the Castillo sisters, would it?" His tone is of feigned nonchalance.

Silas rubs against my legs. Perhaps his magic isn't sure what to make of the man with the blue eyes and fiery red hair either.

I raise a brow at the man. "It would. Are you new around here?" I ask, leaning down to run my hand over Silas's head to calm him.

Slipping his hand out of his pocket and into the inside of his coat, the man produces a badge that gleams in the light. "Detective Declan O'Reilly. Just transferred here from out west."

My gaze moves from his badge back to his face. "O'Reilly, huh? Irish?"

His eyebrows raise, and his eyes roll in the direction of his hair. "Take a guess."

I laugh, and the corner of his mouth tips up again. "Well, what can I get you, detective?"

"Actually, I'm looking for Carolina and Camila Castillo. Can you tell me where I might find them?" He runs a hand through his hair, tousling it and causing a swath of wavy hair to fall onto his forehead. He doesn't move it away, and I can't stop staring at it.

I drum my fingertips on the counter, if only as a way to get my magic to settle. A detective looking for Camila and me probably wasn't a good sign, but my magic didn't seem wary of his presence.

"What's in it for me?" I say finally, drawing my eyes back to his.

His jaw twitches, trying to prevent a smile. "What do you want?"

My gaze floats across his face. His jaw is coated in stubble, and his hair is cut short but long enough to...*What was going on with me?*

I inwardly shake it off. "Hmm, I'm not sure. A favor from a detective could go a long way." He looks me over, and I can feel my skin heat where his gaze lingers. "Why don't you tell me what brings you to Grove Meadow, Detective O'Reilly?"

The detective reaches into another inner pocket of his jacket and pulls out a newspaper. He spreads it out on the counter and turns the paper so it faces me. I don't have to read it. I already know what it says.

GROVE GAZETTE

VOL. XCIV   Sunday, October 13, 2024   NO. 40

GRAVE DANGER IN GROVE MEADOW

Another mortal has gone missing, making five in the last two weeks, and the police didn't have any leads.

Camila and I tended to avoid human problems, but when my dreams started and the weather shifted, we thought they might be related this time.

We'd been following the investigation from afar...and close

up, more recently. Camila had delivered fruit and pastry baskets to the families of the victims, hoping to get a better read on the situation. Her visits had all but diminished our stock of the veritas potion, but it was the only way the families would talk to a Castillo sister. Besides, a little truth serum in a baked good never hurt anyone.

From the information Camila had gathered, the disappearances seemed to be random. The victims didn't have anything in common except that they lived here in Grove Meadow.

"You're investigating the disappearances," I say.

It wasn't a question. It was the only reason the Grove Meadow police force would bring in someone new.

"That's right." He confirms, picking up the paper, folding it, and placing it back in his pocket.

"And you want to talk to the Castillo sisters." I lean forward on my palms, fingers wrapping around the counter's ledge.

"Just have some questions for them." He doesn't shift under my gaze like the rest of the humans. *Maybe there is something strange about him.*

"You don't think they're involved, do you?" I ask, tilting my head at him curiously.

He gives a slight shrug, but his eyes are alight with interest. "Just have some questions for them."

"Because of their history?" I arch a brow.

I didn't take him as the kind of person who would believe rumors without doing some investigating of his own. But then again, maybe that's precisely what he was doing.

"Just have some questions for them," I say at the same time he does. "*Right,*" I nod, untying my apron and putting it on the counter.

He looks amused. "So, do you know where I can find them?"

"Carolina Castillo, at your service detective, and I don't answer questions without a lawyer present."

If he's surprised, he doesn't show it. "You're not being charged."

I tilt my head, my mouth twisting wryly. "Not yet, anyway."

I don't miss the way the corners of his lips twitch. *He is amused.* "And why would you think you would be?"

I was born at night, Detective, but not last night.

I roll my eyes, lifting the part of the counter that separates the workstations from the seating area. I walk through so I'm standing in front of him.

My arms cross over my chest, and my jaw tenses harder than usual. "You think I don't know how this goes?" I ask, my voice taking on a biting but level tone. "People go missing, and we're the first place you turn."

"And why do you think that is?" His gravelly voice sounded like it was truly interested in my logic, but I knew better.

I smirk, and his demeanor shifts. His eyes are narrowed on me now, and his posture has become rigid.

"Because witch hunting is this town's favorite pastime, and they're a little overdue for a hanging."

His eyes don't leave my face, and he doesn't recoil at the savagery in my tone or my words. If anything, he's leaned in closer to me.

Detective O'Reilly's voice is low when he says, "My partner won't come into this shop because he says your family worships the devil. Now, I don't know about that." His penetrating gaze moves across my face and then down my body before locking onto my eyes once more. "You seem pretty reasonable to me."

"The two aren't mutually exclusive, Detective. I could worship the devil *and* be reasonable."

Silas lets out a *meow* that sounds more like choked laughter. Detective O'Reilly's brow furrows as he leans over the counter to get a better look at the black cat.

He shakes his head and looks back at me. "Look, I'm not from here. I don't know your family's history with this town, and I'm not on a witch hunt, but I am trying to find *five* missing people. The way I see it, you can help me with that by answering some questions here, or we can do it down at the station."

"Respectfully, *Detective*, I've already answered too many of your questions. So, unless you're detaining me, I have a shop to run."

His eyes move over mine again, left to right like he's reading them, reading *me*. Then they drop to my mouth, lingering for just a moment before he says, "We're not done here, Ms. Castillo; I'll be back. Maybe you'll be more amenable after you've had your coffee."

"Unlikely," I say quietly but loud enough that he pauses as he passes me.

Detective O'Reilly lets me have the last word as he exits the shop. The bell jingles just as it had when he entered.

Silas hops on the counter with a hearty, "*Me-ow.*" I roll my eyes and watch Detective O'Reilly get into a car with one last nod at me through the window. "You going to hex him?"

"You know we don't do that..." I say, turning back to the counter, "*anymore.*" Silas is perched beside the register, licking a paw. "Do you need to do that right here?"

His large eyes fix on me as he continues his ministrations. "Yes."

"Well, okay then." I pull out my phone to call Camila but pause before I can unlock the screen.

"What are you going to tell Camila?" Silas asks, pausing his grooming.

I glance at him. "What are *you* going to tell Camila?"

"Carolina, you wound me. I would never say anything you didn't want me to," he says, standing and flicking his tail this way and that.

I slip my phone back into my pocket and look at the cat incredulously. "Sorry, did you become *my* familiar, and I forgot?" My eyes narrow, and I don't wait for him to answer because his kindness can only mean one thing. "What did you do?"

"Oh, nothing." He says before leaping off the counter and strolling across the cafe.

Cauldron brew me. "Where's Luna?" The black cat doesn't answer, and I contemplate turning him into a scratching post. "Silas," I growl in a low voice.

"Luna can't come to the phone right now."

"Silas, I swear to Lucifer, where is Luna?"

But he doesn't respond before leaping into the painting. *Charmingly familiar, my ass.*

4

DECLAN

"Well?" My partner, Sebastian Blackwell, intones when I get back in the car.

His body language is relaxed as he lounges in the passenger seat, but I can tell from the bright red skin around his nails that he's been picking at them in my absence. It's his nervous tell.

My eyes flick over his shoulder to the shop's window, and part of me expected that she'd still be there watching me.

"Definitely a witch," I deadpan, leaning my head back against the driver's seat.

Bas's dark brows raise in surprise, and he goes slightly pale. "Seriously?"

I have to force my eyes not to roll in incredulity, but I shake my head in exasperation. "Obviously not."

I loathed small towns and their gossip. Towns like this one, where everyone knew each other, did not have a heavy workload, but the cases were personal. It's why they brought me in.

Carolina hadn't been wrong when she'd called this investigation a witch hunt. The police captain wanted the Castillo sisters in a cell with multiple life sentences, and he wanted the case to be airtight. They were looking for anything to pin on them and needed someone to make it stick. The best way for them to do that was to bring in an unbiased outsider.

I was meant to be a fresh set of eyes for the investigation, but it was hard to get a straightforward story out of anyone here, even Bas—who refused to enter the shop because he "wasn't interested in a plague upon his house."

Carolina hadn't been what I expected, at least not initially. She had been described to me as the "scarier" of the sisters, but it wasn't until she found out why I was there that her disposition shifted into something harsher.

It was like a switch flipped in her eyes. That sharp gaze that could slice through steel had landed on me, and for a moment, I wondered if I'd stepped into something far more dangerous than I realized.

"Were they both in there?" he asks, looking over his shoulder at the shop and then abruptly turning back around.

"Just Carolina."

He grimaced. *Would he have done the same if it was Camila?* "Well, what'd she say?" Bas asks, running a hand through his product-laden dark hair.

I wondered if the police captain assigned him to this case or if he volunteered. It was 50/50. On the one hand, he seemed just as wary of the sisters as everyone else and might want to see them behind bars. On the other hand, Bas didn't seem to want to touch this case with a 10-foot pole.

"Nothing useful. She won't talk without a lawyer anyway, so it's not worth bringing her in unless we've got something concrete."

I had no reason to trust her or anyone in this town, but I had a feeling in my gut that she wasn't involved in this. Her sister could be another story, but–

Bas clicks his tongue. "See, that's suspicious."

I frown and raise a skeptical eyebrow. "Is it? A cop shows

up at your work and asks you about people disappearing, *knowing* the town has a ridiculous vendetta against you and you...what? Stick out your wrists, Bas? You'd roll over just like that?"

Bas stares at me for a beat, probably because he didn't expect me to defend her. I didn't expect to defend her either because even though my intuition told me she wasn't the answer to this case, my intuition also told me not to trust her entirely.

It was a strange balance—feeling like someone was innocent but knowing they were still dangerous. Carolina wasn't directly responsible for the disappearances, but she knew something. Of that, I was sure.

"That family is up to something, O'Reilly. The whole town knows it, and you'll realize it too."

Shaking my head again, I turn the key in the ignition but immediately flip it back into its starting position.

"One second," I say, getting out of the car.

"Where are you–"

I slam the door on Bas's question and jog over to the shop door, pulling it open so quickly that the bell's chime is sharper than before. From behind the counter, Carolina's brows over her deep brown eyes raise in surprise at my sudden entrance. I've noticeably caught her off guard.

"Detective," she says, her lips pulling into a thin line. "Forget something?"

The sight of her is just as captivating the second time, but I try to shake it off. "Just had a question about the menu."

Her eyebrows move impossibly higher as she glances back at the blackboard frames above her head. "The menu?"

"Everything on this board is written in white—your coffees, your teas, your pastries. But this section," I walk closer, pointing at the bottom of the sign. "This section right here is written in different chalk. It's a lavender color." *I sound crazy*, I think to myself, but I know there's something there, so I continue my tirade. "They sound like drinks, but they're not, are they?"

I watch Carolina's mouth tug up on one side as if my observation amuses her. "Camila just likes lilac, Detective. They're drinks." Her eyes light up, a spark that hadn't been there before, as she says, "What else would they be?"

It's distracting. The twinkle in her eyes, that is. *She's* distracting, but I don't know why. It's making it hard to remember why I was interrogating her about this. Why I'd come into the shop again.

Trying hard to clear my head and remind myself why I'd stormed back in here, I shift my gaze back to the menu to look anywhere but at her. "But they're not coffees."

"No," she replies easily. I can feel the forcefulness and speed with which my brow raises at her response.

"And they're not teas." I glance back at her briefly, but it's still too long.

The smile she gives me before answering *feels* condescending, and her posture—leaning against the work counter along the back wall, arms folded across her chest—solidifies that she's indifferent to this conversation.

"Teas are created by infusing herbs and plants with hot water, Detective. By definition, they are teas." She says it in a way that tells me she could have this discussion all day, and her answer wouldn't change.

My eyes rove over the purple items called "Medicine Ball" and "Pick Me Up."

"You're not thinking these are...*potions*, Detective, are you?" Her voice is sickly sweet, and I can almost hear her laugh in my head. I could practically feel the sound roll around on the backs of my eyes, but she hadn't made a noise.

Did I think they were potions? No, but—

I blink rapidly but keep my eyes on the board, willing to find some other explanation for what they could be. "Now, why would I think they're potions, Miss Castillo? You run a coffee shop."

"Why, indeed." She's toying with me like a cat with a mouse. She knows why I'm asking these questions and wants to see if I'll say it. If I'll accuse her of something impossible... something the town has been saying to me since I arrived.

I make the mistake of looking at her again. *Why do I keep doing that?* I swallow deeply under her gaze that seems to have direct control of a tightness that's begun percolating in my chest.

Clearing my throat, I try to get my bearings on my senses. It works momentarily, just enough that I finally form a question. "Miss Castillo, are you selling these to the town under the ruse that these drinks have magical abilities?"

She smiles widely, and a laugh as mellifluous as I had imagined in my head moments ago bubbles to the surface.

"No, Detective. I can assure you we are not."

My jaw ticks because I sense the half-truth. Some of her response is a lie, but I'm unsure which.

There's a pull in my core to stay here and try to decipher the enigma that is Carolina Castillo and her coffee shop with the strange paintings and teas. Still, I have no real reason to think that they and the disappearances are related—at least not at this moment. If she wanted to sell teas that the townspeople believed were imbued with magical healing powers or whatever else they thought, that was not my concern.

The tightness in my chest flickers again; this time, it's almost unbearable. It's unclear whether leaving or staying will alleviate the feeling, but Carolina's tenacity suggests nothing of use will come from the latter.

"Alright, Miss Castillo. Sorry for taking up more of your time." She nods at me once, and I turn to leave.

"Detective," Carolina says, pulling me to look over my shoulder in her direction, but I refuse to make eye contact. "I do *so* look forward to doing this again."

Her voice is a purr. It's as if she'd touched me when my skin prickles with goosebumps under my jacket and shirt.

I don't respond as I exit the shop. I breathe deeply once out the door, and the outside air hits me. My head clears, like the first morning after a cold, and you regain use of all your senses.

She might not be a witch, but she's definitely hiding something.

5

"That cat is dead to us," I tell Camila when she walks into the shop. The bell's chime seems less harsh in response to her presence.

Even the inanimate objects like her more than everyone else.

She laughs as Silas emerges from the painting as if he hadn't locked my familiar in the storage closet hours before. He lands perfectly on his feet before trotting over to Camila.

"What did he do this time?" she asks, eying her familiar suspiciously, but amusement is still displayed on her features.

"Oh, don't be so dramatic, Lina. Luna could have opened the door herself," the soon-to-be-dead cat says as he rubs himself against Camila's legs, weaving in and out of them in a figure eight.

My fingers twitch to spell him like I did as a witchling and have him coughing up hairballs for a week, but I refrain. *Barely.*

Camila reaches down to pick him up and looks him in the eyes. I swear she couldn't be stern if she tried. "With what hands could a giant snake open a door, Silas? And what was she doing in the closet in the first place?"

I roll my eyes. Camila's definition of punishment was what some might call *gentle parenting*. That approach may have worked if Silas was a child and not a 600-year-old warlock turned into a cat.

Luna and Silas had been with us almost our entire lives. All witches had familiars to protect them from danger and guide them during their training. Witches from particularly strong bloodlines like ours often had familiars at birth, but many didn't receive a visit from them until they started their training.

Witches didn't choose their familiars at shops or shelters as mortals did their pets. Tugged by an invisible string, familiars found their way to their witches. Our mother said that my father's heart almost stopped when he first saw Luna on our porch the day after I'd come home from the hospital. After all, it wasn't every day that an 8-foot reticulated python slithered into your home. He'd been grateful when Silas had been a house cat.

For the most part, familiars were witches and warlocks who had been banished for one reason or another.

Silas had broken every rule in the witch's book before the Council gave him the choice between execution and becoming a familiar.

Luna, however, had grown tired of hiding her magic from the humans and decided becoming a familiar would give her some relief. She thought choosing the form of a large snake might allow her to live in peace without looking after a witchling. Surely, no Fate would forge a bond between a witch-in-training and a python. She had spent four centuries of solitude in a rainforest near the coast of Indonesia before she felt my power call to her.

To Luna's absolute distaste, Silas joined our family when Cami was born. Almost immediately, Silas and Luna developed a strange sort of relationship, one that primarily consisted of Silas aggravating her to no end.

"I told her I thought I saw her breakfast scamper in there," Silas says, a tone of innocence coating his words.

"And did you *actually* see it?" Camila raises a brow at her familiar.

Silas dips his head low, a movement that could be described as a shrug. "Must have been the light." Before Cami could scold him further, Silas changed the subject. "Carolina got a visitor today. A detective."

Camila's honey-brown eyes flash to mine. "A detective?" I give her a quick dip of my chin, crossing my arms over my chest and leaning a hip against the back counter. "Asking about the disappearances?"

"He's new."

Camila nods slowly, pressing Silas against her chest. "Is he..."

"I didn't sense anything magical about him," I tell her and glance down at Silas, who murmurs something too low for me to hear. I narrow my eyes at him when Camila smirks at me.

"So, he was cute, huh?" Camila's voice sing-songs.

I roll my eyes and cross my arms. "*Cauldron*, that's *so* not important here. What did Esme say?"

The humor in her expression dissipates instantly. "She hadn't heard much beyond rumblings, but the City Coven has been talking about a prophecy. They think it might be related," Camila says, placing Silas on the floor.

My fingers grip the counter's edge behind me as a knot forms in my stomach. *A prophecy. Great, that's* just *what we need.*

Camila continues, her voice growing haunted,

> "*When men fall, and the moon replaces the sun, a darkness will return, and a joined power will rule the worlds of might and magic.*"

My breath catches in my throat. "Could that *be* any vaguer?" I say, trying to alleviate the weight in my stomach, but it doesn't help. I clear my throat, "What do you know about this one, Silas?"

He hops onto the counter across from me and settles onto his belly. "It's old. Older than Luna and me, for sure. I think it's part of the First Witch's grimoire."

"Why do they think it's this one?" I ask Camila.

She shakes her head, "Esme didn't know. They won't share that information with an inactive." Her lip twitches in disgust.

Camila and I have always treated Esme like one of our own, but not all magics were as accepting. The City Coven is large enough that they may be more selective in which inactive witches they trust with information, so it's surprising that they told Esme anything, regardless.

I shake my head, pulling my arms around my chest again, but it's no longer a posture of apathy. It's the only thing fighting the growing unease inside me.

"How is she doing otherwise?"

Camila frowns. "She seems okay. I could tell something was bothering her. I think she can sense the same thing we can. I don't like that she's so far from us. I wish she'd move back, especially now. We can't protect her while she's in the city and we're in Grove Meadow."

I chew on my lip. Esme had made it clear that she wanted to get out of our small town for the same reasons I had wanted to, but I had hoped that she'd fall in with a new coven when she moved to the city. It seemed like that didn't happen.

"Any ideas on what to do now?" Camila asks, coming over to scratch Silas's head. A comfort that they both take a moment to bask in as I glance at the hidden door to the sanctum currently housing my familiar.

"We need some time to work through the prophecy, but if

the disappearances are related, we have to dive deeper. There has to be a connection we're missing," I say, tucking an errant strand of hair behind my ear and turning back to them.

I can't help but think that our grandparents would know what to do but immediately shake it off. We can't depend on them anymore. Camila and I were utterly and unmistakably alone now.

Camila sighs and drops her hand from Silas to drum her nails against the counter. "I've gotten all I can from the families. If I bring them any more gift baskets, they're going to call the police."

That's it. I straighten my posture as the to-do list forms in my head. "Camila, I think you should meet Detective O'Reilly."

Her eyes grow wide. "You want me to talk to the police? Who are you, and what have you done with my sister?" Silas lets out a sharp *meow* in agreement.

In any other circumstance, I would also think I'd lost my mind. Getting directly involved in an investigation in which we were the prime suspects was practically asking for a one-way ticket to prison. But, if Camila could get some information from the detective using her truth serum pastries, that could work to our advantage.

"I think you'll find Detective O'Reilly to be...different than the others. He's curious, not suspicious."

Camila frowns at me, a tense crease forming between her brows. "What's the difference?"

For someone who'd grown up in this town, I'd say there was no difference, but my intuition told me Detective O'Reilly wasn't the enemy. In fact, it was telling me that getting to know the detective might be in our best interest and the only way to uncover the mystery behind these disappearances.

"Well, for one, I don't think he actually believes we have anything to do with the case."

Her brows furrow in surprise. "What makes you say that?"

"Just a hunch," I reply, lifting a shoulder.

Camila doesn't ask for elaboration. We both knew better than to doubt each other's intuition.

It does take a moment before she nods. "Alright. Am I just supposed to wait for him to come back to the shop, or did you have some other bright idea?"

"Actually..." I say, tossing her an apron from the hook beside me. "Better get baking, Cam; you've got a visit to make to the new detective in town."

She catches the cloth easily. "Fine, but I'm not making extras for you," she remarks, flicking Silas's nose. When he lets out a hiss in protest, she wags a finger at him, "That's for locking Luna in the closet."

At least *that* was something.

6

DECLAN

"Detective, you've got a visitor," Deputy Stotland says, passing by my desk.

I look up from the photos of a singed patch of earth in the woods behind the Castillos' shop. "Who is it?"

Across from me, Bas lets out a low whistle that has me moving my gaze toward him with an arched brow. "That would be Camila."

I turned in my chair to see the younger Castillo sister talking to the officer at the front desk. She bears a striking resemblance to her sister, but there's a lightness about her. Camila Castillo appeared delicate and ethereal compared to her sister despite their similar sharp features. She's wearing a white sweater and jeans, and her hair is pulled back from her face. Where Carolina bore what seemed like a permanent smirk, Camila's face was lit with a smile.

Camila looked up in my direction as if she could sense my gaze. Holding it for a second longer, she looked back at the officer and pointed in my direction.

I look back at Bas, but he's busied himself with something on his computer. The heels of her boots click against the floor as she makes her way over to me.

I'm not looking at her as she approaches. Instead, I note how the officers at their desks stare as she passes. Their gazes locked on her movements, but not in admiration. Contempt was the best word to describe their expressions. It was one thing to hear about how much the town despised their presence, but it was another to see it. In any other place, the Castillo sisters might even be coveted for their beauty—*and sharp tongue*—but not in Grove Meadow. The sisters had the town scared of their shadows.

"Detective Blackwell." Camila nods, her smile widening ever so slightly. "Nice to see you again." When Bas doesn't respond, she looks at me, holding out her hand. "Detective O'Reilly, I'm Camila Castillo. My sister said you stopped by the shop."

I stand and take her hand in mine. With all the gasps around me, I expect to feel some sort of instantaneous pain, but I don't feel so much as a static shock.

"I did. Thank you for coming in, Miss Castillo," I say, sitting back down in my chair and gesturing for her to take a seat.

"Camila, please." She rifles through the bag tucked under her left arm. "I brought you some samples of our shop's pastries. Carolina said you didn't order anything when you came by," Camila says, pulling out a box and placing it on the edge of my desk. "I hope you like banana bread; it's our specialty."

I blink at her. "Miss Castillo—"

"Camila," she says, pushing the box of sweets toward me.

"Miss Castillo," I reiterate and move the box to the floor, eliciting a frown from her. "I was at your shop earlier to ask you and your sister a few questions about the disappearances."

Camila regains her smile as she drops into the seat beside my desk and presses the palms of her hands against her jeans.

"Of course, Detective. That's why I'm here. I want to help however I can, though I'm not sure how useful I'll be."

"I'm so glad to hear that." I lean forward to pull a file from the corner of my desk and flip it open. "Miss Castillo, how well did you know the victims? Were you friends with any of them?"

She shakes her head slowly. "No, I can't say I was. When Gemma got back to town, Carolina and I offered for her to host some of her art classes at the shop until she found a studio space."

Gemma Dawson, 25. Gemma had recently come back to Grove Meadow after art school and opened a studio in town. She went into her space late one night and never came out. She rents the studio from Hazel Whitman, 42, who owns a bed-and-breakfast on the outskirts of the town.

"Were you friends with Gemma before she left?" I ask, jotting down Camila's mention of Gemma in the file's notes.

"No, Gemma is a few years younger than me. I was the same year as her older sister, Winnie. We didn't keep in touch once Winnie went to college."

I nod as I continue writing. "So other than Gemma, no real contact with the other victims: Owen, Miles, Vivian, or Felix?"

Owen Donovan, 32, town librarian. Miles Kensington, 28, works at the bookstore. Vivian Monroe, 35, event planner. Felix Hayes, 45, owns the hardware store. They're all different ages and have no obvious overlap in victimology other than their place of residence.

"No, Detective. I don't spend a lot of time with the other people in town. Just Carolina."

Bas lets out a snort from his desk to my left, and I turn to glare at him.

"It's okay, Detective. Bas is just upset that I know a secret about him." Camila's voice carries a teasing lilt, and Bas turns a gnarly shade of green.

As I turn back to Camila, my mouth tips up in an amused half-smile. "Care to share?"

"Oh, no, Detective. That's between Bas and me." Her eyes don't leave his, as if she's looking at something deeper than the surface.

I hear Bas stand from his chair abruptly. "It's Detective Blackwell, *Castillo*. We're not friends."

Something akin to satisfaction purses her mouth as she watches Bas storm away.

"Sorry about my partner, Miss Castillo," I say, leaning back in my chair and tenting my fingers together.

"Camila," she corrects, directing her gaze back to me.

"Just one last question, Camila." She nods, encouraging me to continue.

I lean forward again to flip the case file to the back and open it to a series of printed crime scene photos. "If you didn't talk to Vivian Monroe, why did she have your necklace in her belongings?" I ask, placing the photo of the gold necklace that reads *Camila* in a scripted font.

Camila's gaze moves to the photo in the file, and her lips part. Her brows furrow and her hand absently reaches for her neck, which is very clearly missing a necklace.

"I—" she shakes her head slowly, eyes narrowing at the photo. "I don't know. I didn't even know it was missing."

I close the file, and she leans back in her chair, seeming like she just had all the air knocked out of her. Her eyes remain on where the photo had been.

"You didn't know it was gone?" I ask, my pen hovering over my notepad, poised and ready to take notes...or write down a confession.

"Detective, I don't know how or why Vivian had that. I...I

keep that in a jewelry box on my dresser. My grandparents gave that to me, and I haven't worn it since they passed. I have no idea how long it's been gone." Camila's ever-present smile was no longer on her face. In fact, her baffled frown appeared to be so deeply set into her skin that I wasn't sure if it would ever reappear.

I set my pen down. "Miss Castillo, I want to believe you. I want to believe that you and your sister have nothing to do with these disappearances, but I need a better answer than 'I don't know.'"

She finally looks back at me, her eyes showing nothing but a confused sincerity. "I'm sorry, Detective, but I don't have one. I truly don't know why Vivian would have it. She doesn't come into the shop at all, let alone into our apartment above."

I stare at her for a beat longer, searching for some sign that she's hiding something. If she is, it's not about this. Not from what I can tell.

"Okay, Miss Castillo. If you can think of anything, anything at all," I grab a business card from the drawer beside me. "Give me a call. Any time of day," I tell her, passing her the card.

Her fingers shake as she pulls it from my hand. "Sure thing, Detective." She gives me a tight smile as she stands and turns away from me.

"Oh, Camila?" I say, and I know I'll regret it later. "Tell your sister I look forward to seeing her again *real* soon, would you?"

Camila's lips pull into a thin line, just like her sister's had earlier when I'd said something she didn't like. But unlike the elder Castillo sister, she merely nods at me and walks out of the precinct.

Despite the necklace that had been found after my visit to the shop, I didn't like the sisters for this. It was too coincidental. The necklace had been sitting on Vivian Monroe's dresser for anyone to see. Her husband hadn't remembered seeing it there before today, and he didn't know where she'd gotten it. The clasp hadn't been broken or replaced because it had the same coloring as the chain, so it wasn't forcibly removed. The color was beginning to tarnish as if it hadn't been worn for as long as Camila had implied.

Raking a hand through my hair, I pull up the photos of the scorch marks on my computer again. It was as if something had been in the center, and whatever had happened occurred around it. I'd never seen anything quite like it—a perfect untouched circle.

The disappearances were becoming too frequent, and we didn't have a single lead. No matter how much the Captain, Bas, and the rest of this town wanted it to be the Castillos, there had to be something we were missing. Something *I* was missing.

7

CAROLINA

"Lina! We have a problem!" The panic in Camila's voice rings clear, and I almost drop a tray of scones in response. I steel myself and place them on the counter before we end up in a bigger mess. Camila makes it three steps into the shop before abruptly turning and flipping the *open* sign to *closed*.

Silas hops onto the counter, and we share a concerned look. "Bad time with Detective McStuffins?" he asks.

Camila shakes her head, but instead of telling us what happened, she holds out her hand for me to take. Typically, I'd roll my eyes at her dramatics, but the look on her face tells me it might be warranted.

Brow furrowed, I take Cami's hand and let her memories of earlier flow into my mind. It's second nature to me at this point. A muscle that barely has to flex to activate.

This is my power.

Recalling the past and seeing the future.

It's out of my control in my dreams, and the need for physical touch to do it is nonexistent. Whether it's my power reaching out and searching for people's memories or futures or the memories are reaching out to me isn't clear.

Before I'd gained control over it in the waking hours, I would brush my hand against someone's, and I'd see their whole life splayed across my vision whether I intended to or not.

The first time it happened, I was pulled out of school for a week until I could get a handle on it. Sometimes my magic went rogue and overruled me if it felt something was off, but for the most part it allowed my friends and family privacy from its desire to see their futures.

On the outside, my eyes glaze over and my body stiffens, seeing memories instead of what's right in front of me. The power prickles in my hand in a way that I find comforting. Camila says she can't feel it when I do it, but the change in demeanor tips her off.

Internally, it's like scrubbing through a movie. I can go forward and see life as it's currently set, but people's ever-changing decisions make it possible things will change. It's harder to see a witch's future, and Camila and I have both agreed that it would be bad to look too far into ours anyway.

Lowering the shield I have up on my ability, I mentally flip the pages of Camila's memories working backwards from the present moment to find her arrival at the police station.

I see Sebastian Blackwell and Detective O'Reilly at their desks through Camila's eyes. I roll my eyes at Bas, just as she had. Then I see the necklace—the cause of Camila's panic.

"*Fuck*. How did they get that?" I ask, dropping her hand like it burned me.

She's already walking to the door of the magic room. "I don't know. I didn't even know it was missing."

Silas and I follow behind her, and Luna startles from her perch in the corner of the room at the abrupt entry.

"What's happened now?" she asks, slithering along the floor towards me.

"Camila killed someone," Silas says, hopping onto the table.

"Silas!" I swat at him, and he lets out a hiss in response.

"One day, they're going to let me eat you, furball," Luna says as she coils herself around one of the trees we magicked in a decade ago.

"Vivian Monroe had Camila's necklace in her house, which is even more ammunition against us," I explain, taking a seat on the couch as Camila paces along the room.

Declan finding that necklace doesn't prove anything, but how did Vivian get it? Camila keeps it in her jewelry box on her dresser. She hasn't been able to wear it since our grandparents died. The only way someone could get to it is if they broke into her room, but surely we would know if someone got past our protection wards. If someone could get past them without being detected, we had a much bigger problem on our hands.

"You're sure it's yours," I ask.

Camila nods. "I checked upstairs before I came to the shop. It's gone. I tried summoning it back to me as soon I left the station, but I couldn't. It was like something was blocking my magic from getting it back."

The weight of that confirmation hangs heavy in the air. Someone was in our apartment. Someone who knew how to get past our charms or was strong enough to deactivate them without alerting us. Someone who could block our magic.

"We need to get that necklace back," Luna says. "Caro could try using her power to see who took it."

Camila pauses wearing a hole in our floorboards to look at me. "You can't read inanimate objects...can you?"

The more a witch trains their powers, the stronger they become. Luna and I had been working on using my powers to view object histories—where they came from, who created them, and things like that. It would be helpful for dating some of our family heirlooms (and avoiding any cursed ones) if we knew more about them.

I lift a shoulder. "I've been trying it out in passing. I've been able to do it with some of our family objects, but there are flashes here and there. Never the future, though."

Ever since our grandparents died, Camila and I haven't been as close, and we certainly don't talk about our magic anymore. At first, it was because it all reminded us of them and how alone we truly were. Then, it became normal. We worked alongside each other in the shop and lived in the same place, but we had different lives.

Camila nods and leans against a table we use for potion making, drumming her fingers on the edge. "Then it seems like a good time to tell you I've been working on the astral projection spell." My brows raise in surprise.

Astral projection allows a witch's spirit to be in one place while their body remains in another. It was our mother's power, and she had written a spell that would simulate the power to a lesser extent. We hadn't tested the distance or how long the spell would last...or at least *I* hadn't, but perhaps Camila had.

"Okay, so...what are you suggesting? I astral project into the police station and see if I can read the necklace? We don't even know if I can use my power while in astral form."

I try not to let it show how hurt I am that she'd been practicing our mother's power without me knowing. It wasn't important right now.

Camila shrugs. "Isn't it worth a shot? If we get a chance to find out who's involved in these disappearances and trying to pin it on us, don't you think we should at least try?"

She has a point. Luna's voice filters through my thoughts.

I glance over at my familiar, but she's looking at Silas. I

wonder if he told her that Cami was working on the spell. I wonder if she feels just as betrayed.

I swallow the knot in my throat. "Okay."

"Tonight, then?" Camila asks.

"Tonight."

"Alright, I think this should work," Camila says, placing the last crystal in position on the ground.

I'm standing at the center of a chalk-drawn five-pointed star, each point adorned with an amethyst crystal. *I think this should work* didn't exactly sit well with me, but we also didn't have many other options.

"Did we have to do this in an alley?" Silas asks, sniffing beside a dumpster and instantly recoiling at the smell.

"Well, you and Camila weren't sure about the distance, so we had to get as close as possible. Stop complaining. We didn't ask you to come."

Silas doesn't respond, but he settles on the ground and watches us with his wide eyes that seem to glow in the dark.

"Ready?"

I nod, unfolding the spell Camila transcribed for me and taking a breath.

> Separation of body and mind,
> Different places at the same time,
> By will and word, I now ascend,
> To realms unseen, where spirits blend.
> My form at rest, my soul shall roam,
> Returning whole when I call it home.

Camila and I used to cast harmless spells when we were in high school after we'd graduated our basic witch training—spells to make us relax before a test in school or clean our apartment when we were too lazy, even one to grant us a little bit of luck on rare occasions—but we've never used magic for something like *this*.

My heart twinges as I wish my *abuela* and mom were here. They would know what to do, and they wouldn't be trying to break into a police station for something that might not work.

"Carolina?" Camila's voice brings me back to the matter at hand.

"Sorry, right." *Here goes nothing.*

As I speak the incantation into the night, I focus on Camila's necklace in my mind's eye to guide my magic.

I want my spirit to go where it's hidden. I want to find it. I want to retrieve it from where it's being kept. It belongs to us, and we want it back.

In a blink, I can no longer see Silas and Camila, and the world feels like it's zooming past me. In another blink, I'm in a dark room with metal shelves lined with boxes.

The room feels stuffy, and I'm sure I'd be sneezing right now if astral forms could have allergies. The door's frosted window is the only light source and shines only on the first few rows of shelves. It's practically pitch black from my position in the back corner of the room. In order to see the boxes back here, I'd have to summon a witch's light, but I don't want to risk that quite yet. Not unless I absolutely have to.

My body feels strange in this form. I feel solid but weightless, like I'm almost floating. At least some of this plan worked.

I hear voices in the hallway outside and hasten my search. The row in front of me is easier to see, but there's no order to the madness, and I'm half convinced that it's to prevent people like me from having enough time to steal whatever they're looking for.

Refocusing on Camila's necklace, I let my intuition guide me to its location instead of wasting time trying to decipher the careless chicken scratch on the boxes. My eyes zero in on the box sitting on the shelves nearest the door. Before I can walk over to it, the door handle jiggles from someone putting their key in the lock.

I drop to the floor where I am, still between the shelves where it's the darkest. I should go back to my body, but I've come this far, so I stay firmly planted in my position.

I seal my lips when the lights flick on, and I catch a glimpse of Declan. We didn't think he'd still be at the station at 11 p.m., but apparently, we were very mistaken. Any hopes I had that he wouldn't be going for Vivian's box are dashed when he stops in front of it and pulls it out of its spot.

On his way out the door, box in hand, he pauses and turns in my direction. I'm confident he can't see me, but the longer he stares, the less sure I feel.

I don't wait to see if he walks over because I'm already back in the alley.

"Mission failed," I say, stretching out my limbs. "Declan's got the box. We'll have to try again another time."

"What's Declan doing here so late?" Camila asks.

I shrug. "His job?"

Camila and Silas both roll their eyes at me, and we clean up the crystals. A thought in the back of my mind presses into me. *Was it a coincidence that Declan came in, or did he know somehow?*

It's a crazy thought. I must have lost my mind in the transition back to my body. Of course he couldn't know...right?

8

DECLAN

I blink at the back corner of the room before placing Vivian Monroe's evidence box back on the metal shelf I grabbed it from and walking over to the furthest metal shelving unit. As expected, nothing is there, not a box out of place, but in my years on the force, I've learned to trust my gut, even when it seems fruitless.

Grabbing the box again, I flip the light switch off and head back to my desk. I don't even know what I'm doing here this late. Bas went home hours ago, and I know exactly what's in this box, but here I am, rifling through the contents again, searching for anything that might spark a new line of questioning.

I pick up the plastic evidence bag with Camila Castillo's necklace and study it closely. Turning it over in my hand and running my thumb over the scripted lettering, I wonder again why this necklace had ended up in Vivian Monroe's belongings.

It seemed too obvious to be a real clue, but my colleagues seemed to disagree.

I know that in most cases, the obvious suspect is usually the answer, but you can't fake a reaction like the one Camila had to seeing her necklace on my desk. The way her face contorted into equal parts sadness and confusion. Whoever put the necklace in that house must have done it to send us to the Castillos.

Abandoning the Monroe box, I turn to my computer and open the file created for the Castillo sisters. I've studied this file to exhaustion.

I could probably draw their pictures from memory. I knew the curve of Carolina's lips and the placement of the dark freckle just above the right side of her mouth. The exact shade of brown that made up her eyes was permanently etched in my mind.

I've combed through the reports of the fire that killed their parents 20 years ago, because my interest in them had turned obsessive. They had been at their family's cabin in the woods up near Tully Lake when the fire broke out.

According to the reports, their father, Jeremiah Mason, got the girls out and went back in for their mother, Sonia Castillo, when the cabin collapsed. They never made it out.

Volunteer firefighters from the nearby town showed up to put out the flames after a neighboring cabin called it in. The firefighters found a nine-year-old Carolina and seven-year-old Camila alone in their pajamas, staring at the burning building. The girls moved in with their grandparents, and the fire was ruled an accident caused by faulty wiring.

Almost three years ago, they lost both their grandparents to old age and some health complications. Nothing unusual there.

On paper, they were ordinary town residents with a particularly somber past, and the only thing that seemingly connected them to this case was Camila's necklace.

By the time I was done reading their file again, I couldn't help but feel sad for them. They'd lost everything except each other and the shop, and the town had a vendetta against them for seemingly no reason.

Or maybe there was a reason, and it just wasn't documented in these files.

"CAROLINA CASTILLO IS THE REASON I'M DIVORCED," A WOMAN TELLS me the next day.

My pen hovers over my notepad before I flip it closed. I've been interviewing the town for the last two hours about the Castillo sisters, and so far, I've gotten reports of stolen high school boyfriends, strange cases of unusual illnesses, and food poisoning from a town event they didn't even go to, but divorce is a new one.

"She brainwashed my husband into sleeping with her," she says confidently.

"Any proof of that?" I ask, pocketing my notepad on the inside of my jacket.

"He told me so."

"Right. Thank you for your time."

It was obvious I was wasting my time talking to these people, and I was growing more frustrated by the second. I move to the empty park bench two over from the woman and stare out at the pond in front of me.

A sharp breeze hits my cheeks and sends a shiver down my spine. It makes me realize just how cold it is outside. There aren't that many people out—only a few runners loop around the frog pond, and a small group of moms push strollers on the walkway. It seemed my town interviews would have to wait.

There's a prickling of the hairs on the back of my neck. "I

didn't, you know," says a voice from behind me. "Brainwash her husband," Carolina clarifies, sitting down beside me.

She's a sight for my sore, tired eyes. Her dark hair is pulled back from her face, and her nose is tinged pink from the cold. The shadows under her eyes are not unlike my own.

"Just a regular affair, then," I assume, turning my body toward hers.

Carolina wrinkles her nose and pulls her jacket tighter around her. "Definitely not. She was married to Zachary Carstenson, and he was sleeping with several women. None of them me, but I'm an easy scapegoat," she says with a shrug.

I look at her and wonder what she's thinking—about me, the town, this whole situation. What must it be like to be constantly accused of every bad thing that happened in this town?

"Something on my face, Detective?" she asks, turning to look at me.

I shake my head. "What brings you out to the park? It's kind of chilly out."

She pushes the shorter pieces of hair that escaped her hair tie behind her ear. "Just taking a walk. Trying to clear my mind. Our parents used to bring us here. This time of year is my favorite."

A laugh escapes me. "The time of year when everything is dying? That's your favorite?"

I catch a ghost of a smile spread across her face. "Mostly the colors and how still everything feels. Summer feels like everything is always in motion. There's something about autumn that makes you reflect on things."

Considering her words, I reply, "I don't think I've ever thought about seasons like that. I don't think there's a time of year that feels more thoughtful than others."

"It's my grandparents' fault, probably. They were very... organic."

"Organic?" I laugh again.

"'In tune with the Earth' feels even more silly to say. They just loved nature but not in the hippie way. In the way that made you really sit with the elements. The changing seasons. The rise and fall of the tides. The phases of the moon. It was their thing."

"Witchy," I say. She smirks but doesn't respond.

Looking back at the pond, Carolina nods and fusses with her hair again.

"I'm sorry about your grandparents...and your parents... and for reading your file."

The corner of her mouth turns up. "All part of your job, I assume."

"Yeah, but still." I ask suddenly, "Who do you think is doing all this?"

She raises her dark brows at me. "Who do *I* think it is?" I nod. "Isn't it your job to find the culprit, Detective?"

Fair point. I laugh. "I've hit a dead end on new leads."

She crosses one leg over the other. "Any prime suspects?" she asks casually.

"I'm not sure. After you two, no one else makes sense." It's out of my mouth before I can stop it. I shouldn't be talking to her about this.

We're both quiet, and I'm searching for something, anything else, to say.

"The banana bread was good" is the only thing that comes to mind. At least it's the truth. "What's the secret?"

"Family recipe. I'm sworn to take it with me to the grave," she tells me.

Carolina's gaze is on the people who walk past us, staring.

When they make eye contact with her, they look away and whisper to each other.

"Did you always want to own a shop with your sister?"

She blinks and looks at me like she only now remembered I was here. "No. Camila and I were always competing with each other when we were younger. We can never really agree on anything, but our grandparents left us the place and...well, we couldn't just sell it. Camila loves baking, and I love coffee shops, so it seemed like a good compromise."

How normal. Utterly and completely normal.

"And who owns the cat that wanders around?"

Carolina rolls her eyes, either because she thinks my question is ridiculous (it is) or because she hates cats (me too).

"Silas is Camila's. We've had him since we were kids, but he gravitates toward Cami."

"I'm not much of a cat person," I tell her, and she smiles at me.

"Me either," Carolina says and checks the time on her phone. "Looks like I've got to go, Detective, but it was nice chatting with you. Hope you get a lead soon."

I watch her walk through the park in the direction of her shop and wonder how on earth I'm supposed to find new leads when I'm constantly distracted by Carolina and whatever secret she's keeping.

9

DECLAN

C*up & Cauldron* is never busy like the other shops in town. It operates as if they have a one-customer-at-a-time town-imposed rule. Some customers walk into the cafe like it's part of their routine, and others enter slowly, looking around to see if anyone's watching before they enter. I note the ones who look like they have something to hide to look into later.

I'm still not convinced that Carolina and Camila have anything to do with the disappearances, but I am sure they're hiding *something*.

Bas has given up staking out the place with me, but it's become part of my workday. I've done it three mornings in a row, but unlike the other times, the younger Castillo sister leaves the shop. I shift in my seat to see where she's headed, one hand on my keys to start the car in case I have to trail her.

With a coffee and a paper bag in her hand, she looks both ways before crossing the street and heading in my direction. *So much for a low profile.*

Camila is smiling as she taps on my window, and I have to turn the car on to roll it down.

"Thought you could use a pick-me-up," Camila says with a smile. "Black coffee and a lemon loaf."

"Appreciate it." Camila lingers even after I've taken the items from her. "Can I help you with something, Miss Castillo?"

"Camila." The correction leaves her lips without hesitation. "I was just thinking that it's probably much warmer in the shop than in your car. If you wanted to...do whatever it is you're doing every morning inside the shop, that would be okay."

I try to reconcile the Camila I've heard about with the one in front of me, and I'm sure they've got the wrong sister. She's far too hospitable.

"Would I have to order something?"

Camila laughs, and I'm convinced the sound gets her out of a variety of precarious situations outside this town.

"Only if you want to, Detective," she says as she turns back to the cafe.

The next morning, I took Camila up on her offer because I'd learned nothing from observing the shop from the outside. I brought my laptop and case files to work on, so at least I wouldn't be loitering.

If Carolina's surprised to see me in her shop, she doesn't show it.

"What can I get for you, Detective?"

My eyes roam over the blackboard menus above her head, and I contemplate ordering one of the teas I am positive are *not* teas out of curiosity, but I don't. "Coffee, black."

Her nose wrinkles almost imperceptibly as she pulls a to-go cup from beside her and rings the order into the register.

"For here, actually."

That gets her attention. "For here?"

Her dark brown eyes bore into mine, and I knew she wanted to know what I was up to, but she didn't ask.

I planned to work here for the day, telling Bas I wanted to get an up-close and personal understanding of who the Castillo sisters were. That was part of it, of course. The other parts were difficult to explain. Call it more of my curiosity.

"How do you stay in business if it's always empty?" I ask aloud and then consider how rude of a question it was.

"Deal with the devil," Carolina replies apathetically as she fills the mug.

"Naturally."

She's turned away from me, but I see the corner of her mouth turn up.

"You know, I don't think you're beating the witchcraft allegations with the word 'cauldron' in your shop's name."

She raises a shoulder. "We decided to lean into it. Actually, around this time, the shop gets quite busy with tourists because of it."

I laugh. "Tourists? In Grove Meadow?"

"Oh, just you wait, Detective," she says, looking over her shoulder at me, "things get real spooky here in the Grove."

Carolina is different from her sister. I feel like I have to work to earn her smiles, whereas Camila's seemed to come more easily. The older Castillo sister seemed more guarded...more mysterious, and the thing about me was that I loved a good mystery.

Our fingers brush as Carolina passes me the cup of coffee, and I jerk back at the surge of static electricity that races up my arm. In contrast, Carolina stiffens, and her eyes seem to glaze over.

"Carolina?" My voice doesn't seem to shake her, but a sharp meow that comes from behind the counter gets her attention.

"Sorry," she says, putting the mug down on the counter and sliding it toward me. "I was just thinking about something...never mind. Here's your coffee, Detective O'Reilly."

My eyes don't leave hers as I try to discern what just happened, but she breaks away before long.

"Thanks."

I settle in at the table in the corner of the shop, furthest from the window, and dive into the files Bas sent over late yesterday. We recently gained access to Gemma's computer, and I've been sorting through the files on it.

Her finances seemed to be in order. She had a lot of student loan debt, but that was normal. She paid for her studio space by teaching art classes for all ages, hosting regular "Paint & Sip" nights, having artists from outside of town sell their work in her studio gallery and taking a commission percentage, and selling her own paintings.

If I isolated her disappearance, it still didn't make sense. Gemma was a prominent member of the community. The town seemed to like her, and she hadn't made any enemies. Gemma, by all accounts considered, was a low-risk target.

Her digital calendar flashes on my screen. It's filled with various colored boxes. A recurring event on Wednesday evenings catches my attention. Unlike the other events on her calendar, it doesn't have a title or location. There are no other invited guests, and it's much later than her usual studio community events.

What could Gemma Dawson have been doing on Wednesday nights?

"Carolina?" I call. She turns to me, pausing in her filling of the pastry case. "Does the town do anything on Wednesday nights? Around 8 p.m.?"

She thinks for a moment. "No, not that I know of. Greg Morris used to host Bar Trivia in the summer, but not anymore, and that was on Tuesdays. Nothing in town tends to go that late. Most shops close by 6:30."

"Thanks."

I return to my computer. It was a long shot, but it was the only thread I'd seen in days.

Pulling out the paper case files from my bag, I locate the transcribed statement from Felix Hayes's wife. I skim the document until I find...

"Felix was home every night at 6 p.m. sharp except Wednesdays when he had poker night with some of the guys from town. Then, one night, he just never came home."

It could be a coincidence that Felix and Gemma had an event on the same night, but my gut told me to dig deeper.

I quickly pull out Owen Donovan's file and look for any mention of a poker night. I find nothing and make a note to check with his family about it.

Then I find Miles's file and don't find a poker night either, but I do see that he attended a book club every Wednesday night at Hazel Whitman's inn. A bookstore owner attending a book club should be the least suspicious thing in the world, but the logistics are brow-raising.

So whatever meeting it is they're all going to, at least one person is lying about it. I continue to pull on the thread.

When I look at Vivian's calendar, I see the same time and day blocked off, but there's no note as to what it is.

What could a librarian, a bookstore owner, an event planner, a hardware store owner, and an artist possibly have in common? In theory, nothing. Maybe they *were* in the same book club, poker night, or whatever.

I startle at Carolina's sudden appearance by my side.

"Sorry, you looked stressed," she apologizes. "I just wanted to bring over this banana bread. Seemed like something Camila would do."

I laugh, still reeling from the connection I just found. "Thanks."

Her gaze narrows at a document behind my computer, and I shut the laptop screen to see what it is. "Are those where they disappeared?"

"Uh, maybe. We're not sure. Each place has a weird marking, but it could be unrelated. I thought there might be something there if I put them on a map."

She touches the map with her index finger. "It's a pentagram."

"What?"

Carolina turns the map so it faces me. "Well, almost. You're missing a point, see..."

Her finger glides across the page to draw the five-sided shape, but the last point is missing. We haven't had a reason to send anyone to check that location, but if nothing is there, it could be our *next* crime scene.

"Five missing people, five points," Carolina murmurs.

I glance up at her, and her eyes are glazed over again.

"So if they're related, there might not be any more disappearances because they've completed the pentagram," I surmise.

Her lips part slightly, and her brow furrows. "Maybe. If they're trying to use some sort of ritual, then they'll need to activate it."

I don't question how she knows that. It's inconsequential to me right now. I can interrogate her later, even though her disclosure of this information makes me less likely to think she's involved. Simulating some sort of weird witchy ritual is exactly what someone would do if they wanted to frame Carolina and Camila, given their reputation.

"How would they activate it?"

"Hmm?" She blinks, coming out of her daze.

"If they wanted to activate the symbol or whatever…how would they?"

"Oh, uh…hypothetically…I'd guess by doing whatever they're doing in the center of the shape. I think it'd be roughly around here, but you'd need to map it out more accurately."

"And hypothetically…to activate it, they'd need to perform the ritual again?" Carolina nods slowly. "So that might mean another missing person?"

"I don't—"

I stand abruptly, causing Carolina to take a step back. She was close enough that I could smell the cinnamon and vanilla scent coming off her skin, but I needed to go.

I had to check out the fifth possible location to determine where I'd need to be posted this evening. My gut was telling me this was the *something* I had been waiting for. The first real lead since I got here.

"Thanks for your help," I tell Carolina as I pack up my things and head toward the door.

"Uh, no problem."

10

DECLAN

I sent a patrol car to the missing fifth location on the map while I made my way over. A pair of officers, who were already near the area, confirmed that similar markings were left behind, and they closed off the scene.

At their confirmation, I felt equal parts relief and dread. Carolina had been right about the pattern, and I had a feeling she might also be right about another disappearance. If that was true and the final disappearance followed the pattern of the previous ones, I had until nightfall to pinpoint the location.

The urgency was gnawing at me. Every case I'd worked taught me one thing: when patterns emerge, they almost always lead to a climax. And that climax rarely ends well for the victims. This was no exception.

My phone rang as I turned off the road and onto an unpaved, marked drive that would take me to where the patrol officers closed off the scene. I put Bas on speaker.

"Find anything?" he asked.

"Just pulled into the drive. Not sure yet. I'll let you know if I do," I tell him, parking my car and shutting off the engine.

The trees swayed slightly in the wind, their branches casting long shadows over the dirt road. Something about the place felt off—not just physically, but emotionally like the weight of every missing person's fear was lingering in the air.

I knew how Bas would feel about taking tips from Carolina, so I hadn't told him about the working theory, just that I wanted to investigate this area based on the relative distance to the other places. He seemed to buy it. I most certainly wasn't going to tell him about my plans to stake out the center of the pentagram.

I would say that the thought alone was insane, but this wasn't my first rodeo. Not by a long shot.

A few years ago, I'd worked a handful of cases in desert towns where it seemed like someone was emulating pagan rituals using animal sacrifices. The amount of blood found at the scenes alarmed the county police so much they called me in, but it turned out to be a bunch of teenagers causing trouble out of boredom. Apparently, a summer blockbuster about a cult had just released and gave them some ideas.

That case, though harmless in the end, left me with the knowledge of how quickly people could adopt the macabre for fun. Or worse, how easily they could cross a line they didn't even know existed.

Those cases made me wary of small towns to begin with. When I was called into this one, I knew there might be another explanation for the disappearances. A quiet town, non-existent crime rate, and low-risk targets? There had to be something more to them.

Of course, someone could be abducting these people. The entire police force had been searching for them around the clock while Bas and I tried to put the pieces together. If we could figure out the pattern and predict the next disappearance, we could trace it back to the source.

Still, nothing about the physical evidence pointed to a clear abduction scenario. No forced entry at homes, no witnesses to strange vehicles, no ransom notes—just people vanishing without a trace. It's what kept me up at night. There were no loose ends to pull, only vague patterns on a map.

But given the situation—the town, the victims, the rumor mill—it may be just as likely that these "missing" individuals were holed up somewhere together, trying to draw media attention to their small town to garner more tourists.

I had considered that theory seriously for a while, but after talking to the families of the missing, their devastation seemed too raw to be faked. Besides, media stunts usually came with announcements and clues left for reporters to follow. Here, there was only silence.

Town scandals, especially stories about witches making people disappear around this time of year, tended to draw a crowd. But in this case, it felt like the town was retreating, almost as if they were hoping the outside world wouldn't notice what was happening. Their reluctance to engage with outsiders, their cryptic answers—it was as if the town itself had something to hide.

No matter what it was, I'd investigate any lead I had to the best of my ability—including ones that came from mysterious coffee shop owners. I'd call Bas if I needed backup tonight, but if I was wrong, no harm done. If Carolina's gut was right—and if mine was right too—tonight would be critical. I didn't want to make the mistake of dragging Bas into something I wasn't even sure about yet.

"Okay. I'll head over after I talk to Owen's family about any late-night meetings he may have been going to."

"Sounds good."

Leaves crunch under my feet as I make my way over to the yellow police tape. "Detective Declan O'Reilly," I say to the officer, flashing my badge.

He nods and lifts the tape to let me under. "Over here,

Detective," calls Specialist MacDonna from the Crime Scene Unit.

"What do you have?" I ask, crouching beside her as she points to a familiar pattern on the ground. The same one found at the other scenes.

"Scorch marks in the grass are perfect circles like the other locations, but some of the leaves, over where Officer Bragg is, have some residue that we didn't find at the others." She passes me an evidence baggie. "Smells like sulfur; we're having it tested in the lab."

I nod, studying the bag containing a small amount of fine pale yellow powder. "Why would we find sulfur here and not the other locations?"

"It's possible there was, and we missed it. I can send CSU back to the other places and have them widen their search."

"Okay, thanks. Anything else?" I ask, passing her the evidence bag back.

She nods, standing and pointing in front of us beyond the circular markings. "There's only one set of footprints coming into the circle. None going out or coming from any other direction. It's like whatever was here just vanished."

I raise a brow at her. "Do you really believe that?"

MacDonna shrugs. "I don't know what to make of it. I think that's your job, Detective."

"Right. Thanks. Let me know when the sample comes back from the lab."

"Will do."

I took a long breath as I walked away from the scene. The sulfuric residue was strange, but even stranger was the lack of any sign of struggle or movement beyond that one set of footprints. It was as if whoever or whatever entered the circle ceased to exist once they reached the center. I couldn't shake the feeling that something—some force—was pulling these people into thin air.

But that was a crazy thought. Impossible, even.

No, this case had an explanation, a reasonable explanation for everything. Unfortunately, finding this last location had given us more questions than answers.

When I get back to the station, Bas is still out. I spread my map out on my desk and mark the fifth location.

"Here's that compass you wanted, O'Reilly," Deputy Stotland says, passing it to me. "Think you have something?"

I don't know why I didn't want to tell the Deputy what I was doing, but something in my gut was warning me against it. "Maybe. Probably nothing."

He nods and continues to his desk as I position the pencil into the tool. I estimate the center, knowing I'll have to adjust it, and line the pencil up with one of the five marks. After some trial and error, the circumference of the circle crosses each mark exactly.

I tap my finger on the point in the center of the circle. "Gotcha."

A chill runs down my spine as I stare at the center point on the map. This was it. Whatever was going to happen, it was going to happen here.

11

CAROLINA

His death plays on repeat in my head.

Declan walking into an alley. The lampposts are flickering and a pungent smell fills my nose like I'm really there even though it hasn't happened yet. A figure moves in the darker part of the alley, and Declan's head whips in its direction. He's shouting at someone…something. Declan's hand goes to his gun, holstered on his right hip. Before he can draw it, it's over. Blue light illuminates the alley, and he's gone.

I don't see him fall to the ground; the light is blinding, but I *feel* it. I feel an emptiness spread throughout my body, and I just know.

He's going to die.

While he worked at the table in the corner, I tried to pinpoint when and where it would happen. I tried to look for any indication of which back alley it could be as I scrubbed the counters with far too much vigor.

I needed more information, needed to examine his future more closely, so I brought him a pastry to try to touch him again. That's when I saw the map.

The pentagram.

For centuries, Grove Meadow only had one supernatural

family to worry about, and now someone was using penta-grams to summon...something.

What the *fuck* was happening in this town?

None of it made sense. Who would be using dark magic? How did Camila and I miss someone with powers? And what exactly were they trying to summon to the Mortal World?

Millennia ago, witches were cursed to the Mortal World by some greater beings. The stories are never consistent; some-times, it was the Fates who wanted to punish witches for trying to change the fabric of time and other times, it was the Gods who were worried our kind was becoming too powerful. No matter who you blamed, it was always the same. Witches were to walk the Mortal World undetected, separate from the rest of the supernatural world.

Sometime after the banishment, a collective of witches and warlocks came together to try and return to their world. They tried to unite their powers and summon a being so powerful that they could overthrow the Gods. But they failed, and the Gods punished them by creating a world meant to imprison them for good.

Over time, the Underworld has become home to dark witches and warlocks that we call demons because they sold their souls to dark magic for more power. A power that exceeds that of common witches and warlocks.

Personally, I thought shoving all the powerful dark magic in one place seemed like a very bad idea, but that opinion was well above my pay grade.

So if the figure I saw in Declan's future *was* a demon, then someone had opened a portal to the Underworld, and that would be...well...very bad.

Anxiety surges through me the moment Declan leaves the shop, and I'm inundated with the panicked thought that I have just sent him to his death.

But the map gave me a better idea of where it might happen. The center of the star is the alley behind the church. It's an estimate, but my intuition tells me I'm right and so I trust it.

Declan going to confirm the last location would buy me some time, but not much. It was night in the premonition, but I had no idea what it was that attacked him and thus I had no idea how to save him without getting myself killed in the process.

"Luna!" I shout, coming into the magic room as soon as Declan drives away. "Luna!" I shout again when she doesn't respond.

I try to convince myself that it's the terror of the Underworld being open that's affecting me so much and not that Declan might die. I need to remind myself that Declan O'Reilly is just another mortal. He's just another mortal, and over the years, I've learned to let lives run their course.

But this was different. A door to the Underworld might be open, and Declan might die because of it. Because *I* sent him there. If I hadn't said anything, Camila and I could have gone on our own to figure out what was going on, but it just slipped out.

Like I'd fallen into a trance, the words fell from my lips without much control. Fulfilling a prophecy by telling Declan about the pattern.

Luna slithers out from under the couch, one of her usual napping spots.

"What happened now?" she asks grumpily.

"I think someone's opened a portal to the Underworld, and I'm pretty sure I just sent Declan to the demon who's going to kill him," I tell her rapidly, opening the trunk with my family's grimoire.

All witches have a grimoire. Ours is a large leatherbound

book with our family crest embossed on the cover. Spells, charms, and anything magical we'd need to know are in this book. Passed down from generation to generation, this book is not just magic—it's history. History has a way of repeating itself, and the best thing a witch can do is write it all down and save the next generation from making the same mistakes in an endless cycle.

When Luna doesn't say anything, I look at her after closing the trunk. If snakes could blink, I was sure she'd be doing that.

"Declan?" she asks finally.

"The detective," I clarify as I set the book on the table and begin searching for anything that might help me save him and stop these disappearances. Any record of a demon that can summon blue light. Any potion or spell that might kill one of them. *Anything.*

"Carolina, you know better than to interfere in mortal deaths." Her quiet scolding irks me, and I can feel the sands of time ticking down on Declan's life.

I shake my head. "*Something* kills him, Luna. That something is *not* mortal, and it was my big mouth that sent him to it. Also, did you miss the part when I said someone's opened a portal to the Underworld?"

"I didn't, but I'm ignoring it because that's not possible. The younger generations always catastrophize things. You and Camila in high school for example. How many times did you claim the world was ending when, in fact, you both seem to be very much alive? *Oh no, Steve from the debate team didn't call me back after I accidentally turned him invisible,*" Luna mocks. "As if a little memory spell wouldn't right things."

I roll my eyes and get back to searching. "I am *not* being dramatic, and this is more than just Camila's idiot high school boyfriend, Luna. I saw it. I touched him, and I saw his future."

I send her the vision in my mind using the mental link between a witch and her familiar.

"See?" I say when it's over, like I really am in high school again and want to prove her wrong.

Camila comes into the room with Silas on her shoulder. "Lina, you left the shop completely empty...what's happening?" she asks, looking between Luna and me.

"We don't know for sure that it's a demon, Caro. Just that *something* kills him."

"Kills who?" Camila asks, setting Silas down on the ground.

I scoff. "I've never seen an active witch or warlock with the power to produce a ball of blue light with their hand and *throw* it at someone, Luna."

"Kills who?" Camila asks again, coming to sit beside me.

"Declan." Luna and I both snap.

"The detective?" Silas asks, and I break my staring competition with Luna to glare at him, but then he offers actual insight. "Blue lights are energy demons. They basically gather energy from light sources and channel it into a semi-permeable form."

I narrow my gaze at him. "How do you know about demon abilities?"

"Just because the Gods don't want witches learning about demons doesn't mean there's no way to get to the Underworld. Someone has to keep an eye on them."

Silas has never explicitly said what it was he did that earned him his life sentence as a familiar, but I'm pretty sure the word "classified" barely scraped the surface.

"And no, I won't be elaborating."

Right.

Camila grabs the book off my lap. "Okay, then either demons have figured out how to get to the Mortal World, or someone has summoned one or more of them here to Grove Meadow. And it can't just be a mortal messing around with some charms or potions. If someone did summon them, it had to be by someone with a Wiccan line. Right? That's what *abuela* said." Silas nods his head at her. "But either way, this is somehow related to the disappearances."

I pull the book back petulantly, earning an annoyed tongue click from Camila, and continue searching for anything that could help us. "I think so."

"It would explain some things," Silas adds. "Like, who could get past the wards to get Camila's necklace."

But why would a demon break into our apartment and just steal a necklace? Why not attack us when we're least expecting it?

That's the question, indeed, Luna says in my mind.

The necklace had to be a diversion. Whoever was behind this wanted Camila and me distracted long enough that they could finish the summoning.

"Wait, if a demon kills Declan, where is he?" Camila asks, bringing me back to the immediate problem.

"Checking out the last disappearance location. If I'm right about the hunch that I had the locations form a summoning pentagram, then we'll be able to triangulate the center of it. That's where the demon will be. I think we have until after sunset tonight, but it could be another night. I'm not sure."

Camila nods as she processes the new information, but wisely decides that now is not the time to ask about the minute details.

We comb through the grimoire, and Silas continues to tell us what he knows about energy demons, which isn't much. If we wanted something to...exterminate our demon problem, we'd have to start from scratch, and unfortunately, we didn't have much time for that.

Camila's leafing through another spell book that *abuela* kept in the trunk when she pauses and suddenly looks up at her familiar.

"Silas, what do you know about trapping demons?" Camila asks, looking intently at her familiar and I just know whatever we're about to do won't be good.

12

DECLAN

S takeouts are notoriously dreadful for most people, especially if you do them by yourself, but I've never minded them. In fact, I would rather do them on my own. When Bas gave up on joining me during my stakeouts of *Cup & Cauldron,* I was more than grateful.

Why? Because most people hated sitting in silence, but I preferred it.

I didn't care about the trials and errors of Bas's dating life or whatever other inane town or work gossip he wanted to share with me. Bas had a habit of filling the air with unnecessary chatter, his voice always breaking into my thoughts when I needed silence the most. With him around, it was like being trapped in a never-ending podcast of someone else's life.

Of course, my not telling Bas about this hunch is what left me completely alone this time, sitting in my car across the street from the opening of the alley behind the church with the windows down.

My morning stakeouts of *Cup & Cauldron* had prepared me for the bite in the air, but the cold was sharper in the evenings —a bitter edge that seemed to creep into my bones. Grove

Meadow had a chill that wasn't just temperature; it carried a heaviness, like the town itself was holding its breath.

I'm bundled in a thick jacket, scarf, and toque, but I can still see my breath every time I exhale. Another breeze passes through the car and sends a shiver down my spine.

"Waiting for someone, Detective?"

I jump, my hand instantly reaching for my gun, but I immediately stop when I meet Carolina's gaze outside the passenger side window. Her eyes, dark and piercing, lock onto mine, and for a moment, it feels like she's seeing more than just the outside of me. There's something unsettling about how quietly she approached, like she belonged to the shadows.

"God, didn't anyone tell you not to sneak up on someone with a gun?" I breathe, exasperated and trying to get my heart rate back down.

"No," she says simply while she opens the door. Even with all the windows down, it's hard to miss how much she smells like vanilla and autumn spices. The scent is intoxicating, and it takes me a second too long to focus again, my thoughts spinning as if the smell itself was wrapping around me, warm and soft.

I frown. "What are you doing here? Where's your coat?" The last question I ask while roughly pulling my coat off my body to give to her. The sight of her in just a thin sweater and jeans makes me wonder if she feels the cold at all. She doesn't seem to, but there's no way I'm letting her freeze out here.

"I'm fine," she asserts, pushing the jacket back at me.

I shove it back at her. "If you're staying, you're wearing this."

Before my mind can catch up with my actions enough to question why her staying here is even an option, she slides her arms through the sleeves. The coat swallows her, looking oversized on her small frame, but she doesn't seem to mind. In fact, it almost suits her, as if she could make even the most mismatched pieces look deliberate.

"Happy?" she asks, a frown that likely matched my own on her face.

"Ecstatic," I deadpan and look back at the alley, doing my best to ignore Carolina's presence...and not freeze to death.

But ignoring her is harder than it should be. Her proximity feels like it's altering the air itself, making it heavier, more charged. Her presence is an unnecessary distraction.

"You really shouldn't be here," I say after five minutes.

"Noted." Carolina tucks her hair behind her ear. "So, how are you liking Grove Meadow?"

Sighing, I turn back to the alley. "It's something." She lets out a *hmm* in agreement. "It's weird. I've never been here before, but I feel like I have. It's familiar."

I blink. I didn't know where that came from, but it was true. I'd had the recurring feeling of déjà vu almost everywhere I went, but I was sure I'd never even come near this area of the East Coast before.

"Our town is strange that way," she says, picking a piece of fuzz off my jacket. Her fingers linger on the fabric a second too long, like she's thinking of saying more but chooses not to. "Lots of people say that. I think they just watch a lot of television."

"Maybe. It's different. It's just a feeling," I explain, trying to keep my gaze on the alley, but I find it drifting back to her.

My eyes move on their own accord, drawn to the curve of her profile, the way the dim streetlight casts a soft glow on her skin.

This is why stakeouts are better alone.

"Why did you come here?"

She inspects her nails, even though they're perfectly manicured. "To see if I was right." She glances at me. "I like to be right."

A laugh escapes my mouth. "You like to be right so much you're willing to potentially watch some sort of satanic ritual with me?"

"Well, at least you'd know I had nothing to do with it. If I'm here with you, you can keep your eye on me."

I open my mouth to respond, but the words die before they reach my lips. My eyes drop to her mouth instead, lingering longer than they should. I blink out of my daze when I realize it. *What was wrong with me?*

"Right. So, where did this whole *the Castillos are witches* thing come from?"

Carolina sighs and faces forward, her gaze trained on the windshield. "It was a long time ago. When my grandparents moved here, they opened an apothecary shop. *Abuelo* was a doctor in Veracruz and specialized in herbal remedies and homeopathic practices."

I nod. "So naturally, they thought it was witchcraft."

She tilts her head back and forth slightly. "It wasn't really that, so much as they were Hispanic, and they moved to a predominantly White small town in New England."

"Ah."

That single sound carried more weight than I'd intended. Small towns like Grove Meadow could be places where old prejudices festered, and the Castillo family, it seemed, had borne the brunt of it.

"They really doubled-down on the witchcraft when my mother and father got together."

My brows knit together in confusion when Carolina hesitates in her explanation. She looks away, her eyes distant as if recalling something painful. There's a flash of something—

maybe anger, maybe hurt—but it's gone as quickly as it appeared.

"They said that she *bewitched* him like it was the only way he would have been interested in her. If my father hadn't been part of the founding families, I think it wouldn't have been so bad, but…"

Her face is solemn, like she's trying to pretend that she doesn't care about what she's saying, but my chest constricts for her. The way her voice tightens when she speaks of her family, the quiet pain that seeps through—it hits me harder than I expect.

"That must have been hard on you and Camila."

She shrugs. "Our family was close, but when our parents died, it got harder. The town tried to distance themselves from us more…like we were cursed or something." She says it with a laugh, but it's a harsh sound.

I learn more about her every time I talk to her, but just when I think I'm chipping away at a layer, another one presents itself. Opening up so that she can close herself off more tightly.

"Carolina, I'm sor–"

Just then, a sound from across the street catches my attention, and I see someone walking down the sidewalk across from where we are. They're wearing a hoodie and jeans. I try to make out who it is beneath the hood, but I don't recognize them.

"Elijah Thorton," Carolina whispers. "He's a little eccentric but harmless. Calls himself an *inventor*, but mostly is employed as the town's handyman."

He might be looking for discarded scraps to repurpose, but I had to be sure. Something about the way he's walking doesn't sit right with me. It's too purposeful, too focused.

"Stay here," I tell Carolina as I grab my walkie-talkie and open my door. "I mean it."

Carolina's eyes are wide as she stares at me, but I don't have time to wait for a verbal confirmation that she'll listen to me. Though I have a niggling feeling that she won't.

Slamming the door after me, I quietly jog across the street to the entrance of the alley, but it's empty when I get there. The space is lit by intermittent lamposts, two of which are out, and one flickers in my periphery. The darkness feels heavier here, pressing in from all sides. It's like the air has thickened, and I can feel the hair on the back of my neck stand on end. I squint to try and see better into the darkness.

Why would Elijah come down here?

A familiar sinking feeling settles in my gut—the same feeling I get when I know something's about to go wrong. I hear Carolina's footsteps approaching behind me. Of course, she didn't listen.

"I told you to wait in the car," I say without looking at her, my gaze darting to all of the dark corners of the alleyway.

"I thought you could use some backup," she whispers back at me.

I don't have time to fight her on this if Elijah could be involved in the disappearances. "Just stay behind me."

Carolina's presence looms closely behind me as we move further into the alley. There's a strong odor that coats my nose, and I recognize it as rotten eggs. *Sulfur.*

The smell brings with it a sense of dread, creeping up my spine and settling between my shoulders. Something is here, something dangerous. The muscles in my back tighten, and I put a hand on my gun, prepared to draw it if things go south.

The alley leads to a dead-end, a cement wall that separates the town from the woods. I know we're only a few steps away from seeing Elijah unless he's scaled the wall.

When he comes into view, I stop dead in my tracks. I'm surprised to find him just standing there in the middle of the alley, facing the dead-end. He doesn't move. Doesn't turn around. It's like he's frozen.

I swallow the sense of foreboding lodged in my throat and the urge to tell Carolina to run. My instincts are screaming now, louder than ever, and all I can think is that she shouldn't be here. I wish she would've stayed in the car. *Hell, I wish she would've stayed home.*

"Elijah Thorton," I call out to him, straightening up and trying to block Carolina from view.

He turns his head over his shoulder. I can see his mouth moving but can't hear what he's saying. It's like he's whispering to someone just out of sight, but there's no one else here.

It's Carolina's gasp that makes me notice his eyes.

They're pitch black. No whites. No pupils. Just an endless, empty blackness that seems to swallow what little light is around us.

"*Fates,*" Carolina breathes.

"Elijah Thorton, my name is Declan O'Reilly. I'm a Detective with the police department, and I'm going to need you—"

My words get cut off because I see something gathering in his hand. The alley somehow gets darker, but a light begins to glow from Elijah's hand.

"Now!" Carolina shouts, and three things happen at once.

I reach for my gun at my hip. Carolina darts in front of me, tossing something onto the ground in front of us. Elijah's hand moves suddenly, and I feel a sharp pain in my lower abdomen.

I hear Carolina's voice again as I drop to my knees, but I don't feel it when they make contact with the ground beneath me. I don't feel anything.

13
CAROLINA

I see the energy ball of blue static leave Elijah's hand, the crackling sound echoing through the alley like the crack of a whip. It pulses with unnatural power, twisting the air around it.

Everything moves in slow motion. As if by the Fates' design, the moment the energy ball passes across the perimeter of the crystal cage, charged strands of golden light emerge from the five crystals Camila and I placed around the alley and unite at an apex above Elijah's head.

Then, time seems to speed up again. The alley is filled with a hum of magic, so thick it feels like it's pressing against my skin. I feel the energy woosh past me, locked on its target. It's too fast for me to do anything about it. *Bullseye.*

"No!" The word is a choked plea as I try to catch Declan before he drops to his knees.

He's a dead weight against my body, and I struggle to hold him upright. I do my best to gently guide him to the ground, summoning my magic for a bauble of extra strength. The air crackles with static energy, a tangible tension that almost feels alive. It buzzes in my ears, mixing with the frantic pounding of my pulse.

My emotions are too chaotic for me to try to do more than that. I can feel my magic flickering inside me, chaotic and desperate, as if it's trying to fight against the inevitability of what just happened.

No, no, no. This wasn't supposed to happen. My being here was supposed to prevent all of this.

Why did I lose everyone? My parents, my grandparents. It's like the Fates brought people into my life just to take them away.

"Camila!" I yell while trying to pull Declan's upper body onto my lap. Camila would heal him, and everything would be fine. He would be fine, and the giant hole burning in my chest would go away.

There's a grunt from behind me. "A little busy, Caro! I could use a hand!"

A crushing sense of sadness spreads throughout me that I can't explain. I don't even know him, so why was this affecting me so much? I should be more preoccupied with helping Camila trap the demon 10 feet away from us.

My hands pull at Declan's sweater, trying to find where the energy ball hit him. Aside from a patch of red, welted skin, I don't see any other injuries. Fingers pressed against his neck, I feel his pulse slowing, and I panic all over again.

"Carolina! The sooner you help me, the sooner I can heal him." Camila's voice has a tone of desperation that wasn't there before.

Right. Focus, Carolina. I close my eyes, inhaling deeply, trying to force the panic down. *Demon first, detective later.*

"I'll be right back," I whisper to him, like he can hear me. Maybe he can. I *hope* he can.

As soon as I turn to her, I see the problem. Elijah—or rather, the demon inside him—has completely lost control. His eyes are wild, black pits of malice, and his movements are frenzied. Relentlessly attacking the cage, he's firing energy ball after energy ball at it without tiring. Each hit rattles the cage, the golden strands trembling but holding. I wonder just how much of a toll their magic takes on them and if it's anywhere near ours.

I cringe at the sound a particularly large blast at the cage makes.

"I don't think we can transport it while he's doing that," Camila says. "I'm worried it's not going to hold him."

I chew on my lip and flex my hands at my side. My magic pulses beneath my skin, desperate to do something, but it's divided. Half of it is pulling me toward the demon, the other half tethered to Declan, lying unconscious behind me.

"Think we can use a spell to knock him out?"

Camila shrugs, but I can feel the anxiety radiating from her. "Worth a shot."

My hand closes around hers as we begin an incantation our grandparents used on us more times than we can count. Before our magic came in, we thought it was just a lullaby our family would tell us. Safe to say, we felt pretty betrayed when we got older and learned they'd been spelling us to sleep.

By the stars that softly gleam,
Let them drift into a dream.
Eyes grow heavy, breath so deep,
Fall now gently into sleep.
Whispers of peace, soft and slow,
To the realm of rest you go.
Restful night until the morn,

Wake refreshed when day is born.

In the cage, Elijah's movements slow with every line we recite. His arms drop to his sides, his head lolling forward as if the weight of the world has finally caught up with him. His eyelids grow heavy, and he stumbles, fighting to keep himself upright. He loses, collapsing to the ground.

The second I'm sure he's not going to pop back up, I turn back to Declan. The pull to him is magnetic, overpowering. I'm by his side before I even realize I've moved.

I swallow the growing feeling of apprehension and try to stay calm as Camila crouches beside him and places her hand on his chest. The seconds stretch out, feeling like hours. Every beat of my heart is excruciating as I wait for Camila to work her magic.

I'm holding a breath that I only let out when I see the steady rise and fall of his chest resume. The red-marred skin doesn't heal, but Camila removes her hand.

"I don't want to over-heal him. It'll have to wait until he's conscious," she says, standing.

Camila's powerful enough that her magic targets anything that might eventually decay. It's like watering a plant—give it too much water, it'll drown.

For that reason, Camila tends to assess injuries in piece-meal ways, but in this case...

"Unless you think there's a way to explain this situation without telling him," she says when I don't respond.

I shake my head slowly, resigned. "No, I know we'll have to." Now that Declan is breathing, I can think more clearly. "Let's get them both back to the shop. We'll put Declan in the pantry and Elijah in the attic."

I wave my hand over him and allow my magic to guide his

body into the air, and a flick of my wrist allows me to shimmer his visibility. I can't see him anymore, but I can sense him.

Camila does the same to Elijah before collecting the crystals from the ground.

"Silas and Luna will be so proud," she says as we begin our trek home. Our hostages floating silently behind us, non-existent to the naked eye.

"Babies' first demon," I laugh.

We settle into a silence, and we're halfway home before Camila breaks it. "Are we going to talk about…"

"No."

"Got it."

My reaction to Declan—that's what she wants to talk about. Even if I did want to talk about it, I wouldn't know where to start. I can't explain the way my magic reacts to him, the way it pulls me toward him like a magnet. Since he first walked into the shop, my magic had called out to him for some reason.

It had grown attached to him. Comfortably alive in his presence.

Whatever its reason for wanting him, I couldn't give into it. He was here to solve the case and go home. Whether he knew we were witches or not, I wouldn't get involved with him.

I'd never been a curious child. I didn't wonder about why things were or how things happened. I stuck to rules and routines. They were there for a reason, and I found no reason to deviate from them.

Camila had been the wild child. Restless. Always exploring and interested in testing boundaries.

No doubt, if she were in my position, she'd have climbed the detective with the blue eyes and scruffy beard like a tree already.

Like calls to like, my magic whispers to me again.

I roll my eyes.

No.

There would be no climbing. No exploring. No curiosity. Not with him.

I'd already almost gotten him killed once. That was enough.

14

DECLAN

There's a pulsing in my lower left abdomen and pressure on my chest. It's uncomfortable, like something heavy is sitting right on top of me, making it hard to breathe. I groan as I open my eyes, blinking them rapidly to clear my vision.

Where the hell am I?

As my eyes adjust, I realize I don't recognize anything. The ceiling is not the same white popcorn one I wake up to every morning. This one is high and has wooden beams that run across it.

As I try to shift myself into a sitting position, I see the cause of my chest problem but wince at the pain that shoots through my side. Sharp, immediate, like a knife digging into my skin.

A black cat on top of me blinks slowly like it's trying to understand what I'm doing here. *Same.*

"Oh, good, you're awake," Camila Castillo says from across the room. Her voice startles me. I didn't even realize she was there. "Silas, get off of him," she snaps at the black cat.

It doesn't, but it does narrow its eyes at me, and I feel judged. *I hate cats.*

"How's your side doing?" Camila asks, walking quickly toward me with a glass of water.

Her eyes are bright with concern, but there's a casualness to her movements like she's used to dealing with this kind of thing.

I look around at the room, wondering if I've somehow ended up in the Castillo sisters' living room. It's ornate and decorated with large pieces of antique furniture. An array of Persian rugs is tastefully layered, one on top of the other. The room is bright, and it drastically contrasts the colors of the coffee shop. I wonder if it was Camila's doing.

"Uh, hurts a little...where's Carolina?" I ask, attempting to sit up again, but I give up when the pain flares again. The cat, still perched on my chest, meows loudly.

"She's dealing with a problem upstairs," she says, setting down the glass on the table in front of the couch I'm lying on. "I'm supposed to wait for her to come back downstairs before I help you with that injury, but we also thought you'd be out longer."

I frown at her. *How could she help me?* "What happened?"

Trying to piece together the fragments of my memory wasn't going well. It's like trying to grasp smoke—every time I think I've got a piece, it slips away. Carolina and I had followed Elijah Thorton into the alley, and then...nothing.

I should check in with Bas, but based on a quick check of my pockets, I don't have my phone on me.

"Uh...best to wait for Carolina. She should be back any second." Camila's face and voice are apologetic.

I'm battling two sides of my personality. The one that wants all of the information immediately and the one that knows that the truth has a way of revealing itself when the time calls for it. I want to give her the benefit of the doubt, so I reorient to the cat still sitting on my chest.

"This must be Silas."

Camila gives me a small smile, possibly because she's grateful for my forced patience. "Yes, he's our cat."

I raise a brow at her. "Carolina was very clear that Silas is your cat." I drop my voice to a whisper like he can understand me when I say, "I don't think she likes him much."

Silas rears back on my chest. His eyes narrow into tiny slits, and for a second, I'm almost convinced he understands every word I'm saying. "Well, she's no peach either."

I blink and realize I must have hit my head, because it sounded like that came from the animal in front of me. I watch him as he leaps onto the table and slinks away.

Camila laughs nervously. "Yeah, Silas is an...acquired taste."

"Right." I don't know what else to say. Everything feels slightly off, like I'm missing some crucial detail that would make sense of this entire bizarre situation.

When the door opens behind her, Camila lets out an audible sigh of relief.

"Thank the cauldron. Everything go okay?" she asks, turning to her sister who looks like she just went three rounds with a wild animal. I almost jolt forward, but the pain reminds me there's a reason I'm lying here.

Carolina wipes her right eye with the back of her hand and frowns. "Well, I'm alive, so by all accounts—Oh, hi," she says when we make eye contact.

I *definitely* must have hit my head because Carolina's eyes soften under my gaze, which has never happened in any of the times we've been in a room together.

My eyes dart from her to Camila to Silas, who's found a new resting spot on a large table across the room. The entire scene feels surreal, like I've stepped into an alternate universe where cats talk and Carolina Castillo actually seems to care about me.

Perhaps the only explanation for this situation is that I did actually hit my head in the alley and landed myself in a coma.

That would make sense. Coma dreams are supposed to be weird, right? A rather unfortunate one if I'm still feeling this pain in my side, but now that I've realized it's a coma, maybe it doesn't—*Nope, still hurts.*

Carolina hurries to my side at my grimace. Her movements are quick, almost frantic, like she can't stand to see me in pain. It's unnerving.

"Camila," Carolina says.

I'm not the only one who thinks Carolina is acting differently because even her sister shoots her a confused glance at her concern. Camila's eyebrows lift, and she looks between the two of us like she's missed some crucial development. *Me, too.*

"I was waiting for you."

"He's in *pain*," she replies like Camila should have obviously been trying to help me. Aside from offering me an aspirin, I'm not sure what exactly she could be doing.

Camila blinks slowly at her sister, and her eyes move to me and back again. It's like there's some silent conversation happening between them, something I'm not privy to.

"Sorry," she finally says and turns to me. "I'm going to finish healing this for you, but you must be very still. It will feel a little strange, but it shouldn't hurt."

Healing? Did she just say healing? If I'm not in a coma, I'm in a dream, at the very least. There's no other explanation for the strange things coming out of her mouth. Carolina hovers above me, watching her sister as she pulls up my sweater and places her hand against my skin. I jolt at her cold hand.

"*Camila.*" Carolina's voice has more than a hint of impatience.

Camila rolls her eyes. "If you're going to fuss, go away. I've done this a million times, Caro. When you become an expert healer, you can scold me. Until then, *zip it.*"

Healer?

I've given up tracking this conversation. It is too confusing and nonsensical to follow, so I let them continue their bickering until something pulses inside me. The sensation is strange—like a warmth spreading through my body, soothing the pain but leaving an odd tingling in its place.

It occurs to me then that if I wasn't dreaming, I should be asking quite a few questions. Namely, "what are you doing?"

"Healing your wound." She says it so simply, like this is something totally normal.

"Right...and where did this wound come from exactly?"

Camila glances up at her sister, and they share a silent exchange. "It's a long story," Carolina says at the same time Camila removes her hand from my stomach. "You should be able to sit up now."

I suck in a breath to prepare for the pain, but it doesn't come as I push myself into a sitting position. I'm shocked—there's no pain, no residual ache. It's like the injury never existed.

"What do you remember?" Carolina asks. Her voice is soft, but there's an intensity to her gaze that makes me pause.

"Not much. Everything after following Elijah into the alley is a blank." I try to recall more, but the memories are foggy, still just out of reach.

"And what do you think happened?"

All three of them are watching me closely. "I must have fallen and hit my head."

Silas narrows his eyes at me, and Camila lets out a relieved sigh before looking at her sister. Carolina shakes her head slowly in return.

"Is that...not what happened?" I ask hesitantly.

Camila and Carolina are locked in a staring contest. The tension between them is palpable, like they're arguing without saying a word.

For a moment, I think they didn't hear me, but then Camila stands abruptly.

"We'll let you two talk. Come on, Silas," she says, leaving out the door Carolina entered through with Silas tucked against her body.

The air in the room shifts once Camila is gone. It's like all the tension left with her, but something else lingers—something between me and Carolina that wasn't there before. Just like in the car, I feel drawn to Carolina, but the feeling has grown impossibly more desperate.

I want to touch her, but I don't.

A part of me knows I should be wary, that I should be searching for my phone to call Bas or my walkie-talkie to radio someone at the station. But that part of me is minuscule, almost non-existent.

The rest of me feels safe and unconcerned.

Right, coma.

This dreamlike state explains everything. I read somewhere that there are no phones in dreams, so it makes sense that I wouldn't have mine. My tongue flicks over my teeth to make sure they haven't started to fall out. *Classic anxiety dream.*

All my teeth are firmly planted, but Carolina's behavior also makes more sense this way. Only in my dreams—or a parallel universe—would she look at me like she cared.

She sighs, her mouth setting in her usual pout, but her eyes still hold that semblance of warmth. I hold onto it like a lifesaver.

"You didn't hit your head, Declan."

Declan, she said. Not *Detective*. I was *Declan* now. I want her to say it again.

"I didn't?"

She sits on the edge of the table in front of the sofa I'm on, crossing her arms over her chest. She's in the same tight black sweater and jeans that she had on in the car. Despite everything, despite the insanity of this situation, my eyes can't help but follow the curve of her body.

Even in a coma, I didn't have a crazy imagination. *Bummer*.

"No, you were...attacked."

My brows dip low. "Attacked? By whom?" Maybe I was wrong about the imagination thing. "Elijah?"

"Technically," she says, her eyes rolling toward the ceiling like there might be something inscribed there to help her with this situation.

"Carolina."

There's the sigh again. It's becoming a pattern now, this reluctance to say what's really going on. "I haven't been... honest with you."

My skin starts to prickle, and I swallow a bulb of dread that has made its way up my throat as possibilities for what she's about to say filter into my head.

My mind races through the options, none of them good. Was she behind these disappearances after all? Did she know who it was? Had she come on the stakeout with me for another reason?

"You see..." she starts, her eyes glued to her fingers pulling at a loose thread on the stitching of her jeans. "Camila and I are..."

I start to laugh. I can't help it. The tension is too much, and the only logical explanation is something ridiculous.

"Carolina, if you're about to say that you and Camila are

witches, I will have no choice but to confirm my theory that I am in a coma."

She frowns at me. "What? Declan, you're not in a coma. You are very much awake and alive."

"Well, that's good." *I think.*

Her lips pull together as she considers her words again. "But, it's true. Camila and I are witches. You're here because a demon attacked you, and Camila had to heal the wound on your stomach. You did almost die."

I'm staring at her more intensely than I ever have, looking for any indication she's lying to me.

The laugh that leaves my mouth this time is different. It's a hollow sound, filled with disbelief. "Yeah...sure, you are, Carolina."

"You don't believe me?" she asks, standing and looking... annoyed that I'm doubting her.

I stand, too. Surprised that there isn't any pain that flares again.

"Well, it's just a little...ridiculous to think you and your sister have magical powers. Don't you think?"

She frowns. Her expression darkens, and for the first time, I feel like I've actually offended her. "Camila just healed you. How do you explain *that*?"

Well, I wasn't entirely convinced Camila "healed" me. I didn't remember being injured and sure, my skin was a little red, but I could have just bruised it. There was hardly enough evidence to label them as *witches*.

"Maybe I tweaked a muscle, and it relaxed while I was lying down."

Carolina scoffs. "Unbelievable. This town has been trying to get us to admit this for decades, and when I do, you don't even believe it." She's shaking her head at me now, and then she stops, her eyes lighting with an idea.

"Carolina—"

My warning falls short as we're blanketed in shadows that fill the room.

15

CAROLINA

I don't even need to wave my hand to do it. Summoning shadows has always been second nature to me, as easy as breathing. Closing myself off to the environment. Encasing myself in darkness and not letting anything break the shroud. The shadows respond to my emotions, curling around me like a protective blanket, muting the world beyond us.

The shadows stretch and swirl, filling every corner of the room like they've been waiting for this moment. Declan and I can see each other, but the room beyond the shadows is hidden from sight. It's as if the space between us and the rest of the world has dissolved, and nothing else exists outside this cocoon of darkness.

Declan sucks in a breath. I probably could have warned him.

His blue eyes are wide as they move around the room. I'm watching him try to find an explanation for it in real time. His gaze fixates on the corners of the room like a fog machine is going to appear suddenly.

He's waiting for some logical reveal, but I can see the exact moment when it dawns on him that this is real, that he's in my world now.

I don't rush him. I don't even roll my eyes. I just wait for him to say something.

When he finally does, his voice doesn't hold the fear I expected but rather a blanket of awe that wraps around me.

"God, you're a *witch*. A real, honest-to-God witch. I thought..." He blinks, scratching the back of his head. "I don't know what I thought."

"Probably that I was crazy," I say, lifting a shoulder in a half-shrug.

"Something like that. Camila? She can do the..." He waves his hand around in the air, searching for words, "...the shadow thing too?"

"*Declan*, a witchling could 'do the shadow thing.'"

He looks offended. "Sorry, I didn't realize encasing a room in shadows was *infantile*, Carolina." There's a playful defensiveness in his voice, but beneath it, I can still hear the awe.

I couldn't believe we were arguing about this. He's taking this far better than I thought he would. Most people would've bolted by now. I tell him as much.

"You're taking this pretty well." I drop the shadows around us. The room brightens instantly, like the shadows were never there at all, but the shift in the atmosphere lingers between us.

"I'm not entirely convinced this isn't a dream, but in the event this is real, I'd like to remember being cool about it in the future." Declan's head swivels around the room, his hands reaching out to touch shadows that were long gone. "So, Camila..."

"Witch."

"Parents?" he asks, his eyes finally settling on my face. There's a seriousness in his expression now, a need to understand more.

"Mom was a witch. Her parents were witches, too."

"And your dad?"

"Just a white man."

"Typical," he says. Then his eyes widen when they drift down my body. "Uh...Carolina..."

It's then that I notice Luna has coiled herself around my body. Well, I noticed when she did it, but I'm only just now realizing that her existence is quite frightening to other people.

"You said you'd stop doing that!" Luna says, unwrapping herself from my body. "Do you know what it's like to be napping under the couch just to be suddenly catapulted into complete darkness? You awful girl," she hisses.

I ignore her squawking. Luna has always had a flair for the dramatic. "Luna, this is Declan."

"Oh good, you see the snake, too," he says, his voice raising multiple octaves and his skin paling. "Good, good, good. I just—"

Declan falls back on the couch, seemingly passed out from shock. I don't even try to catch him—it's clear that the combination of shadows and a talking snake has been too much for him.

"Well, that's embarrassing," Luna remarks.

I raise my eyebrows at her. "That's embarrassing? You're almost 800 years old and afraid of shadows."

"I. Was. *Sleeping*."

"Right," I say as the door opens.

Camila walks in with Silas close behind her. The energy in the room shifts again, lighter now that Camila is here. She always has a way of bringing calm with her.

Her eyes widen when she sees Declan sprawled on the couch. "Oh, dear. Luna, you scared him."

"You owe me $10," Silas gloats, hopping onto the potion table.

"Silas," Camila hisses and then looks at me with a guilty

expression. "Sorry, I thought the shadows would have got him."

I glare at her. "How did you know I would use the shadows?"

"Oh, just a hunch. Anyway, did you get anything from the demon upstairs?"

She thinks I used the shadows because that's how Mom told Dad she was a witch. Of course, she had planned to tell him, and they'd been on a date while I was just desperately looking for some way to prove I was telling the truth—a totally different circumstance.

I cast a weary glance at Declan, but I know he's fine where he is on the couch. He'll wake up soon enough, and then the real questions will start.

"Not much. Lots of obscenities, not a lot of answers," I shrug, walking over to her. I can still hear the demon's growling voice in my head, but nothing useful came out of him. "Is the veritas potion almost done?"

Camila nods. "Yes, it just needs to simmer. It should be done in the next hour or so. What are we doing about the Declan situation?"

The Declan situation. "Not sure. I think once the initial shock wears off, he's going to have questions, and we'll either need to wipe his memory or answer those questions."

Confusion crosses over Camila's face. "If you were just going to cast a memory spell, why bother telling him in the first place?"

Why, indeed.

Like calls to like, my magic whispers.

Enough with that, I tell it.

)　)　)　●　(　(　(

"I don't understand. There are bad witches called 'demons,' and they're the ones who are kidnapping all of these people from town?" We've relocated to the shop, where he's sitting at one of the tables asking us questions while Camila and I are working on the veritas potion behind the counter.

When he woke up again, we returned his phone to him, and for some reason, that was what made everything real to him—not the shadows or the talking cat and snake...the phone.

"So you do understand," I say, tossing an herb into the pot with the potion in it.

"But *why?*"

"We're not exactly sure, but there's this prophecy, and we think they're trying to summon this super evil being and take over the Mortal World." Camila's voice is dripping with her usual sunshine, and it dramatically juxtaposes her response.

"Oh, is that all." Declan's sarcasm is back, but there's an edge to it. He's trying to keep up, but I can tell this is more than he bargained for.

"I mean, probably not, but it's all we've got."

"But that's why," Camila starts, uncorking a small glass bottle and ladling the liquid into it, "we have this. Let's get some answers, shall we?"

Declan follows silently behind us as we climb the stairs to the attic.

He doesn't point out that, structurally, we should not have an attic. So, I don't have to tell him that magic has a way of being deceptive to the untrained eye.

He *also* doesn't point out that, technically, we've taken

Elijah Thorton hostage, which is most definitely a crime. So I *also* don't have to tell him that the demon has taken over Elijah's body *and* that if the demon is able to extract Elijah's soul and complete whatever summoning they're working on, it would probably lead to the downfall of man, not just Grove Meadow. Assuming the prophecy is right, that is.

Getting Elijah "settled" in the attic had been a battle. Once he'd come to, he resumed his attacks on the reformed crystal cage. The golden strands of magic shook with every collision. I cast a reinforcement spell for good measure.

When we get to the attic, Elijah is sitting in the center of the cage with his eyes closed and his legs crossed underneath him. It's eerily calm. Too calm. The kind of calm that makes my skin crawl.

When Silas walks in front of the enclosure, Elijah pops one solid black eye open and appears to track Silas as he walks across the room.

"Silas, good to see you." His voice is different, deeper, more guttural. It's a jarring reminder that Elijah is no longer in control.

The three of us don't react, and Camila throws the veritas potion into the cage. The magic of the crystals lets the vial pass through it and shatter on the ground in front of Elijah. The liquid turns into a gas that fills the space, stopping at the boundaries of the crystals, and then clears a moment later. Both of Elijah's eyes are open now, but he's fixated squarely on Camila.

"What's your name?" she asks.

He tilts his head at her, and it's difficult to separate this creature from the Elijah we'd grown up around—the one who tinkered in his garage with the door open so he could chat with his neighbors as he worked. Kids used his driveaway at the end of the cul-de-sac as a loop, and when tires needed air or chains needed realigning, he did it happily.

The man who had always been so kind, so present, was now just a vessel for something dark and twisted.

I hoped when this was over, there was a soul left to save. The thought of losing him completely gnaws at me, but I can't dwell on it now.

"I have many names, but the one your familiar might recognize is Nightcrawler."

The name sends a chill down my spine. I don't know why I expected demons to have normal names. John. Damien, perhaps.

Silas turns his head to us. His eyes are sharp, and I can tell he's already figured it out. "He's a lower-level demon. They're sent to do higher-level demons' dirty work."

Nightcrawler hisses at the comment, and I frown. The sound is like nails on a chalkboard, grating and unnatural. It is far too late to *nope* out of this whole thing, but dissociating from all of this is looking pretty good right now.

"Who sent you?" Camila asks.

The veins on his neck appear to jut out, and he looks like he's having trouble breathing. I wonder if the truth potion hadn't been strong enough when his skin starts to turn an interesting shade of purple.

"I do not know their names," Nightcrawler finally bites out.

"But there are two of them?" I ask, stepping forward. "Two demons?"

His fingers dig into the skin on his face and drag down his cheeks, leaving deep scratch marks behind. The sight is grotesque, and I feel bile rise in my throat. I grimace at the sight of blood streaking from them and hear Declan's sharp intake of breath, but I don't turn to look at him.

"Not demons." Nightcrawler's voice has become more panicked and desperate. There's fear in his voice now, and that scares me more than anything else. *Not demons? Were witches doing this?* "I will not betray them. They are trying to save our kind."

Just like in the alley, an energy ball begins to form in his hand, blue light illuminating the air around him. *What is he—*

"No!" I shout, but I can't do anything to stop him.

Nightcrawler launches the energy at the cage with enough force that it bounces back at him, and his entire body goes up in flames. The smell of burning flesh fills the room, and his screams echo in my head. It's over in seconds, but the image of him engulfed in fire is seared into my mind.

All that's left of the demon is the pile of ash on the ground in the crystal cage. The silence that follows is deafening.

"So...that's not good," Camila whispers from beside me.

Silas circles her legs in a gesture of comfort. "Well, at least we stopped the summoning."

"Right, but they'll try again," I note, kicking the crystal out of place and breaking the cage that once held Elijah. My foot nudges the ash, and the finality of what just happened sinks in.

Declan looks grim when I look at him. "Are you okay?"

His blue eyes seem less like pools of cerulean and more like hard sapphires now, an edge to them. "I will be when we catch who's behind this. We should all get some rest and start fresh tomorrow."

There's a weariness in his voice that wasn't there before. I want to ask him how he's really feeling, but it's not the time, and he doesn't seem to feel like sharing. He's pulling away, retreating into his thoughts.

I also don't want him to leave, but I can't say that either. I know it's my magic and its weird obsession with him, but it's distracting me from the present danger here in town.

On our way down the stairs, Declan says, "I can take the couch."

Camila freezes on the second-floor landing. "You're going to stay here? Even though you just watched a demon kill itself upstairs?"

"My chances of survival are probably better with two witches, a giant snake, and a talking cat," Declan explains like it couldn't be more obvious.

"Fair enough," Camila nods and continues her walk.

I ignore the feeling of my magic rejoicing at the news that Declan will remain nearby. It swells inside me, warm and satisfied, but I push it down.

Don't even say it, I warn my magic, and for once, it listens to me...which is never a good sign.

16

CAROLINA

The dream feels like it's moving in reverse. I can hear warped sounds and voices, and the world wooshes around me like a rollercoaster that only moves backward until I'm suddenly living a memory.

The air around me is hot, and my back is pressed against something...a wall, maybe. The surface is hard and uneven.

My hands are in his hair, and his mouth moves against mine like he's going to devour me. I haven't opened my eyes yet, but I'm sure it's a *him* based on the growing hardness against my thigh.

I want him. I want him so badly that my magic feels like it's prowling under my skin, waiting to explode. I need to control it, so I squeeze my eyes shut more tightly and focus on not unleashing my power on whatever unsuspecting room we're in.

Working against me, the emotions I'm feeling are so strong that I know this is a past life and not just an errant memory that's invaded my dreams. I feel wanted, cherished...loved. The feeling is unmistakable in my throat, in my mind, and in my body.

It's also foreign to me.

Being worshipped by someone isn't something I've ever experienced, but I'd imagine it feels like this.

Whoever this is belongs to me just as much as I belong to him.

One of his hands leaves my face and drops low on my body. Even through my clothes, it's like he's touching my skin when he presses on the most sensitive part of me.

My lips part, and I sigh when his mouth moves to my neck. His teeth scrape against my pulse, and his other hand tugs at my hair, tilting my head away to give him more access to my skin.

More. I want more from him. I need it.

Abruptly, he turns me around, and my eyes fly open as my hands come up to steady myself against the wooden wall. His fingers are quick to unlace the corseted back of my dress. His lips are at my neck again, and his fingertips drift along my spine before pulling the bodice down my body.

I feel, more than notice, my eyes closing again, trying to savor the feeling of him against me. His hands are at my breasts, and when they pinch my nipples, I suck in a sharp breath.

"Scream for me," he demands, his breath leaving goose-bumps in its wake.

When he tugs my nipples again, I let out a gasp, and that seems to appease him because he diverts his attention to other parts of me. His hands are firm on my skin, and I almost moan for him to be rougher with me.

"Grady Asher said you used your magic to get him into bed with you," his voice is low, threatening, but I don't need to tell him that Grady Asher is a liar. He already knows.

"And how did you take that?" I ask as my dress pools on the floor at my feet. My voice is breathy, and I grow impossibly wetter with the feeling of his gaze on my body.

There's a sharp sting against my rear as his hand makes contact. A moan slips through my lips as he kneads the flesh there.

"I told him even if you had magic, you'd never use it on him." I smile to myself when I hear the sound of his clothes hitting the floor. The anticipation of what's to come tightens the knot in my core, and I pull my bottom lip into my mouth. "That you're too busy sucking me off, and I don't share."

I feel my cheeks flame at his words. There's no possibility he said that to Grady Asher, but I'm tightening at the thought of him in my mouth.

It's then that I dare a look over my shoulder at him.

Mentally, I freeze, but physically, I'm already on my knees in front of Declan.

I peer at him from beneath my lashes and run my fingers up his thighs, my nails digging into his skin. Taking him in my hand, I squeeze his length, and he bucks forward in my grip.

His hand laces in my hair and pulls my head forward. I smile against his head as he lets out a frustrated murmur of my name. My lips wrap around his tip, and my tongue flexes against him while I create a seal with my mouth.

I feel like I'm going crazy. Everything about this makes me want him even more than before, but I'm still reeling from seeing him.

Another life. Another version of us was together. Another version of him loved me irrevocably.

His head tips back as I draw him further into my mouth and dig my nails into his thighs even more like I'm desperate to mark him as my own.

I can tell he likes it because he sucks in a breath, and his fingers press into my scalp, working me further down his shaft. He hits the back of my throat, and my eyes water, but I don't pull back.

If he wanted to devour me, I'd return the favor.

At least, I try to before he pulls back and sets me on top of what looks to be a desk.

I still have no idea where we are. I can't even be sure *when* we are, but it's inconsequential.

There's a sense of urgency to his movements that I write off as desire, but I should have looked closer.

His hands force my thighs open so he can step between them. He notches himself inside me an inch at a time, and my body accepts him readily. I wish he'd move faster. I wish he'd slam against me so hard that I feel it in every part of me.

I want him to ruin me.

He must sense it because his hips are suddenly moving at an unforgiving pace. It feels like he's using me for release rather than something more, and I love it.

Maybe because I know that after this, he'll return to himself. That we drive each other so wild that we forget there's more than just this moment in time.

His fingers dig into my waist, and I groan, tipping my head back. I'm so close. I know he can feel it, with how tightly I'm clenching around him.

His hand skims up my body and rests against my neck. It's just a light squeeze, but I explode around him, and he grunts at the sensation and grinds himself further against me.

It's starlight and shadows behind my eyelids, and it feels endless. I'm suspended in this moment in time and so lost in the experience that I can't remember when it started or how long it's been.

When I come down, his pace picks up, and it's only a moment before he stills and pulses inside me.

My magic flickers, and I'm made aware of its presence for the first time in this dream. Usually, I can feel it throughout a memory, but not this one.

Our breathing is rough. We're both trying to control it, but he kisses me anyway. His mouth moves against mine urgently, biting down when he pulls my lip between his. It makes me warm and wanton all over again.

When he pulls away this time, he rests his forehead on mine, and I feel my magic pulse again at the connection it senses between us.

His eyes lighten even more like he can feel it too, but that's impossible. Dream me doesn't feel concerned, and so neither do I. Instead, we're locked in this silent exchange that is somehow more erotic than what we just did.

The sound of people approaching from the outside snaps us out of the heady silence, and he quickly slips out of me, a look of panicked acceptance flashing across his features.

"It's us in every lifetime," he whispers, pressing my hand to his lips. "We'll find each other again, my love. I swear it."

"By the old Gods and the new," I hear myself tell him.

The banging on the door begins, and the smell of smoke finds its way into my nose. It's only then does the weight of what's about to happen press against me.

We're about to die.

17

DECLAN

When I first saw the old alarm clock with bright red digits beside the bed in the Castillos' guest room, I thought it was charming. Now, at 2:45 a.m., it's mocking me. The bright red numbers are like eyes staring at me in the dark, taunting me with every minute that passes. While the rest of Grove Meadow sleeps, I keep turning over the day's events.

I can't stop my mind from racing, going in circles around the same impossible truths.

Carolina Castillo is a witch.

So is her sister, and they have a talking cat and a reticulated python as pets.

Elijah Thorton is dead, and it's likely all of the other people who went missing are too.

We still don't know who's behind the disappearances, but a demon under a truth spell said it wasn't other demons, which left...humans or witches.

Carolina Castillo is a witch.

The thought loops in my head like a broken record. Again and again, the cycle turns in my head, even when I beg it to stop. I try to think rationally, to piece it all together like a puzzle, but every time I get close to clarity, another piece shifts out of place.

I should be afraid of Carolina and Camila, but I can't bring myself to be. It was clear that if they wanted to harm me, they would have done so already.

Or, at the very least, if they wanted to keep me away from them, they could have cast a spell on me. But they didn't, and Carolina told me her secret. *Showed me* her secret. That had to mean something.

Trust. That's what it had to be. Why else would she have let me in on a world I didn't even know existed?

Maybe they trusted me.

Not that I'd given them a reason to. I'd come here to interrogate them and close this case. While I was getting closer to doing the latter, I never imagined investigating the girls would turn into...this.

When the mocking red digits turn to 3:00 a.m., the screaming starts, and I jump out of bed. The sound rips through the silence, sharp and panicked. My heart jumps into my throat, and adrenaline surges through me before my brain even registers what's happening.

I grab my gun from the bedside drawer and slowly walk to the door. Every muscle in my body is tense, hyperaware of the smallest sounds. I grimace when a floorboard creaks under my weight but continue down the hallway and end up in front of Carolina's door—the source of the cacophony.

Her screams are like nothing I've ever heard before—raw, guttural, like she's being torn apart from the inside. I don't knock before opening the door.

The room is dark, but the curtain in front of her window is open, so it lets in some of the light from the moon, and I can make out her shape in the bed. Carolina's screams have turned to wails of agony, like something is hurting her, but there's nothing in the room, and she's asleep.

Just a nightmare.

Relief floods through me, but it's short-lived. If this is what her nightmares are like, I can't even imagine what she's been through.

Placing my gun on her bedside table, I see she has the same alarm clock, and I wonder if it plagues her as much as it does me. That same red glow, unfeeling, as if it's mocking both of us now.

"Carolina," I whisper, sitting on the edge of her bed and reaching out to grip her arm to wake her from her dream. My hand hovers for a second before I touch her, unsure if this is the right way to help, but I can't just sit back and do nothing.

But when I touch her, I'm not in her bedroom anymore. Everything shifts. The air changes, and suddenly, I'm somewhere else entirely, somewhere that feels too warm for comfort. Heat presses down on me, stifling and thick, like the walls are closing in. I tug at my shirt, but I'm not wearing one, and I'm looking down at Carolina, who's pulling on a dress.

Her hair is different—longer, maybe. Her face is familiar, but there's something...older about her. This isn't the Carolina I know.

I don't mean to move, but I'm suddenly helping her lace up the back with an expertise I didn't know I had. My hands move with a skill I've never learned, tying the intricate laces with precision. It's like I've done this a hundred times before, but I know I haven't.

The room we're in is quickly filling with smoke, but I feel oddly calm. The smoke should make me panic, but it doesn't. There's a sense of resignation settling over me, like this was always going to happen.

The emotion is opposite to the one written on Carolina's

face when she turns to face me. There's fear in her eyes, but there's something else—urgency.

"You need to leave," she says quickly.

And then, just like that, everything snaps back into place. The clock blinks 3:03 a.m. in its big bright red digits, and Carolina is staring at me with a look of horrified wonder, our faces inches from each other. I'm close enough to feel her breath against my skin, and for a moment, I forget how to move, how to think.

Her breath fans across my face as she tries to regain control of her breathing.

"You were screaming," I explain, pulling away from her and choosing not to tell her what I saw. I wouldn't even know how to begin.

I register that I shouldn't be able to see her this clearly, but there's a floating orb of light that wasn't there when I first entered the room. It hovers above us, casting a soft glow, but I don't remember it being there before. My mind is spinning too much to focus on it.

My gaze goes back to her as her big brown eyes search my face. She's still trying to get her breathing under control, and I notice the thin sheen of sweat that covers her skin. The way the light catches on her damp skin makes her look almost ethereal, but there's a fragility to her in this moment that makes my chest ache.

Whatever I saw must have been different than whatever she saw, and that made everything much more confusing. The fear in her eyes isn't the same as mine. We weren't in the same nightmare, that much is clear.

Carolina puts a hand to her chest as if feeling herself inhale and exhale will help her force air into her lungs. Her breaths are shallow, shaky, like she's still trapped in whatever nightmare gripped her. I know nothing I do will help her, so I just study her expression.

It's an amalgam of things. Confusion. Terror. Concern. It's like she doesn't know how to process what just happened, and neither do I. But my presence here…I'm not sure it's helping her calm down.

"I get nightmares. I should have warned you. Camila sleeps with earplugs in most nights." Her voice is quiet, almost apologetic, like she feels bad for disturbing me.

The idea of her going through this, night after night, alone, twists something inside me. "Do you want to tell me about them?"

"Not really." Her hand trembles slightly as she runs it through her hair, and I notice how exhausted she looks. It's like she's carrying the weight of a thousand sleepless nights.Her hair is loose around her oversized T-shirt-covered shoulders, but the baby hairs on her hairline stick to the sweat on her forehead.

"Can I get you anything?" She shakes her head. "Okay," I reply, standing.

"What are you doing?" Her voice is that of startled confusion.

I raise my eyebrows at her in question as I situate myself on the floor beside her bed. "Going to bed."

"On the floor? Why?"

Her flustered confusion makes me want to laugh, but I hold it back. It's not like I had a grand plan here, but I wasn't sleeping in the other room, so I might as well stay here. I didn't feel like going back to that guest room with its mocking alarm clock. Being near her, even in silence, felt…right.

"In case you need me." The words come out without much thought, but there's truth in them. I don't want to leave her alone tonight. She frowns at me and looks like she's going to argue, so I say, "And it's good for my back."

Carolina leans back in her bed, and the mysterious floating light extinguishes. Even though the floor is cold, possibly giving me a splinter, and I'm only in a T-shirt and boxers, I'm already more comfortable than in the other room.

The tension that had been coiled so tightly inside me begins to unwind, and I can feel the pull of sleep tugging at me. It's now a struggle to keep my eyes open, and when I finally give up, I dream of Carolina.

The next morning, I don't wake up on the floor of Carolina's bedroom; I wake up in her bed. She's not in it, though. I'm sprawled out on my stomach in the middle of the mattress. The scent of her—cinnamon and vanilla—lingers on the pillows and sheets, wrapping around me like a cocoon. I let myself sink into it for a moment, savoring it.

My mind affords me the luxury of basking in the scent before it propels me into the previous day's memories, making me realize I have no idea how I got into this bed in the first place.

I probably shouldn't be getting hard over a witch's scent. That's probably not good. Especially Carolina's, who I was pretty sure wished I would just go back to the West Coast and forget everything about Grove Meadow.

But I can't forget her. And that's the problem.

Begrudgingly, I drag myself from the bed, flip off the clock that reads 8:46 a.m., and go back to the guest room to shower and dress. I'll have to stop by my place to get fresh clothes before I go to the station and figure out what to do about Elijah and the rest of this situation.

I should go straight to get my car still parked across from the alley, and then to the hotel where I'm staying to change my clothes, but I go into the shop anyway.

"Morning, Detective," Camila says as she pulls an espresso shot for someone I don't recognize. Her smile is bright, her voice cheery, but I can't help but feel a little disoriented by how normal everything feels after last night. "Lina had some errands to run, so just me here. Can I get you a cup to go?"

"Sure, I'll try one of those medicine balls, finally."

Camila shakes her head and passes the to-go cup to the waiting customer. "Here you go, ma'am. Thanks for stopping in."

The woman leaves, and Camila fixes me with a stare. I grin at her. "They're not teas, are they?"

"Obviously not." Camila rolls her eyes while she pours a drip coffee into a to-go cup for me.

On my way out the door, I glance over at one of the paintings on the wall. It's one of those pieces that looks simple at first, but the more you look, the more you notice. It's a landscape painting of a park during the fall, but a snake is wrapped around the branch, and a cat is swatting at it. I narrow my eyes at it, just like I had the first time I saw it, but this time, I know what I'm looking for.

"Bye Camila...and Silas and Luna."

"Goodbye, Declan." Camila's laughter follows me out the door, light and easy, like everything is perfectly normal.

Why couldn't I like the nice sister? It just *had* to be the one with the snake. Fate was cruel.

When I get to the station, Bas is deep in investigation mode. His desk looks like a crime scene of its own—files and papers scattered everywhere, his phone pressed between his ear and shoulder while he types furiously on the keyboard. His cuticle beds are jagged and bright red.

"What did I miss?" I ask when he hangs up the phone.

"Elijah Thorton is missing." There's an edge to his voice as he shuffles through his files. "No one knows where he was last night, so we can't figure out where he might have disappeared."

"Who called it in?"

As far as I knew from Carolina and Camila, Elijah didn't have anyone checking in on him. I thought it would be at least a full day before someone reported him missing, if not longer.

"I did," Bas says, leaning back in his chair and running a hand through his hair. There's so much product in it that I'm surprised his fingers don't get caught. "I went to Owen Donovan's house to ask his family about those Wednesday meetings like you asked me to, and it turns out he was going to AA meetings at Hazel's Inn with the other victims. They didn't tell us about them originally because they were embarrassed, but they admitted it when I asked specifically about those nights. They also mentioned that they knew Elijah was also attending them. So, I went over to Elijah's last night, and he wasn't home. I went back again this morning, and there was no sign of him. No one's seen him since yesterday afternoon when he was tinkering in his driveway."

I raise my brows. "And it's not normal for him to go visit friends or family in a neighboring town? We're sure he's missing?"

If this were anyone else, we'd need to wait 48 hours to issue a missing person report, so the fact that Bas wasn't waiting was curious. Unless he knew something about Elijah that other people didn't.

"It's not likely. He doesn't have any family, and I don't know of any out-of-town friends."

"Well, who saw him last?"

Bas flips open the report and passes it to me. I glance at the notes, each one a confirmation of what I already knew. Elijah had been alive yesterday. A number of people saw Elijah working on something in his garage in the afternoon. His garage door was closed after sunset, and no one saw him after that.

I slide the file back onto his desk. "We should definitely investigate, but this might not be our next vic, Bas. Weird shit is happening in this town. He might just have wanted to get out of dodge."

He shakes his head at me in frustration. "You're all about your gut, right? Intuition?" he asks, leaning forward and pressing his index finger on the report. "Well, *my* gut is telling me that something's wrong here, and we should be looking for Elijah."

My stomach feels like it's bottoming out. I'd seen my share of victims and missing person cases, but to know that someone wasn't coming back and having to lie about it...

"Okay, Bas," I say with a resigned sigh. "You take lead on this."

Bas nods. "Thanks, O'Reilly," he says, grabbing his coat off the back of his chair and heading out.

My hand twitched to call Carolina and give her a heads up about Bas, but no doubt her phone records would be evidence if she ever ended up in a trial.

It didn't matter. All that was left of Elijah Thorton was a pile of ash anyway.

I grab Elijah's file from Bas's desk to look over, and underneath it is a business card I hadn't noticed before.

I quickly type "Esme Briarwood" and "Thorn & Thistle" into a search engine, and a storefront in New York City pops up. From what I could gather in this initial search, Esme Briarwood was a botanist who sold exotic plants.

Why would Bas have this?

I replace the business card and file on his desk. Maybe

Sebastian Blackwell was a closet plant lover. I'd been working in shades of grey the past 24 hours; I drew the line at investigating my partner.

18

CAROLINA

"**Y**ou can come out now. He's gone." Camila's voice is teasing as she pokes her head into the magic room where I'm trying (once *again*) to make sense of the prophecy Esme gave us.

It's like everything else around me has stopped mattering, except for this prophecy. The words keep haunting me, spinning in my head like a riddle I can't solve.

> *"When men fall, and the moon replaces the sun, a*
> *darkness will return, and a joined power will*
> *rule the worlds of might and magic."*

A joined power will rule the worlds of might and magic...

I chew on my lip, turning the words over in my mind. What the hell does *joined power* even mean? Is it two people? Two forces?

Nightcrawler said there were two someones behind the disappearances.

Two someones...that could be the joined power. *But who?*

We'd bought ourselves some time by stopping Elijah's summoning, and maybe it was time *they* didn't have. In which case, they'd either be moving quickly to regroup, or they'd missed their opening. I had a feeling it wouldn't be that easy.

My mind was working overtime on all of these things: compartmentalizing Elijah's death by reasoning that he would have died anyway, figuring out what "darkness" is about to return to the Mortal World, and very carefully trying to avoid thinking about what my magic was telling me about Declan (especially after last night). It was proving difficult to fight my magic, mind, and body at the same time when all they wanted to do was replay the sight of a sleeping Declan in my bed.

I scoff at Camila and turn the page in our grimoire. If only it were as easy to flip through this mess of emotions as it was to turn pages. "I wasn't *hiding* from him."

Not really, anyway. The more distance I put between him and my magic, the more I could think clearly. With him so close last night, there was no way I was going to fall back to sleep. My powers felt like a fidget spinner on a bender.

I gave myself an hour of staring at my ceiling before I slipped out of bed and levitated him into it. Seeing him on the floor had stirred something in me—something protective. The man had almost died. The least I could do was let him sleep somewhere comfortable. The ease in which sleep found him on the floor concerned me.

Maybe his profession made him used to finding sleep where he could. Or maybe his body was so desperate to find sleep after the day he'd had that the moment he closed his eyes, it didn't matter whether it was a mattress or the warped floorboards of my bedroom floor.

A part of me worried that Camila missed something in her healing, but I knew she didn't. She was thorough. Perhaps his body just needed to recover more completely.

It was trivial, of course. Considering all of the other things we had going on. The more pressing worry was his reaction to the news about our magic. I had prepared myself for him to haul us down to the station, but he hadn't. Why not?

He had every reason to, and then he got several more reasons when he watched Elijah disintegrate into a pile of ash. But instead of running out of our apartment screaming, he stayed over.

I absently rub at my chest and ignore the thrumming of my magic.

Like calls to like.

Like calls to like, I mock back to my magic.

Carolina, Luna's voice invades my mind since she's in my bedroom sunbathing by the window, *please do not mock the only thing that's going to keep you alive should demons choose to try and kill you. Thank you.*

I was surprised witches didn't go crazy more often. Between listening to their families, their familiars, and their magic, there wasn't a single ounce of privacy to be found.

"Whatever you say. If he comes back, should I let him know you've fled the country?" Camila's voice pulls me from my thoughts, and I realize she's still standing in the doorway, grinning at me.

I turn another page, pointedly avoiding looking at her. "Well, that would be suspicious to the other police officers, don't you think?"

She perches on the arm of the sofa next to me. I can feel her eyes on me, waiting for me to crack a smile or engage in her teasing. But I'm not in the mood.

"Why do you even keep looking at that prophecy? It's not going to tell us anything else. There's not even an eclipse due soon, so I don't know how the moon will replace the sun to begin with."

Between my lack of sleep and all of the other things I had to worry about, Camila's comments were less than welcome.

I slam the book closed and look at her. "Do you have a *better* idea, Camila? Is that what you've been doing this morning—working on some foolproof plan to bring back everyone who has gone missing and stop whatever evil that's set up shop in Grove Meadow?"

Her jaw ticks, and a shadow passes over her features. I know I've struck a nerve, but I don't care.

"Why do you have to be so mean all the time?"

Outrage flares through me. "*Mean*? You think I'm *mean*? I'm trying to *save* us, Camila. I'm trying to make sure we can protect ourselves. If you think me being irritated that you aren't taking this seriously enough makes me *mean*, then you need to grow the fuck up."

Carolina! Luna scolds.

"Oh, you know it's true, Luna," I snipe aloud as I watch Camila blink back tears.

The sight of them, brimming in her eyes, sends a pang of guilt through me, but I shove it down. I can't afford to be soft right now. She knows if she lets them fall, it gives me more ammunition against her, so she fights them back. I know it's cruel, but I can't stop the words. They spill out before I can rein them in.

"She's waiting for one of us to figure out a plan so she can get back to baking pastries or whatever else it is she does all day."

Camila storms out of the magic room and slams the door behind her while Silas looks at me from his corner of the room.

"Someone woke up on the wrong side of the bed," he says in his usual apathetic tone, but I know he's mentally consoling Camila. He's trying to make light of the situation, but I can feel the disappointment in his voice.

I shake my head and open the book again. "I don't want to talk about it."

Hours later, I'm still poring over abuela's magic books, trying to find anything useful. My eyes burn from reading so long, but I can't stop. If I stop, the weight of everything will come crashing down on me, and I'm not sure I can handle it.

"Silas, what's a demonic bounty hunter?" I ask him, my voice hoarse from hours of silence.

He hops onto the couch beside me. "Where'd you see that?"

I point to the page with a brief mention of the role, which only explains that they were witches and warlocks employed by the Fates. I hadn't realized the Fates had expense accounts. It feels like there's so much more to this world than I even know, and I've been a witch my entire life.

"They're professional narcs," Silas hisses. His ears flatten slightly as he says it, like the very idea offends him.

I blink at him. "Come again?"

"When the Fates want information about what's going on in the Underworld, they strike deals with demons or witches and warlocks to investigate and report back to them. Sometimes, it's the promise of more power, time off a sentence, whatever they think will entice them to do their dirty work."

I look down at him curiously. He's not telling me everything. Silas, usually a terrible gossip, seldom shared anything about his life before becoming Camila's familiar. There are stories locked inside him, secrets I've never asked him to tell. I wonder what else he's keeping from us. I wasn't sure if it was because he was ashamed of it or because he thought we might judge him for it.

"You sound like you have experience with them..."

"It's a story for another time," he says, kneading a spot on the couch cushion. His claws extend, pulling on threads. There's a tension in his movements, a wariness. I grimace but don't say anything because I have a feeling he could redirect those weapons at me...or my clothes. Besides, I know better than to push Silas when he's not ready to share. But that doesn't mean I'm not filing that little nugget away for later.

"Ookay…well, do you think one of these bounty hunters might know something about this prophecy or the disappearances?"

Silas pauses his kneading and drops onto his belly. "It's a definite possibility. Even if it's not being widely advertised down there, the bounty hunters have an inner circle where they exchange whispers. I…*may* have a contact. I haven't talked to him in a few years, but he might still be down there."

A contact? Silas has contacts in the Underworld? I raise a brow at him. *Of course, he does.* I shouldn't be surprised, but it's still jarring to hear him talk about it so casually. Why would Silas have a recent contact in the Underworld? Perhaps that was *also* a story for another time.

"Can we bring him here? Summon him or something?" Because there's no way in hell I'm going down to the Underworld without knowing all the details.

Silas shakes his head. His tail flicks in annoyance, as if the very idea is reckless. "It's dangerous to summon a bounty hunter to the Mortal World, especially if they're on assignment. The Fates will intervene if someone compromises their informants. If you want to talk to him, you'll have to go to the Underworld yourself."

My stomach drops. Just a few days ago, I didn't even realize there was a way to enter the Underworld, and now we might have to go there.

"You think it's a good idea to send me to the Underworld… where all the realm's demons live?"

"I didn't say that. If you think that getting information from someone who is constantly privy to the inner workings down there will get you the information to put an end to all of this, then maybe it's the only way."

Luna?

I wait, hoping my familiar will chime in with some wisdom that will get us out of this mess.

He's right, I fear.

I let out a deep sigh, leaning my head back on the couch. The very thought of stepping foot in the Underworld sends a cold shiver down my spine. But what choice do we have? We're running out of options, and time isn't on our side.

"So how do we get down there? Is there a demonic taxi service or something?"

Silas huffs in the judgmental way that only cats can master. "I know how to open portals, Carolina. No need to take your bad attitude out on me. Just because you're having sex dreams about Detective Do-Gooder and won't acknowledge what's happening between the two of you doesn't mean you need to push everyone else away."

What?

My cheeks heat. I can feel the blush creeping up my neck, all the way to my ears. "I'm going to kill Luna."

How dare she share that with Silas? That thing I said about privacy? Yeah, it's suddenly much worse than I expected. How many other things has she told him about me?

You're awfully quiet, traitor. I send the mental jab toward Luna, but there's no response from her.

No response from my familiar.

"Don't blame her. You're the one pretending like you're not thinking about it when you know she has access to your mind." Silas stretches out, his claws retracting as he speaks, clearly enjoying my discomfort. He lives for moments like this, where he can throw my emotions back in my face.

I shake my head in disbelief. I couldn't believe we were talking about this. "Can we go back to the visiting the Underworld thing?"

Silas slinks over to the door. He's clearly had enough of teasing me for now, but I know he'll bring it up again later. He always does. "I'll get Cami."

As he leaves, I exhale deeply, trying to push away the mess of emotions swirling in my chest. But it's harder than I'd like to admit.

Because Silas is right. I am pretending. I've been pretending that whatever is happening between me and Declan isn't real, that my magic isn't pulling me toward him like a magnet. But I can't ignore it forever.

"Remind me again why you two think it's a good idea to go anywhere called *The Underworld*?" I ask, my tone dripping with skepticism in a torrid attempt at hiding my growing concern.

When I'd gotten back from the station to check in with them at the shop, the girls had filled me in on their plan. They said it so casually, like a trip to the Underworld was no different than a quick run to the grocery store. Meanwhile, my brain is short-circuiting, trying to figure out how this is all my life now. They're the experts in this particular domain, but even the idea of them walking into a world of demons made my stomach knot uncomfortably.

Camila laughs from her spot on the couch. She's furiously scribbling something into a notebook. A spell from the book on her lap, maybe.

That was a thought I never expected to have.

"Are you worried about us, Detective?" Camila asks, her voice clearly amused.

My face heats when Carolina's curious gaze meets mine. Looking away, I cross my arms and lean a shoulder against the doorway to their cafe. "It's my job to be concerned about the general welfare of others."

I haven't asked about the logistics of visiting the Underworld because I'm afraid they might actually tell me. What if they can't come back? What if something goes wrong down there? And why the hell am I standing here, pretending like I'm okay with this?

"Right. Well, if we want to figure out who's behind all of this and stop them, we need information from someone who knows what's going on down there," Carolina says, vigorously shaking a vial of a light purple liquid.

Her movements are methodical, calm, but there's something underneath her exterior—something nervous, maybe. Or maybe I'm projecting.

"Do you even know if your powers will work down there? You might be entirely unprotected." I gesture at the cat lounging beside Camila. "Why can't Silas go?"

His head lifts, and he squints his green eyes at me until they're just slits. I'm familiar with them enough to know that's cat language for *fuck off, or I'll maul you.* "Can't. I'm banned from the Underworld. Has to be them."

Somehow, this information doesn't surprise me. Of course Silas has been banned from the Underworld. That tracks.

Luna slithers over to me and starts to scale my body. My body freezes instinctively, every muscle locking in place. My entire life, I've tried to avoid situations where I'm literally wrapped in a snake. Yet, here I am. The sound of her chuffing fills my ears. *Oh good, the snake is laughing at me. Perfect.*

"Why is he here again?" Silas asks, and I glare at him even though I'm pretty sure that the only reason Luna is climbing me is to prevent Silas from attacking my face. It's a strange kind of comfort. The snake, weirdly, feels protective, and I'm not sure how I feel about that.

"I think the concern is cute," Luna says, perching her head on my shoulder. Her voice is oddly soothing, despite the fact that she's a literal serpent wrapped around me. My life has gotten very strange, very fast. "But, the girls will have their magic, don't worry."

I grimace and look at Carolina again. Her mouth is slanted down, but her eyes are lighter than usual. Somehow, between the talking cat and barista witches, *I* have become the comic relief. *Wonderful.*

The irritation is short-lived when another question comes to me. "If you don't know who you're looking for because Silas won't be there, how do you know where to look? Is there some magical *Find My Demon* app?"

"Clever," Silas says, though clearly not amused. His tone tells me he's about one sarcastic comment away from scratching my face off, snake or no snake. "It's more like…a sensor. I've given Camila an item given to me by my contact for emergencies. Her magic will help guide them to the item's owner."

A magical tagging device. Great. Sounds foolproof.

"What am *I* supposed to do while you two are gone?" I hate feeling useless, but in a situation like this, I'm not exactly the guy you call to fight demons.

Camila tears out a piece of paper from her notebook and closes the spell book before standing. She moves with a casual confidence, like this is just another day at the office. "You mean while we're busy doing your job, what should you be doing?"

I know she means it as a joke, but I roll my eyes anyway. My job was to solve *normal* disappearances. Human-on-human crimes. Supernatural happenings were above my pay grade and outside my jurisdiction.

"Camila," Carolina says, her tone borderline scolding.

I didn't grow up with siblings, but I watched enough sitcoms to be able to identify a clear sisterly hierarchy.

"Keep Bas away from us," Carolina continues. "The more you can keep him out of our path, the better. We'll call you when we're back."

That's something I can do. I can keep Bas in the dark long enough to buy them some time. But the idea of just...waiting while they dive into the Underworld? That doesn't sit right with me.

"And when will that be?" I ask, straightening and then realizing Luna is still firmly wrapped around me.

Somehow, Luna's presence has become more comforting than off-putting, something I hadn't imagined ever happening. To be fair, the last 24 hours had been a little...overwhelming.

"Don't be clingy, Declan. It's unbecoming," Silas says between lapping at his paw.

Camila bops his head with her palm. "Hopefully not long. I don't want to be there any longer than absolutely necessary. Got the emergency escape potion?"

"Yes, ma'am." Carolina shows her the vial before slipping it into her pocket. The small gesture gives me a strange sense of relief. At least they're going in with a backup plan. "Got the spell?"

"Check."

"Good." Carolina gives a satisfied nod, then turns to me, her expression softening slightly. "Look, Declan, I know this is outside the norm for you—*way* outside—but we've got this. We need to do this."

Camila slips the last few items into her weathered satchel, her movements precise. "It's the only way to get ahead of whatever's happening. We've hit a dead end up here. I hear you know what that's like."

"Are you making fun of me because my investigation did

not initially include the possibility that demons were kidnapping the people in this town?"

Camila grimaces. "Yeah...I didn't think that one through."

I can't help but smirk a little at that. At least she's honest about it.

"Okay, enough of this. Camila, bring the book over to where we'll do the spell," Carolina orders while rummaging through the drawers of the antique-looking desk.

"On it," Camila replies, grabbing the book she'd been copying and carrying it to a wall that was devoid of decoration.

When Carolina joins her sister, I watch them prepare for something straight out of a fantasy novel. They face the stark, unadorned wall, their concentration palpable in the cool air of the room.

Carolina holds a piece of chalk in her hand—not just any chalk, I note, but one that emits a faint, ethereal glow. It catches the light in a way that makes it almost otherworldly. I can feel the magic humming in the air before they've even started. Camila, with the ancient-looking book propped open in her arms, directs her sister where to start.

"Make sure every line connects perfectly," Camila instructs, her finger tracing over the page as if she could transfer the spell through her touch alone.

"I know how it works, Cami," Carolina snaps, but Camila doesn't react. Either she's used to it, or she's aware of how stressed her sister is. There's an underlying tension between them, one I haven't fully figured out yet.

I watch, fascinated, as Carolina begins. The movements are precise, each stroke of the chalk deliberate. It's like watching an artist paint something only they can truly understand.

The chalk touches the wall, leaving luminescent lines in its wake. She draws with a steady, practiced hand symbols and shapes that are foreign yet oddly mesmerizing. The symbols seem alive somehow, each line pulsing with energy the moment it's drawn. A large circle first, then intricate patterns that filled the inside, each stroke adding to the complexity of a glowing mandala.

As the final line is drawn, the air around us seems to charge, the hair on my arms standing on end. Camila steps forward, her voice strong and clear as she begins to recite the words that she'd written on the piece of paper.

> Shadows gather, night unfurl,
> Open the gate to the Underworld.
> By the echo of ancient chimes,
> Grant passage through the veils of time.

The words hang in the air, and as she speaks, the symbols on the wall begin to glow brighter, pulsing in time with her voice. As Camila speaks the final words, the chalk lines on the wall ignite with a soft, silver glow. The symbols pulse as if breathing, and the air in front of the wall shimmers like heat above a flame. Slowly, the center of the drawing seems to dissolve, revealing a swirling vortex of colors that beckoned them forward.

"Whoa," I breathe.

Carolina looks back at me and gives me a tight smile. Her eyes are still filled with that same determination, but there's something else there too—something I can't quite place. Maybe it's concern. Maybe it's regret. "We'll be back soon."

I can't help but admire their resolve, even as the dread gnaws at me. "Just...be careful, okay?" I say, feeling suddenly inadequate with only my concern to offer in the face of their magical expedition.

The corner of her mouth tips up as she dips her chin in a

short nod. It's a small gesture, but it's enough to soothe some of the anxiety roiling inside me.

"Ready?" Carolina asks, holding out her hand to her sister.

Camila stares at it for a moment before clasping her hand around Carolina's. For a second, they don't move, and I wonder if they're as scared as I am. But then they step forward, together, and the magic around them seems to surge in response.

"Ready."

As they step through the doorway, the light seems to swallow them, and for a moment, my heart stops—then starts again as the vortex shimmers and becomes the wall again, leaving me in the silent magic room with Silas and Luna.

"That's normal, right?"

Silas jumps onto the counter, his tail flicking with annoyance or perhaps worry. "Yeah. They'll be alright," he mutters, more to himself than to me. Luna, still wrapped around my shoulders, tightens her coils in what I assume is her version of a comforting gesture.

Left in the quiet, I ponder Carolina's instructions: keep Bas away. It feels like a small, almost trivial task in the grand scheme of things, but it's something I can do. Something within my control.

I check my phone to see if Bas has reached out with anything new and wonder, not for the first time, if I'm in way over my head.

Drawing a deep breath, I set my jaw and prepare for the task at hand. Protecting them from this side might not be as flashy or dangerous as delving into the Underworld, but it's something I can do. Something I must do well. After all, in a world where talking cats and barista witches exist, a determined detective can surely keep one overzealous cop at bay... right?

20

CAROLINA

We step into a colorless, mirror image of the magic room. The room that once contained vibrant jewel tones and a certain aura of warmth and comfort was now shades of grey and felt as welcoming as a morgue.

Silas warned us that walking into the Underworld would be disorienting, but I never expected *this*. Disorienting doesn't even begin to cover it.

Everything feels wrong. It's like I'm looking at a world where all the life has been drained out, leaving only hollow versions behind.

"Weird," Camila breathes out, her fingers drifting over a table in the same place the one we use for potion-making sits. "Okay, it's giving me the creeps; let's just find this guy and get back."

The sooner, the better. Every fiber of my being wants to bolt, to get out of this place and back to somewhere that doesn't make my skin crawl.

Silas explained that doorways in the Underworld acted as a set of interconnected portals. You had to be extremely specific in where you wanted them to take you; otherwise, you could be roaming the caverns of the Underworld for eternity.

"Do you think it'll be like the catacombs in Paris?" Camila asks, hesitating in front of the door that would usually take us to the shop.

"Lined with skulls and full of mole people living not-so-secretly under the city? Maybe."

Camila shivers. "Thanks for that. *Really.* I can't wait to open this door now...any second now...I will open this door."

I roll my eyes and grab the doorknob. The hesitation is getting us nowhere, and I just want this over with. *Bounty hunter,* I think at it before yanking it open.

"Whoa," Camila whispers when we're pulled through the open doorway and propelled into a place far more eerie than a mirror version of our magic room.

The door we'd come through is still behind us. Its wood is a stark contrast to the rock walls it seems to be embedded in. There's a chill in this cave-like structure. The ground beneath us is a mixture of solid earth and loose gravel that crunches under our feet.

I sense Camila's discomfort rapidly growing with each step we take. We're both uncomfortable, but I'm better at hiding it.

My magic wants to cast a protective barrier around us and shoot us straight back to the Mortal World. It's screaming at me to leave, to get us out of here. Every instinct I have is telling me that we don't belong here. Instead, I wrap my arms around myself, a shield of my own making.

The Underworld is meant to distress, according to Silas. Those who live down here are always in a constant state of unease.

I quickly realize that the feeling is not unlike holding your breath for too long underwater. Pressure on my chest and head begins to spread throughout my body. I take a deep breath, trying to shake it off, but it only makes it worse, like the very air down here wants to trap us.

Note to self: I would not recommend this place to people with claustrophobia.

A strong sense of foreboding settles over me as we travel deeper into the winding, maze-like paths of the Underworld. Every corner seems to hide a new secret, and every shadow could be a trap. Soft whispers float past my head, but I can't understand what they're saying—a new form of torture.

I need a distraction, and luckily, I have the perfect one. If we're going to die down here, I might as well get this off my chest.

"I have to tell you something," I say, cringing at how my voice seems to echo off the rock walls.

"*Now?*" she asks, raising an eyebrow at me. "Can't it wait until we're back home? I just want to see Silas's weirdo contact and get out of this place."

Her face contorts warily as her eyes take in our surroundings once more. Her gaze darts between the jagged edges of the walls, and she looks over her shoulder like she senses someone following us.

"Well, we might die down here, so..." We probably wouldn't *die*. Maybe just get stuck down here for the rest of our lives if anything happens to our connection to the Mortal World.

"Comforting, Caro." She lets out a dramatic sigh when I shrug in response. "Fine, go on. It will give me something to think about other than this incessant buzzing. *God*, do you hear it, too?" Camila asks, pulling on her earlobe and flexing her jaw like popping it would get rid of it.

I shake my head as we carry on, letting our instincts guide our way. "The night Declan stayed over—"

Instantly, Camila scrunches her face in disgust and holds up a hand to me. "Ew, no. I definitely don't want to hear this, even when we're back home."

Ignoring her protests, I continue, "I had a *nightvision*. A past life, and Declan was in it."

In my periphery, Camila looks at me curiously. The teasing look fades from her face, replaced by genuine interest. This has her attention. "It's not uncommon to meet people from past lives, is it?"

It's not impossible, but statistically unlikely, to have your timelines match up with someone who could be anyone, anywhere in the world, at any time.

Abuela warned me once that it could happen but that I shouldn't go looking for people in my visions. Something about disrupting Fate and disrupting Fate never ends well. But I didn't go looking for Declan. He just…showed up.

Her warning was enough for me, whatever the reason. I never ventured out to find Camila, though we were sisters once before. She was pleased to find out she was the older one in that lifetime.

"Maybe not, but it's not that he was there. It was what he said." The words still echo in my mind, and every time I think about them, a chill runs through me.

Telling Camila about this was opening a version of Pandora's Box. Once it was out, I'd never be able to get her to forget about it. Even so, I've been driving myself crazy, turning over the dream in my mind.

"Which was?" She presses when I don't say anything right away.

I stop walking, needing a moment to gather myself before I say it out loud. "He said, 'It's us in every lifetime.'"

Her reaction is immediate—shock, followed quickly by excitement. She practically vibrates with it. "Oh my god. *Carolina!* Do you think he's…you know?" Her voice drops to a near-whisper, like she's afraid saying it out loud will jinx it.

"I don't know, that's why I'm talking to you about it." My

heart races in my chest, and the tightness I've been feeling since that night comes back full force. What if he *is* my mirror soul? What if this is real?

Despite our surroundings, Camila's face lights up. Her joy is contagious, and for a moment, I almost let myself feel it too. *Almost.* If only she knew how the dream ended.

"Wow, wow, wow. My big sister found her *mirror soul.* God, I can't believe it. I didn't even know you had a soul under that thick skin."

Ouch. But given what I'd said to her earlier, I probably deserved it.

"Camila," I warn, turning back to our path and resuming our trek.

"Sorry, that was mean. So, what are you going to do about it? I wish Mom were here. I think Dad was her mirror soul. I mean, why else would she be with a mortal?"

Huh. I hadn't considered that.

"I suppose that falling in love the old-fashioned mortal way won't satisfy your weird, hopeless romantic tendencies?"

Mirror souls were Fated. Their souls were infinitely intertwined. When their timelines matched up, they always managed to find their way to each other. This bond was beyond the physical world, threading through the fabric of time itself.

I've spent my whole life not looking for someone like that, knowing it was unlikely I'd ever find them. Now, the possibility feels...overwhelming.

Many witches study the bonds between *mirror souls.* Some think that everyone has a *mirror soul,* but...extenuating circumstances may make it difficult to reunite in each lifetime.

Most witches don't know when they've encountered their mirror soul, but it's witches like me, gifted with the power of foresight, who can recover old memories. Locked away in a vault until initial contact has been made, once a witch with my power meets their mirror soul, they begin to uncover more and more of their memories.

Maybe that's why I'd never been as boy crazy as Camila when we were younger. I knew if I didn't start getting those memories when I was with someone, they weren't meant for me.

It didn't stop me from dating, but it did prevent me from going much further past an initial infatuation.

We begin to hear voices as we move deeper into the cavern (or at least I think we're moving deeper into the cavern).

"Do you hear *that*?" Camila asks, our movements slowing down. There's a barrage of laughter, and we make eye contact. "Silas didn't warn us they might be having a party."

"Can I help you two?" A male voice from behind us freezes us in place.

Camila's eyes close, and she lets out a breath through her nose. Then she nods lightly, and we both turn to face whoever—or *whatever*—has caught us.

The man in front of us has dark hair and even darker eyes. His stubble is slightly overgrown, not enough to be classified as a beard. His black shirt and pants are well-fitted to his body. There's something familiar about him, but I can't place it.

His eyes grow wide, and his face pales. "Camila?"

Cami's voice is bewildered as she says, "Sam?"

The wave of recognition hits me like a wall. This is Sam, the guy who broke Camila's heart. Shock and confusion ripple through the air, tangible as the chill that seeps from the stone walls.

"Camila, why is your ex-boyfriend hanging out in the Underworld?"

21

CAROLINA

"Sam, what are you doing here?" Camila's voice is sharp, her surprise morphing quickly into suspicion. I can feel the shift in her energy, the way she stiffens next to me.

The last she knew, Sam was exploring remote areas of the Mortal World, cataloging unclassified flora. His presence in the gloomy depths of the Underworld was utterly out of place.

After Camila graduated high school, Sam came to do research under our grandparents before embarking on a year-long study abroad of sorts. He had been tasked with leading a team of other magical scholars on an expedition. After a whirlwind summer romance, he'd invited Camila to come with him, but she declined, bringing their relationship to a screeching halt.

I'd only met him briefly when I had been forced home for a week that summer—magically redirected from a summer internship I was doing.

Camila and Sam had a lot in common: their optimism, overt curiosity, and stubbornness. The latter would surely cause some trouble if he learned what we were doing here.

"I'm here on...an assignment," Sam replies, his voice hesitant, as if weighing each word before speaking it. He glances around nervously, the flickering shadows playing across his face, revealing a tension that seemed out of character for the Sam I remembered.

"An assignment? In the Underworld?" I interject, finding it hard to mesh this image of Sam with the stories of his harmless and, in my opinion, boring botanical ventures. "That sounds like a drastic change of scenery."

He sighs, a sound of resignation escaping him as if he had been carrying a heavy burden. "It is. After the expedition, I stumbled upon...let's just say, a *unique* opportunity that brought me here. I know it sounds crazy, but there's a lot about the magical world that isn't just flora and natural ecosystems. There are deeper, darker layers, and somehow, I found myself working with beings from those layers."

The revelation hung in the air, heavy like the oppressive atmosphere of the Underworld itself. Camila's eyes narrow slightly, her mind undoubtedly racing to connect the dots between the Sam she once knew and the man before us, newly wrapped in mysteries and shadows.

"So, you're telling us you're here on some sort of *mission*?" I probe, trying to understand the full scope of his involvement in this realm.

The idea that he might be the bounty hunter we were looking for flickers in my mind, but I keep it to myself.

"Something like that," Sam admits, his gaze finally meeting ours. "I can't reveal much—there are rules and contracts involved. But I can assure you, my intentions are to maintain a balance, to prevent certain...elements from tipping the scales too far in any one direction."

The pieces were slowly beginning to fit together, though each revelation only led to more questions. Camila's expression softens slightly, a mix of worry and perhaps a flicker of her old feelings for him complicating her thoughts.

"Sam, are you in trouble?" Her voice is softer now, the edges of old affection coloring her concern.

He manages a wry smile, the gesture not quite reaching his eyes. "Aren't we all, in one way or another, when we deal with the Underworld?"

Well, that's dramatic...but not untrue.

Before we can press him further, a distant sound catches our attention—a low, rumbling echo that seems to come from deeper within the caverns. Sam's head snaps towards the sound, his body growing tense.

"We should probably move somewhere more private," he says, his voice dropping low as he presses a palm against one of the cavern walls.

He murmurs something under his breath, and the area to the left of his hand shimmers.

"After you." Sam motions us forward, and Camila and I share a look.

Do we trust him? I try to ask her with my expression.

She glances back at Sam, who is beginning to look panicked at our hesitation. Camila assesses him a moment longer before giving me a slight shrug. *What other options do we have?*

An unnatural magic flickers around us as we step through the shimmering doorway. The magic here is strange, foreign. It doesn't settle the way ours does. It clings to my skin, crawling like invisible fingers. I try not to shudder.

I could just hear Declan's *I told you so* echoing in my ears if we got stuck down here.

We step into a bunker of sorts. The room, if you could call it that, is cramped because of the way the cavern walls slope overhead. I have to duck my head to avoid knocking into them.

It's chillier in here than it was on the other side, and I tighten my arms around my body. If the temperature drops any lower, I'll be able to see my breath.

There's something ominous about the space, like the walls themselves are watching us.

There's a cot with a blanket thrown haphazardly over it tucked against the left wall and items scattered on the floor. Despite the lack of ornamentation, I can tell he's been living here—though *living* might not be the right word. Existing, maybe. Surviving. But not living. The space feels too hollow for that.

I look at Sam curiously.

"Home Sweet Home." He grimaces apologetically. Sam doesn't wait for us to comment before he asks, "What are you two doing here, anyway? I don't suppose you two make it a hobby to explore the Underworld."

Camila sits on the corner of the mattress and looks around. "We're looking for someone. A bounty hunter," she clarifies, her gaze settling on Sam.

His brows lift in surprise, and his body tenses. "A bounty hunter? What for?" His voice is casual, but the sudden stiffness in his posture betrays him. He knows something.

"There have been some disappearances in the Mortal World, and we had a little visit from a demon called Nightcrawler," Camila says, her eyes firmly locked on his face. "Friend of yours?"

His lips form into a thin line. "No. I don't think so." The hesitation in his voice is clear. He's hiding something, and I don't need magic to know that.

"Oh, wait." Camila digs into her pocket, pulling out the crystal Silas gave her. "Missing something?" Like a magnet, the iridescent object propels itself toward Sam, slamming against his chest and hovering in front of him.

The impact is almost comical, but the way Sam's face pales as he plucks the crystal from mid-air is anything but. Whatever connection he has to this place, to this world, it's deeper than he's let on.

A pained expression crosses Sam's face. "Camila, you have to understand—"

"Actually, I don't. It doesn't matter. I don't care what you've been doing or why you didn't contact me when you got back from the expedition. You don't owe me anything." Her voice cracks on the last part, and I can feel the pain radiating off her in waves.

She was hurt, and my heart throbbed uncomfortably in my chest for her. It's one thing to lose someone you love. It's another to find out they've been keeping secrets from you all along.

When I'd been around them that summer, they'd been nearly inseparable. I remember thinking how good he was for her, how happy she seemed. Now, all I can think is how wrong I was.

Camila had *fallen in lust* a number of times in high school, but I had never seen her like she was with Sam. I thought it was nice that Camila had found someone who understood her and our family. But then, as fast as it had started, it ended.

Camila continues, her voice growing stronger as she changes the subject, "Silas sent us here to find out if you've heard anything about two individuals working together to fulfill a prophecy from the First Witch's grimoire."

Sam's mouth drops open and then abruptly closes. He looks more like a fish than a demonic bounty hunter.

He finally says, "There have been rumors...I'm not sure if they're related. The Underworld has been on lockdown. It's almost impossible to get around down here right now."

"Why? What's happening down here?" I ask, sitting beside Camila on the cot.

Sam shies away from me as I pass him, and I wonder if it's because he doesn't want me to touch him and trigger a vision. His avoidance is almost too obvious, and I wonder what he's afraid of me seeing. He leans against a flat part of the wall, further away from me, crossing one ankle over the other like it's a normal position for him.

"It's like the demons are preparing for something. Waiting for something to happen. If it's related to the disappearances and the prophecy, then it's big," he says.

Camila frowns. "Like...*Fates banishing the first demons to the Underworld* big?"

He runs a hand through his hair, and it's then that I realize he's not wearing his glasses. The black-rimmed, 50s-inspired browline glasses made him look more golden-retriever than German-shepherd were no longer there.

Gone was the boyish Sam who'd helped Camila identify varieties of fungi, and left in his place was a man who seemed like he'd go to the ends of the Underworld to keep whatever he was hiding from us.

"Maybe. What's the prophecy say?" Camila recites the prophecy from memory, and he furrows his brow. "You're sure that's what it says? I don't recognize it. You read it in the grimoire?"

My heart sank. If the prophecy was wrong, then we'd been looking in all the wrong places. We'd have to start all over and rethink everything.

I shake my head. "No, Esme told us about it."

A trickle of doubt enters my head. What if the City Coven purposefully told Esme the wrong prophecy because she was an inactive? Why hadn't we considered that before?

"Esme Briarwood?" Sam's face scrunched up in confusion. "How'd she hear about it?"

"The City Coven. She moved to the city after our grandparents died," Camila tells him.

He flinches at the implied dig. He hadn't come to their funeral, and it might have been because he was doing Fates knew what in the Underworld.

"I'm sorry, Camila." His tone does sound apologetic, but it does little to quell the anger coming off of my sister.

She looks at me, ignoring him. "What should we do?"

I sigh, but Sam interjects, "I'll see what I can find out down here and try to get the information to Silas." He passes Camila back the crystal, and she pockets it. "In the meantime, maybe you two should go talk to the City Coven and make sure the prophecy is right."

Nodding, I stand. I want to get out of here. I want to breathe air that doesn't feel like it's choking me. "Is it safe for you to be poking around like that and sending information to the Mortal World? We can try and come back."

Sam shakes his head. "Don't worry about me. I'll do what I can." His face takes on a grim and serious expression. "Do not come back here, Carolina. It's not safe for you. I'll contact Silas when I can."

Camila stands, looking relieved to be leaving this place, but I know she's more relieved to be leaving Sam.

"Emergency button?" I ask Camila, pulling out the vile.

"*Cauldron*, yes. Let's get out of this place," she says, looking around the room with uneasiness in her expression, like the longer she was down here, the more it sucked the energy from her.

"Wait," Sam says, his hand shooting out to grab hers.

She gasps, and I feel Camila's magic flare. Sam drops his hand like he'd been burned.

"What just happened?"

Camila and Sam look at each other. A charged, silent exchange passing between them. Sam gives her a slight shake of his head, and Camila's shock turns into a sadness I have to look away from.

"Camila?" I try again.

She visibly shakes off the situation in front of her. "It's nothing. Let's just go home. We'll tell Silas to be on the lookout for a message from you."

Sam nods as Camila takes my hand.

"Ready?"

Camila dips her head in confirmation, and I throw the potion at our feet.

Everything rushes past us instantly as our magic electrifies our bodies, and we're transported back to the magic room. Silas's head perks up from the couch.

"You're dead to me," Camila says, pointing a finger at her familiar.

I grimace as she storms out of the magic room, and Silas watches her go.

"I take it you found Sam."

My jaw clenches, and I cross my arms over my chest, quirking an eyebrow at him. He knows exactly what he did. "You think?"

22

DECLAN

Just like the alarm clock in Carolina's guest room, the numbers on my phone mock me endlessly. Each minute feels like an hour dragging by in the quiet of the hotel room. I could see the sunlight peering into my room through the slit in between the blackout curtains.

I'd sent Bas on a wild goose hunt, which will keep him buried in paperwork for the foreseeable future. When I was certain he was distracted, I went back to my hotel room to catch up on sleep, but it continued to evade me.

Maybe because I was so anxious about Carolina and Camila going down—I'm assuming it's *down*—to the Underworld. They'd been gone a little over 12 hours at this point.

Whenever I closed my eyes, I saw crime scenes, and the victim was always Carolina. Each dream felt more real, the details clearer, her face frozen in some kind of pain or terror. On the precipice of sleep, the images jolted me awake each time. At this rate, I wasn't sure if I'd ever sleep again.

I should have never let them go, but really, what could I have done to stop them? I was a human, and they had supernatural powers. It's not like I could pull rank on them or use logic when magic was involved. The attempt alone would probably have Silas rolling on his back hysterical with laughter.

I wondered what the extent of their powers were. Judging by the lack of pain I was in, it seemed like Camila could heal people at the very least. I knew they could both cast spells and make potions. Did they have particular special abilities? If so, what could Carolina do, and did it have to do with what I saw when I went to wake her up from her nightmare?

A sudden knock at the door startles me from my line of thinking and erases the image of lacing up Carolina's dress.

I check my phone for the umpteenth time to see if I missed a call from Bas or Carolina. *Nothing.*

"One second," I call while pulling on a pair of sweatpants. I tug them on hastily, my heart picking up a beat. What if it's Carolina? What if it's not her? What if something happened? My mind's spiraling already.

When I open the door, Carolina stands in front of it, arms crossed, looking at me expectantly.

"Up for a trip, Detective?" she asks, her voice casual like she's inviting me to get coffee and didn't just get back from the Underworld.

The breath I didn't realize I was holding releases in a slow exhale. My gaze drifts over her body, cataloging anything different about her. Her long, dark hair cascades around her shoulders, and she's wearing an oversized sweatshirt, jeans that hug her hips just right, and white sneakers. She looks the same.

She was here, alive and standing in front of me. The relief that overcame me was so potent that it catapulted me forward, my arms wrapping around her and pulling her against me.

"Uh, what are you doing?" she asked, mouth moving against the exposed skin of my chest.

What was *I doing?*

My arms drop from her immediately, and I take a step back, but my body feels drawn to her. "Sorry, I don't know what came over me."

Lie. I know exactly what came over me—fear. The idea that I'd never see her again had settled in my gut like lead.

She blinks, her dark gaze roving over my torso. Satisfaction that she's at least slightly affected by me courses throughout my body. I bury the smirk that wants to take over my face deep inside me.

"Come in," I say, turning back into the hotel room and leaving the door open for Carolina. Grabbing a clean T-shirt out of my suitcase, I pull it over my head before turning to face her. "When'd you get back?"

She's looking around the room, and a part of me is embarrassed that I've been using it as a catch-all. Clothes are strewn everywhere, and old takeout containers and coffee cups line most available surfaces. The sight of my mess suddenly feels more exposed, but I catch her eyeing the rumpled bed and the color creeping into her cheeks.

It's the first time I've been truly alone with her since the stakeout, and I wonder what's changed to make her act this way.

"About an hour ago," she says. "What have you been up to?" she asks, leaning her hip against the small table near the kitchenette.

"After I buried Bas in paperwork, I came back here to try and get some sleep."

She nods her head slowly, processing. "Any luck?"

I lift a shoulder. "Not much. Did you find the bounty hunter?"

There's a shift in her demeanor, a flicker of apprehension that crosses her features. "I'll tell you about it in the car."

"Right...where are we going again? I don't think the rental

plan covers miles to the Underworld," I quip, turning back to my suitcase to find a new set of clean clothes.

"New York. We need to visit the City Coven. I figured you might want to come with me." Her voice is overly casual like she's trying too hard to make it sound that way.

Yeah, she's definitely being weird.

"Okay, I just need a minute to shower. Feel free to..." I freeze when I see that the entire room has been cleaned, and there are folded piles of laundry on the newly made bed. "Make yourself at home. You folded my laundry."

Carolina rolls her eyes. "Please, I don't fold laundry. My magic seems to like you for whatever reason."

I can't stop my smirk this time. "Just your magic, huh?"

She shifts her weight to her back foot. "I thought you were going to shower."

"Right. If your magic has time, the water pressure kind of sucks."

The comment earns me another eye roll, but I see her fingers twitch, and sure enough, the water in the shower feels more like a massage than a depressing trickle of water.

CAROLINA HAS SPENT THE LAST 30 MINUTES EXPLAINING WHAT SHE found out from her trip to the Underworld and why we're going to Manhattan at 8 a.m. I'm half convinced that the only reason I'm here is to drive the 3 hours into the city.

"So, Camila used to date a bounty hunter?" I ask, flicking on my blinker to merge onto RT-15 South.

"Well, he wasn't a bounty hunter back then," Carolina says.

We hit a bout of stop-and-go traffic, and I prop my elbow up against the door frame, leaning my head against my fist.

"What did she say about it when you got back?" She looks at me curiously, brows raised, and I raise mine right back at her. "I mean, you asked her about it, right?"

There's a flicker of something—guilt, maybe—that flashes across her face. "It's not like she knows anything about it. She was just as surprised as I was to see him."

I grab my coffee from the center console and take a drink. "No, I know that, but you didn't ask her if she was okay?"

She shifts in her seat and crosses one leg over the other. "Camila and I aren't like that. We don't talk about that stuff."

A laugh slips out of my mouth before I can stop it. "Feelings, you mean? You don't talk about your feelings?"

Another one of the least surprising things I've ever heard. It explains a lot—her walls, her evasiveness. Nothing about Carolina tells me she's exactly forthcoming with her emotions. That must have been hard for Camila when they lost their parents and then again with their grandparents.

Carolina waves the comment off. "Whose side are you on here?"

"I didn't realize I was picking a side."

"Okay, enough judging me. What about you?"

"What about me?"

"Any kids? Pets?"

This time, the laugh is genuine. "No kids, no pets. When I was little, I had a fish. That was the only pet my stepmom would allow."

"Your parents are divorced," she says.

I lay on my horn when someone merges in front of us abruptly without signaling and roll my eyes when they flip me off in their rearview mirror. "My mom died when I was a kid, and my dad got remarried to his secretary a few years later. She has pretty bad allergies, so no pets."

"And no kids?"

"You're really adamant about the kid thing. Do you know something I don't?" I glance over at her to see she's trying to hide a smile. "Never married. No kids. I'm only 30, Carolina. Not nearly old enough to have a whole family."

She tilts her head at me. "Why not?"

I shrug. "I travel a lot for work. Never met anyone I was serious enough about for me to settle in that place." When she doesn't say anything, I turn the question on her. "What about you? Any demon ex-boyfriends or ex-boyfriends of other magical varieties?"

She hums to herself, thinking. "I dated a vampire once, very briefly, but just humans before that."

Naturally.

"Why'd you end it? Bad kisser? Too much teeth?" I ask, hopefully sounding unfazed, even though I'm internally reeling over the idea of the existence of vampires.

Which versions of them were right? I silently hoped it wasn't the shimmery ones, but for the good of the world, those might be the best ones. And what other kinds of creatures existed if witches and vampires were real?

Her laugh fills the car, and it's like it solves all the world's problems. Even the traffic in front of us clears up.

"No. I wouldn't consider converting."

I almost slam on the brakes at the statement. "To vampirism?"

She laughs again. "No, he was Jewish. I'm Catholic. *Cauldron*, not everything has to do with magic, Declan."

"That's cute. *Cauldron*," I murmur under my breath.

"Nice to know you think I'm cute," she says.

I raise a brow but don't look at her. "Not what I meant, but you should know that I find you to be much more than *cute*, Carolina."

"Anyway," she says, changing the subject, her favorite

pastime with me. "When we get to New York, we'll need to visit Annabelle. She's the leader of the City Coven. She'll either have the First Witch's grimoire or know where we can find it. She might also have an idea about who's behind all of this."

My forehead wrinkles in confusion. "Then why haven't you talked to her before this?"

She hesitates before answering. "Well, the other reason Camila isn't here is because they don't get along. Difference of...opinions."

"Oh?" Astonishment coats my voice because I wasn't sure that I could imagine Camila not getting along with someone... but then again, her ex-boyfriend is a demonic bounty hunter, and they seem to be on uneven footing.

"*That's* a story for another time," Carolina sighs like it's one she'd rather avoid telling altogether.

23

CAROLINA

Abuela died of a broken heart. My dad died trying to save my mom because he couldn't bear the thought of losing her. Camila's adventures in love had caused her more heartbreak than anything else. As far as I was concerned, love was just another way to give someone the power to hurt you.

I must have been a junior in high school when Camila claimed she'd had her heart "ripped out of her chest and stomped on" by her then-boyfriend. With red-rimmed eyes, tears streaming down her face, she sat at the kitchen counter while *abuela* made *pozole* for dinner, Camila's favorite food, to comfort her.

When Camila's sobs quiet, she drags herself upstairs for a pre-dinner nap.

"I'm never going to fall in love," I tell *abuela*, helping slice radishes and other garnishes.

She looks over her shoulder at me as she continues to stir the soup with a wooden spoon. "Is that so, *cariño*?"

I nod, returning to my task. Fingers curled against the tiny red vegetable; my knife cuts were methodical. In the kitchen with *abuela* was my favorite place. It was easy to find a role to fit into, and we never talked about magic while we cooked. *Cooking was its own form of magic*, she'd often say. Though, we both agreed baking was more of a science and left that for Cami.

"It seems like it's more trouble than it's worth. Just look at Camila." My voice is confident, decided.

Abuela hums in thought while she covers the soup with a lid. The humming is a habit of hers that Camila told me I'd picked up recently. It irked her beyond reason.

"Carolina, I'm going to tell you something I don't think you'll want to hear." *Here we go.* "But I'm going to tell you anyway because I think you'll need to hear it one day."

"Why can't you just tell me then?"

Her hand reaches in front of my field of vision from across the island counter. She covers my hand, and I set down the knife to look at her.

Abuela looks like me. Her frizzy (but somehow in a neat way), wavy hair is parted down the middle. Her eyes are a deep brown, and there are wrinkles in the outer corners that you don't really notice until her smile is wide enough to make her eyes squint. Even though she moved to a place that seems like it's under a constant cover of clouds, her skin is still a deep tan shade, and it makes my light caramel coloring pale in comparison.

She holds my gaze almost sternly like it's imperative that I listen closely to what she's about to say, but there's a sadness in the set of her mouth.

"Because one day, I might not be here to tell you when you need to hear it, so I'm telling you now." I swallow a lump in my throat that emerges at the thought of her being gone one day. "You're not like your mother and Camila; you don't wear your heart on your sleeve. No," she shakes her head slightly, "you keep it locked inside your chest, just like *abuelo*. He told *papá*

Miguel that he was never going to get married in a million years." She says it like it's the funniest thing in the world, and I can see the crinkles appear by her eyes.

She's told this story to Camila and me a thousand times, but I don't tell her that because I like that she doesn't seem so sad anymore.

"I know, I know. You know this part," she says, reaching out with the hand not holding mine to smooth the crease between my eyebrows. "But what you don't know is what *papá* Miguel told *abuelo*."

"What did he say?"

Her smile is warm, and it makes my chest feel lighter. "Love, *mijita*, is like our magic. Sometimes subtle, sometimes overwhelming, but *always* a force of nature." Her thumb strokes the back of my hand in soothing circles. "You may see the future, Carolina, but there are still things in this world that may surprise you. No matter how much you try to avoid them. When that day comes, remember, even the most powerful of witches can find themselves bewitched in ways they never imagined."

I let her words sink in as she pats my hand and pulls the cutting board to her.

"Now, go set out aspirin for your sister, *mijita*. With all that crying, she's going to need it."

Abuela was right. I never saw their deaths coming, and what a terrible surprise they were.

24

CAROLINA

"Carolina, wake up. We're here."

Declan's voice filters through the cloudy state of being awake and asleep at the same time. I blink my eyes open and lift my head, wincing at a knot in my neck from the position it had been held in. I must have drifted off at some point during the trip.

I glance over at him, noticing the lines etched deeper into his features than they had been before. A stab of guilt pains my chest because he looks like he hasn't been sleeping well, either.

"Sorry, I didn't mean to pass out on you." My voice is still drowsy as I look around at where we are. He must have parked a few blocks from Annabelle's apartment because I don't recognize the buildings immediately.

"Don't worry about it," he says, running a tired hand over his face. His fingers tremble slightly as he rubs his eyes. "I figured we could both use a coffee before heading over."

As a rule, I don't ever turn down coffee, and I was pretty sure he could use an entire vat of it. A coffee and a bagel later, we're walking the three blocks up to Annabelle's townhouse.

To say I was jealous of the City Coven would be a vast understatement. What must it be like living in a city that doesn't hate your existence or even know you exist for that matter? Camila and I couldn't walk down the street without getting at least two glares and one person crossing the street so they wouldn't get too close.

Annabelle lives on a street lined with brownstones. The trees that line the sidewalks are various shades of red, orange, and yellow. Fallen leaves have been pushed into haphazard piles against the gates and stairs that lead to the townhomes' doors. The scent of fresh rain and earth mingles with the crispness of the season, making the air feel alive. Annabelle's stairs are lined with pumpkins of various sizes, and her stair railings are woven with vine-like greenery.

"How festive," I murmur, mostly to myself, as we climb the few steps to her door. "Do you think I should have called first?" I ask Declan as I press on the doorbell.

He laughs. "A little late for that, don't you think?"

Annabelle's voice is startled when she answers the door. "Carolina? What are you doing here?" Her brows scrunch in confusion as she looks at Declan.

She looks the same as when I saw her last at *abuela's* funeral. Annabelle was my polar opposite. Her platinum blonde hair is pin-straight and hangs long over her shoulders. Her eyes, icy and calculating, seem to take in everything in a single glance, like she's already dissecting the situation. The blues of her eyes and the pink of her lips stand out against her fair skin. She's always looked more spritely than witchy, and every bit like a New Yorker.

Annabelle works as a paralegal for a small but well-known law firm, which meant that any time I saw her, she looked immaculate. Today is no exception. Her nails are painted a neutral color, filed, and clipped. Her black trousers are expertly paired with a fitted beige turtleneck, neatly accessorized with gold jewelry. Everything about her screamed effortless perfection, the kind that only someone deeply in control of their surroundings could manage. She made me feel mousy and underdressed.

While Camila couldn't stand her, Annabelle and I had a decent...working relationship. Some might even mistake us for friends. I think I could like her, but my own jealousy gets in the way most of the time, especially a few years ago.

She had everything I wanted and could never have: a life outside magic, outside Grove Meadow. The freedom to move wherever she wanted, though she'd have to give up her position in the City Coven. Even so, at least the city wouldn't drag her back here, kicking and screaming.

"Annabelle, this is Declan. Hope we're not interrupting anything," I say.

She frowns at me, and I know she's reading me. Her eyes flicker between Declan and me, her powers already working overtime.

"I assume you weren't just in the neighborhood. Come in," she says, opening the door further and stepping aside.

Annabelle is an empath. She can read others' emotions and, if they're strong enough, feel them herself. When she first came into her power, her parents sent her to live with us. Being able to read emotions in a city as big as New York...let's just say she went a *little* crazy. Grove Meadow had far fewer people, which made it easier for her to train.

Camila had never told me what really happened between them. I told Declan it was a long story because there were so many versions of it. In reality, I think Camila was just as jealous of Annabelle as I was, except it was because Annabelle was able to learn her powers so quickly.

On the surface, it may seem like being able to read emotions isn't that powerful of an ability, but she was basically a supernatural lie detector. Shifts in emotions, subtle redirections, false expressions of them…she was dangerous if you had something to hide.

"This way," Annabelle gestures us into her sitting room, which is every bit as meticulous and proper as she is.

The fireplace is the focal point of the room. It sits against the far wall, positioned in the center. On the right side, a grey couch is placed against the wall of windows, and on the left, stylish tan accent chairs. A pendant light hangs over the circular white stone coffee table in the center of the room. The entire space feels curated, down to the smallest details, as if she'd personally approved each and every item. Light streams in from the windows, making everything feel bright and airy.

Declan and I sit beside each other on the couch, not quite on opposite sides, but not touching. Annabelle studies the space between us as she settles into one of the chairs across from us. She waves a hand, and coffee and pastries appear in front of us.

"Please." She gestures to Declan, probably sensing his exhaustion. "So, what can I do for you?"

While Declan pours himself a cup of coffee, I lean forward.

"Something is coming, Annabelle. Something big. We've come to ask for your help figuring it out."

She nods slowly, her hand coming to her necklace and fiddling with the charm that hangs from it. The air around her shifts, her expression growing more serious.

"We've been observing the disappearances from afar. Solana detected an energy flair a few days ago; she and I have been investigating its source. We've narrowed it down to somewhere around you and Camila."

"There was a demon." Her eyes widen impossibly. "Called himself Nightcrawler. We used a *veritas* potion to interrogate him, but when we got too close, he kind of…"

"Vanquished himself?" she offers, and I nod. The tension in

the room thickens, and I can feel her attempting to probe deeper into my emotions. "Right, that would do it. Did he say anything useful before that?"

"Just that two people are behind this, and they aren't demons."

"Humans, then?" Her brows twitch in concern.

"Or witches."

At that, Annabelle leans forward, her eyes furrowing even more deeply. "You truly believe that."

And now I *know* she's trying to read me, but I've always been good at burying my emotions, especially from her. After all, we trained together.

"I believe it's possible, but I don't want that to be the case. Camila spoke to Esme about a prophecy, and she said your coven was working on figuring out how it's related."

Annabelle tilts her head. "We were, but we drew up a little short. Esme didn't come to me about it. She must have heard it from someone else."

She waves her hand again, and a book shimmers into sight. Declan chokes on his coffee, placing the cup down on the table.

"Sorry, still getting used to all this," Declan apologizes, coughing again.

Annabelle quirks an impeccably groomed brow at him, humor dotting her features. For a moment, the air between us lightens as Declan's awkwardness slices through the tension.

"Oh, don't worry, you'll adjust. It'll just take a while. When Christian learned about everything he was fainting multiple times a day, but he's very dramatic."

"Christian is your husband?" Declan asks.

Annabelle smiles. "My mirror soul. He's human, too."

Ah, fuck. I let the barrier on my emotions down ever so slightly so Annabelle could sense my warnings not to say anything else.

"Mirror soul?" Declan's brow furrows, and he looks over at me questioningly. I'm looking at Annabelle, practically pleading for her to change the subject.

Realization flickers across her features, and she glances at me apologetically. The empathy in her eyes sharpens, and I know she regrets saying anything.

"Ah, Carolina will explain later. I don't want to keep you too long. Let me just find the..." Annabelle trails off as she flips through the pages of the worn, leatherbound book. Her fingers move with a practiced ease over the ancient pages, tracing the symbols as if they're familiar to her.

The First Witch's grimoire is much bigger than ours. This book alone contains millennia of information about our species, and it's less than two feet away.

"Here it is," she says, passing me the book.

It feels light despite its size, but my magic thrums insight of me in its presence. I find the old prophecy easily, but Sam was right. It's not the same, and it's longer than we'd previously thought.

> *In the stillness where voices once thrived, spirits are*
> *drawn into the void. Between the realms of flesh*
> *and phantom, the threads of fate intertwine,*
> *heralding either ruin or redemption.*

> *When men fall, as shadows eclipse the light, a dark-*
> *ness will return, and a joined power will rule*
> *the worlds of might and magic.*

"They're still alive," I whisper as Declan stiffens beside me. "The mortals that have been taken. Their souls are on a middle plane. That's what Nightcrawler was doing when we stopped him." I look back at Annabelle. "The demon we saw, he'd taken over a mortal's body. They must be keeping them in the Underworld until the summoning is done."

"So whoever's behind this is selling the mortals out to the demons. Getting them to say the spell to open a portal," Annabelle says.

"The humans are calling the demons?" Declan asks.

Annabelle and I share a look. "They'd need to. For a summoning like this one, the mortals need to offer their souls willingly. The question is, who gave them the spell in the first place?"

"And which witches want to summon this power and why now?" I add.

Annabelle stands from her chair. "I'll have Solana see what she can find out now that we know for sure it's the right prophecy. I'll also see if she can pull the police files from the disappearances—what was that?"

"What?" I ask, following her gaze to Declan and then looking back at her.

"Not you, your..." she gestures to Declan.

"Oh, he's a detective," I say, realizing that Declan must have suddenly shifted his emotion at the statement, which drew her attention. "We'll get you the files."

Annabelle's eyes light with humor again. The tension she'd been carrying seemed to melt away for just a moment, replaced by a glimmer of amusement.

"Oh, that's...*convenient*," she says, the corners of her mouth lifting.

Declan mumbles something about *chains of evidence* and *case contamination*, which makes Annabelle laugh.

I stand, and Declan follows. "Let me know if you find anything. We'll go back and talk to Silas and Luna about this version of the prophecy and see if they know anything."

"Sounds good," she says as we walk to the door. "You

know, you could have called instead." I know she senses the unease in my body. She knows I had to see the prophecy for myself. "Well...it was good to see you, regardless," she says, pulling me against her in a hug. "I wish you'd visit more. And Camila, too."

"If we survive this, we'll come up as much as you want," I promise when we pull away from each other.

Annabelle smiles and then looks at Declan. "Good to meet you. Open invitation to you, too, Detective. Christian could use a mortal sounding board. Swap war stories and all that."

Declan looks like he could use a stiff drink, but also like he's slightly relieved that someone might know what he's been dealing with. "Thank you."

"I'll meet you outside, Declan. I just need to talk to Annabelle about one more thing," I tell him. He gives her a tight smile before turning toward the front door.

Annabelle's eyes follow Declan, and I wait until I hear his steps move down the stairs, crunching the fallen leaves, before looking at her.

"I'm sorry for bringing up the mirror soul thing," Annabelle says, looking genuinely distraught. Her empathy must be picking up on the turmoil I'm desperately trying to hide. "The connection between you two was just so strong. I could practically taste it."

I grimace. "Thanks for that imagery, but...you're sure? A mirror soul connection?"

She blinks at me, her expression stilling. "You didn't know."

I fix my gaze on a photo of her and Christian on the wall behind her. "I suspected. I've been having dreams...about him."

"Carolina, this is wonderful. Why aren't you happier about this?" Her voice is excited but perplexed.

She's right. Getting confirmation about what I thought

was true *should* make this one of the happiest moments of my life. Instead, my mouth dries, and I feel my chest tightening uncomfortably. The weight of all the lifetimes where we failed —where we died—crushes any joy that might have surfaced.

She sucks in a breath, reacting to my emotions. "What is it? What's wrong?"

I can feel the sorrow building in my throat. A pain I haven't allowed myself to feel. It's strong enough that Annabelle's lip begins to quiver, but my own is steady. "In those lives...we die. We never end up together."

"Carolina." My name is a whisper. "I'm so sorry. I'm so sorry I said it. I didn't know."

I shake my head. "How could you know?"

Annabelle catches her tears before they fall, using the sides of her index fingers as a barrier. Her usually composed features crumple with shared sorrow.

"It could be different this time, Caro. You have Camila. You have me. We can fight this. You aren't alone in this lifetime. Maybe you were back then, but you have people to protect you this time. To protect Declan."

Her voice is pleading, but I could never ask that of her or anyone else. I wouldn't put any of them at risk for something that was just a possibility. I wouldn't do that to them. I wouldn't do that to Declan.

25

CAROLINA

"Sorry about that. I just wanted to check with Annabelle about something," I say, bounding down the stairs to meet Declan at the gate.

He turns at the sound of my voice and gives me a tight smile. "No problem. I hope you got what you needed."

If he only knew.

"Not really, but it's fine. Solana's a pretty good second, so I'm sure she'll figure out what we can't. I want to stop by this place in the Lower East Side. Is that okay?"

Declan shrugs his shoulders. "Sure thing," he says as we begin our walk back to the car.

"You're being quiet," I note aloud.

"Sorry, I'm exhausted, and it's just a lot to take in. The idea that there's a *coven* of witches gathered in this city is...equal parts remarkable and terrifying. It makes me wonder what else is true, yknow? If witches, vampires, and demons exist, what else does?"

The question is fair, but it's a hard one. Toeing the line between keeping Declan on a need-to-know basis and wanting to be honest with him is more difficult than I thought it would be.

"You don't have to answer that," he says. "I'm just thinking out loud. I am curious about one thing, though." *Please don't let it be the mirror soul thing. Please don't let it be the mirror soul thing.* "You and Annabelle seem friendly. How come you never moved here? You know, before you had to come back to help your grandparents."

A wind whips down the street we're on, picking up the loose leaves on the sidewalk, and I wrap my arms around myself as we walk.

"I tried to leave, actually. I wanted to get out of Grove Meadow more than anything, but somehow, I ended up right back where I started. Kind of like something was drawing me back there...literally."

"Where would you go? If you could, that is?"

I laugh. "Where wouldn't I go? If I could leave, with any degree of longevity, I'd travel the world. My dad's parents would take these long summer trips when he was growing up. Weeks in other countries, learning about enirely new cultures. He would tell me about them like they were bedtime stories, and I ate them up. It's quite the cosmic joke that I have all this power, but I can't leave Grove Meadow for more than a few days, sometimes only a few hours."

Declan slides his hands into his coat pockets. "It's kind of like we're the opposite. You can't leave home, and I don't have one."

He doesn't say it sadly, just as a matter of fact, but that doesn't stop the anguish that expands throughout my body. A pang of empathy flares, unbidden, in my chest. It's strange how different our lives have been, yet in some ways, how similar.

"You don't see your dad and stepmom?"

"Nah. They're doing their own thing. I never fit with them, and then I stopped trying," he says as we approach his car.

Opening the passenger side door, I look at him over the hood of the car. "Sounds lonely."

Declan tilts his head, assessing me with those all-knowing blue eyes. "So do you."

The car ride is quiet but not uncomfortable.

He's a radio guy, and it reminds me of my mom dancing around the kitchen in the morning, listening to a station that only played Spanish music. Her voice would sing along, off-key but full of life, as she moved between pots and pans like she was performing a concert. Those mornings felt like magic, in their own way. When we'd complain it was too loud, she'd turn the dial higher until she couldn't hear our complaints anymore.

He pulls into a spot out front of Esme's shop. Mostly, I want to stop in to have her reinforce our protection wards. The apartment hasn't felt entirely safe since we learned someone broke in to steal Camila's necklace. But now that I've talked to Annabelle, I want to update her on the prophecy and see what she thinks about it.

"Thorn & Thistle?" Declan asks, looking out my window at the storefront sign.

"Have you heard of it?"

His eyes are narrow as he studies it. "Maybe. It sounds familiar, but I'm not sure why."

"Our friend Esme owns it," I tell him. Perhaps he'd come across it in his investigation of us.

"Esme Briarwood?"

I turn to look at him. "Yeah. How did you know that?"

He blinks. "Bas had a business card on his desk. I didn't think much of it, but maybe he's been investigating you more than I thought."

Why would Bas have Esme's business card? He knew Esme from school. Did he really track her down to interrogate her about us? I mean, that sounded like something Bas would do.

"Interesting. We'll have to ask Esme if she's talked to him recently. Come on. The sooner we do this, the sooner we can get back."

The corner of his mouth turns up. "Ironic coming from you."

"Yeah, we'll laugh about it later." I roll my eyes as we get out of the car.

Esme's shop sits between an Italian restaurant and a hardware store. The dark greens and purples of the shop's colors make it stand out from the others. Potted plants line the windows, and the stained-glass window embedded in the door reflects the sunlight at us.

"Another theme," Declan notes as I open the door. "Does she have magic paintings, too?"

Looking over my shoulder, I raise an eyebrow at him. "How do you know they're magic?" He gives me a look that clearly says, *That's a dumb question.* "Okay, we'll talk about that later."

"Just add it to the list," he mumbles. That's when I knew that he most definitely did *not* forget about the mirror soul thing.

"Esme?" I call into the shop. It's hard to see anything further than a few feet in front of you. A glorified bodega of overflowing plants.

"Back here!"

"You guys are really into plants, yeah?"

"It's our grandparents' fault. *Abuela* had a green thumb, and *abuelo* loved a good salve. They became pretty well known for it, and Esme was always interested in charms and potions." My voice drops to a whisper as we move further into the shop. The air feels thick with magic, a subtle hum vibrating through the leaves and vines that seem to pulse in response to my presence. "She doesn't have access to active magic, like Camila and I, but she can manipulate plants and different herbs to mimic a lot of active magic. Sam actually came to stay with us that summer so my grandparents could teach him similar techniques. Camila and I are much more into history and learning active magic."

He looks at me curiously. "So, you can learn how to do additional magic?"

"Kind of? Just like you can get physically stronger by working out, we can strengthen our magic. It's not so much that we *learn* new magic, I guess. It's more like our powers expand."

Declan's face is thoughtful. I can see the gears turning in his mind as he processes everything. There's a certain fascination in his eyes, a curiosity that seems to be growing the more he learns. "What exactly is your power?"

"Premonition," I say, pushing my way through plants that are being drawn to my magic. At least these ones don't have thorns.

"You're a psychic?"

"For all intents and purposes, yes."

He looks like he wants to say something else, but Esme's dark curls come into view. She's hauling a large box onto the checkout counter.

"Carolina!" she cries when she sees me. "What are you doing here?" Rounding the counter, she envelops me in a hug that feels like home. Her warmth is contagious, wrapping around me like a familiar blanket, and for a moment, I forget all the darkness that's looming. "Who's this?"

"Detective Declan O'Reilly, ma'am," he says, sticking his hand out for her to shake.

Her face is delighted as she looks over at me. Esme's green eyes are practically begging for more information.

"It's a long story, but Declan's helping us with the disappearances Camila told you about."

Esme's face falls instantly. The shift in her energy is palpable, like a shadow passing over the sun. "The disappearances? Did you find out anything about the prophecy?"

My magic flares in warning, but I'm not sure why. The sensation licks up my arms, and I wonder if it's trying to tell me not to talk about the prophecy out loud in case someone's listening. With all the portals that have been opened via these summonings, it wouldn't surprise me if one of the demons slipped through.

I'm cautious, just in case. Between Annabelle's coven and the familiars, I'm sure we could work through it without Esme's help.

"Not much. I just talked to Annabelle about it, and the coven's got nothing. But we're here because we need stronger protection wards for the apartment."

Esme's face grows more concerned, the space between her brows puckering. "Did something happen?"

"Someone stole Camila's necklace, so we think someone got past them," I explain, my fingers twitching slightly at the reminder of how vulnerable we've been.

It's unsettling, knowing someone could breach our wards and take something so personal.

Esme nods solemnly, walking around the counter again and pulling a box of crystals out from beneath the register. "Yes, of course. If you want them to charge as much as possible, they need to sit overnight."

Of course. That familiar frustration bubbles up in me, the need for things to happen faster than they can.

"There's nothing quicker?" I ask. It makes me uneasy, leaving Camila at home by herself when there's so much going on.

Esme shakes her head. "If you want wards stronger than the ones you have, the crystals need more time to charge. We can't double up because the wards will interfere with each other. I'm sorry. If I had known you were coming…"

Her apology sounds genuine, but the helplessness weighs heavy on both of us. I can tell Esme wishes she could do more.

"Right, of course. I should have called, but it was sort of a game-time decision."

Esme reaches across the counter and places a reassuring hand on mine. Her touch is warm, grounding me a little.

"We'll figure this out, Carolina. You and Camila will be safe. I'll work on these tonight, and they'll be ready for you by morning."

Declan, who had been quiet during the exchange, finally steps closer. I can feel his presence behind me, a comforting, steady force. "We appreciate it, Esme," he says, his voice calm but resolute.

Esme gives him a soft smile. "Anything for Carolina and Camila. You two have always been family to me."

I nod, thankful for her support but also keenly aware that time is of the essence. "Thank you, Esme. Really. We'll stop by in the morning."

As we turn to leave, Esme's voice calls out softly. "Carolina, wait."

I stop, turning back to face her. There's something in her expression, a flicker of uncertainty but also determination. It's a look I haven't seen on her before—one that makes me pause.

"There's something else I need to tell you," she says, lowering her voice even more. Her eyes dart to Declan, and I know this isn't something she'd normally share with an outsider.

I glance at Declan, who steps back slightly, giving us space. "What is it?"

Esme bites her lip, glancing around the shop as if someone might overhear, even though we're alone. The tension in her body makes me nervous, the air thick with something unspoken. "There's been talk...within the coven. Rumors that someone—" she hesitates as if saying it aloud will make it more real, "someone on the inside is helping these demons."

My blood runs cold. The words settle in the pit of my stomach like stones. "Inside the coven?" I repeat, my voice sharper than I intended.

Esme nods. Her face is tight with worry, the kind of concern that's been festering for a while. "I didn't want to believe it at first. But the evidence is starting to pile up, and it's becoming harder to ignore."

"What kind of evidence?" Declan steps forward again, his detective instincts kicking in. His voice is measured, but I can tell he's just as concerned.

Esme glances at him, then back at me, her fingers twisting together nervously. It's rare to see her this unsettled.

"Small things at first. Spells going wrong that shouldn't have. Wards failing in places they never should have. And then, more recently, the disappearances in Grove Meadow."

A chill runs down my spine. This is exactly what I was afraid of. But there were still things that didn't add up about that. Namely, why Grove Meadow? There were plenty of people here in the city to steal souls from. The disappearances in town felt oddly personal.

"Do you have any idea who it might be?" I ask, keeping my voice steady even though my mind is racing.

Esme shakes her head, looking frustrated. "No. Not yet. But I'm working on it. I've heard Solana's been keeping an eye on things, and I've been discreetly watching the others. But whoever it is, they're good. They're careful."

I nod, taking in everything Esme has told us, but something still feels off. We're still missing something big…and probably obvious.

"Keep us up to date, and we'll do the same if we hear anything. We'll come by tomorrow," I say, turning to leave. Declan follows, but not before giving Esme a reassuring nod.

Once we're outside, the cool air hits my face, and I breathe deeply, trying to shake off the growing sense of dread. The city feels different now, as if the shadows are creeping closer, threatening to swallow us whole.

Declan is quiet as we walk back to the car, but I can feel his mind working through everything we've just learned. It's a lot to process, even for me, and I've been living in this world my whole life. Though, the demon thing is a recent development.

When we reach the car, he stops and turns to me. "Why wouldn't Annabelle mention the possibility of a traitor within the coven?"

"Maybe she didn't want to say anything until she had evidence. It's a terrible accusation if it ends up not being true." Declan considers that and nods. "Sorry for making this an overnight field trip."

"Honestly, maybe it's a good thing," he says, opening his car door. "At least this way, I'll finally get some sleep."

He had a point.

26

DECLAN

I drive us to a hotel that Carolina mentioned she and Camila stay in when they visit. Opting to do so rather than cram themselves into Esme's studio or stay with Annabelle. Evidently, Camila *would rather die* than stay at Annabelle's.

I notice that Carolina has drifted off in the car again when I pull into the hotel parking lot. Her head is tilted slightly, lips parted in a soft sigh, and despite the exhaustion etched into her features, there's a certain peace there. A peace I haven't seen in her while she's awake. I didn't blame her in the slightest; I was practically counting down the minutes until I could get some rest.

"Carolina," I say, hoping my voice is enough to wake her up, but she doesn't so much as shift in her sleep. The rising and falling of her chest remains steady, deep. "Carolina." This time, I reach out to jostle her shoulder.

I gasp at the images that suddenly fill my mind, much like that night in her bedroom. Except there's something different this time. The images flash and change abruptly, like swiping through photos on a phone.

It's all skin. Carolina's mouth on me. My mouth on her.

Tangled sheets. I'm gripping her hips, and she's biting my shoulder.

Just as quickly as it started, I'm back in the car. I blink rapidly, trying to ground myself back in reality, the sudden shift leaving me breathless. Carolina lifts her head and looks at me with a confused expression.

"Declan?" I can feel the heat rising up my neck and into my face. "Are you alright?"

My chest is heaving, and I'm staring at her like I'm seeing her for the first time. Carolina's gaze drifts to my hand on her shoulder and back to my face. I drop my hand and press it to my chest instead.

"Did you...did you see my vision?" Her face is horrified, and her cheeks turn a shade of pink that I don't see on her often.

"Your vision?" I breathe out, but I can't look her in the eye. Shame and confusion war with the lingering heat from images I saw. It was too real, too vivid.

"You did and that's why you aren't looking at me, but how is that possible?"

I think that question is rhetorical, so I don't answer it, opting to exit the car for much-needed fresh air. The cool air hits my face like a slap, but it does nothing to erase the images burned into my mind. Once I'm outside, I keel over with my hands on my thighs. I'm still breathing heavily. I'm not even sure it has anything to do with what I saw...What *she* saw? *Confusing.*

"It's the magic," Carolina says, closing her door and walking over to me. She stands close but not close enough to touch, and I'm grateful because I don't know if I could handle that right now. "It can be overwhelming."

Between heavy exhalations, I say, "It wasn't like that last time."

Her brows knit together in confusion. "Last time? That

wasn't the first time this has happened?" Then, realization dawns on her. "That night in my room. You saw that?"

"Not a lot. You told me I needed to leave. Only lasted a few seconds, I think." The breathing is slowly but surely becoming easier.

She nods. "Seeing the future requires more magic than receiving a *nightvision*; that must be why you're like this. It's also probably why you were able to pass out on the floor after seeing it. Humans shouldn't be able to wield magic. You're not built for it."

You can say that again.

I give her a thumbs-up before putting my hands on my hips and walking around in a circle aimlessly. "So you're probably really fit if you can get those without..." I gesture to myself and my reaction.

Carolina laughs. "Magically, sure. Physically, not so much. I could run up a flight of stairs if it would make you feel better."

I wave her off. "No, it's fine. I'm going to go get rooms."

It would give me a distraction from the memory of the images of her fingernails scoring lines down my back, my hands sliding up her thighs, and her head tilted back, lips slightly parted.

Enough of that.

"I called Camila," Carolina says when I get back to the car. She's leaning against the trunk of the car, arms crossed over her chest, and her hair is pulled up into one of those clips that people shouldn't wear while they drive. "Things seem normal back in Grove Meadow. I filled her in on the new prophecy, so she and the familiars are going to work on that while we're here."

I nod. "Good call. We should try to work through it too, but honestly, I think I'm on the verge of passing out."

Concern flashes over Carolina's features. "Sorry, I shouldn't have asked you to come."

"No, I'm glad you did." I pause, considering my next question. "Why *did* you ask me to come? It seems like you've got everything under control."

Something passes between us when she meets my gaze. It feels like a livewire, charged and unforgiving.

"I'm not sure exactly. I got in my car, and then suddenly, I was parked beside your car in the parking lot of your hotel. Given my track record at being dragged back to Grove Meadow, I decided to bring you along...or at least, my magic decided you were coming along."

"Your magic made you bring me?" I asked skeptically.

She lets out a deep sigh, her arms uncrossing and tapping her fingers against the lid of the trunk. "Believe or don't, but it's what happened."

I narrow my gaze at her, studying her reaction. Weighing whether or not to bring up the thing that's been on my mind since we left Annabelle's townhouse.

What the hell?

"And it has nothing to do with this mirror soul thing?"

Carolina's skin pales, her body stiffens, and her fingers look like they might be denting my trunk. The shift in her demeanor is instant, a wall slamming down between us. Maybe bringing it up wasn't such a good idea after all.

"It has *everything* to do with this *mirror soul thing*," she practically seethes.

I wonder if this usually works for her. She seems like someone who's used to controlling the narrative, deciding when things get discussed and when they don't. Ignoring things until people stop bringing them up. Pretending that things aren't happening when they so obviously are. She'd be a terrible police officer...or maybe a good one, depending on the jurisdiction.

"But we're not going to talk about it," I say stepping closer to her.

"I thought you wanted to rest." She's back to crossing her arms over her chest.

"Will we talk about it after I rest?" My voice is doubtful, and I pause a few inches from her. I'm close enough that her arms brush against the opening of my jacket.

"Unlikely," she deadpans.

"Then now's good." I can feel my mouth quirk into a half-smile.

"Also unlikely."

Carolina's gaze is zeroed in on my mouth, and it sends a heat licking up my spine. I'm not thinking clearly anymore, though whether I was before was already questionable. My hand reaches out to cup her chin, but her arm stops it. The place where our skin touches sizzles, and we both recoil.

"Carolina," I whisper because it's all I can manage.

She's staring at my hand like I might have actually been burned. "Don't. I don't want to talk about it. Let's just get some rest."

There's no arguing with her as she slips past me and heads toward the hotel entrance.

Even if she didn't want to talk about it, I knew one thing for certain: the more she fought whatever connection we had, the more her magic pushed us together.

I COULD WEEP AT THE SIGHT OF THE BED IN THE CENTER OF THE ROOM, but Carolina's surprised and sharp gasp pulls my attention away.

"They only had one room left," I explain. "I can call the front desk for a cot if you'd be more comfortable."

She shakes her head, walks over to a desk under the window across the room, and drops into the chair. "It's fine." Carolina hasn't looked at me since the almost...whatever it almost was.

"You're sure?"

She nods, lifting her hand and moving her fingers in a circular motion in front of her. A carry-on luggage that looks a lot like mine and another duffel bag appears at her feet.

"I need to shower. Care if I go first?" she asks, picking up the duffel bag and rifling through it.

"All yours. I'm going to order room service. Any preferences?"

"Don't bother," she says, waving a hand and making an array of takeout boxes appear on the small dining table in the corner of the room.

Well, that was certainly faster. I mutter my thanks as she walks over to the bathroom entrance near where I'm standing. I don't want to sit on the bed until I'm in cleaner clothes, so she presses against me as she passes, the walkway too tight to avoid it.

"Sorry," she mumbles.

I wonder if she's worried about me seeing another vision. Whatever's been building between us in the past few weeks has to come to a head at some point, and I think that the vision was just proof of that. Proof that she might feel just as insane about me as I do about her.

My magic seems to like you. The thought echoes in my head as I collapse in the armchair near the dining table.

I'm hungry, but not as hungry as I am exhausted. Leaning my temple against my fist, I shut my eyes for just a moment.

My eyes blink open at the sound of the bathroom door opening. Steam emerges from the room and dilutes the light that surrounds Carolina. Her wet hair is already curling, and she towels the ends of it to keep from dripping water on the floor. The oversized pajama shirt she brought hits her mid-thigh, and I can't help staring at the exposed skin of her legs.

"All yours," she says, sitting on the bed with one leg beneath her while the other dangles on the side.

Hoisting myself out of the chair, I stretch out my back, which cracks in at least three places. Because I'm kind—and still half asleep—I don't even smirk when I catch Carolina staring at the sliver of exposed skin from my shirt riding up.

"Be right back."

The shower is the perfect temperature, and the pressure is just enough to uncoil all the knots in my back and shoulders. I practically groan at the feeling, and my eyes close of their own volition.

When an image of Carolina flashes in my mind, I have to brace myself against the shower wall, and my head dips low between my shoulder blades. This is *so* not the time.

My dick hardens to an uncomfortable degree as I fail to stop the images from coming, except now they're mixing with the dream from the other night and more recent ones of Carolina. My lips press together, suppressing a moan that's made it's way up my throat.

I need both hands to keep myself upright as the mental images become overwhelming. If her magic is causing this, I'd like it to stop, and if it's my own imagination, then I'm officially a masochist.

God, there were so many other things I should be thinking about other than this. The disappearances. Bas investigating

Esme. Who planted Camila's necklace. The prophecy. *Anything other than imagining Carolina on top of me.*

On top of me. Under me. Wrapped around me.

This time, I do groan softly as my balls tighten. I couldn't possibly come just by thinking about her...and her body and—I slam my mouth closed to muffle the sounds that bubble into my throat as my dick twitches, spurting lines of cum onto the tile. It seems to go on forever, but all I can do is continue to brace myself, teeth gritted, and pray Carolina can't hear anything that's happening in here.

That would be a first.

I rinse off and realize I didn't grab any clothes. *Great. This was going great.*

Wrapping a towel around myself, I open the door and step onto the carpeted floor. Carolina is sitting at the table with her legs tucked under her, eating something from one of the boxes, her phone pressed to her ear.

"Yeah," she says, and then takes a sip from a drink in a Styrofoam cup with a red straw.

She glances at me when she feels me staring and almost drops her cup. "Sorry," I mouth, walking past her to grab my suitcase.

"W- What was that, Annabelle?" Carolina stutters, which fills me with a strong sense of satisfaction. "Well, let me know what you find out," I hear her say as I head back into the bathroom to change.

When I emerge again from the bathroom, Carolina's still sitting at the table, but her phone is beside the takeout box. "Annabelle says she hasn't heard any rumors, so either someone's trying to throw us off, knowing that we've been talking to Esme, or they're keeping it from Annabelle."

"You don't think Annabelle could be lying?" I ask, pulling down the sheets.

Carolina looks over at me. "She could be, but I don't think so."

"Why not?"

"The prophecy suggests that someone powerful will take over the Magical and Mortal Worlds. No one with a mirror soul would want that to happen. A witch's mirror soul is their human half. Mirror souls are created for balance. They're granted to powerful witches as a way of reminding us that we're supposed to be living in harmony with mortals. Christian is Annabelle's mirror soul, and she'd sooner die than allow the possibility of...It doesn't matter. Annabelle wouldn't risk Christian."

She says it with such certainty; it sounds like she knows exactly what that's like.

27

CAROLINA

Declan's gaze is searing as I explain why I *know* Annabelle doesn't have anything to do with this. Things were getting too tense between us to avoid this subject for much longer.

I'd almost kissed him, for *Fates' sake*. That could not happen again.

"So is that it, then? What's happening between us?" he asks from his place by the bed.

There's something so strangely...domestic about this conversation. Like if we were normal, we'd be about to argue about something mundane before bed. Except, it's 3 in the afternoon, neither of us has slept in two days, I'm a witch, and I'm about to tell him why we can't ever be together.

I shake my head. "No. There's nothing happening between us, Declan."

It hurts me to say it, and I feel a part of my heart fracture at the lie. My magic doesn't like it either, and it seems to retaliate by making my fingertips prickle, mirroring the feeling of static shock.

The energy crackling between us is undeniable, and I know he can feel it too. I can sense the pulse of my magic trying to push against the walls I'm so desperately trying to build, and I'm afraid it'll betray me.

His brows raise, and he scoffs. "That's such bullshit, Carolina, and you know it."

It's anger that propels me out of the chair and to the opposite side of the bed. My heart is racing, and the tension between us feels like it could snap at any second.

"No, I don't *know* it, Declan. I don't know anything except what my dreams tell me."

Declan holds out his hands like the point he's arguing is tangible, sitting right in front of me, but I'm still missing it.

"And your dreams, at least the ones I've seen, tell you that we should be together." His voice is level, but there's an edge of desperation to it.

He's hoping he can reason with me, I'm sure, but I've already seen him die too many times to forget what will happen when this inevitably ends poorly.

The visions flash behind my eyes—the smell of smoke, the sound of screams, the moment I watch the life drain from his eyes. My throat tightens just thinking about it.

I shake my head again. "Well, you haven't seen how they end, and you're lucky for it. They're not just *dreams*, Declan. My power is foresight, but it also shows me my past lives. Throughout history, we're thrown together time and time again, but we always end the same way." My hands are splayed out in front of me, pleading for *him* to understand.

"Outside the car, you said what I saw was the *future*. The things I saw us doing are supposed to happen. *We're* supposed to happen, Carolina." His legs are bringing him closer to me, but when I take a step back, he freezes.

"The future can be changed, Declan. I've changed it before, and I can do it again."

A flash of hurt passes over his face, and it says more than

he ever could. *Why would I want to change us? Why didn't I want us?*

"Then show me," he says. This time, the desperation rings clear. His voice cracks slightly, and for a moment, I see the vulnerable side of him. The side that's just as scared of this as I am. "Show me how the dreams end."

My mouth drops open and closes again. Swirling in my fingertips again, my magic doesn't like that suggestion either. It wants to protect him from the visions. But maybe it's the only way to convince him that we'll never work. That it really is for the best we don't give in to some predetermined Fate.

"If you're so sure that I'll feel the same once I see what you have, then show me," he says again, but more confident.

His eyes bore into mine, challenging me to prove him wrong. I know this isn't just about us—it's about him needing to understand the truth I've been keeping from him.

"Fine," I relent, climbing on the bed and sitting cross-legged.

"Fine?" He's staring at me as if I'm kidding.

"Get on the bed. I'll show you how that dream ended." My voice is steady, but inside, my stomach churns with nerves. I've never shared something this personal with anyone, not even Camila.

He joins me a moment later, matching my position. The bed is a king, but his legs are so long that our knees touch. I want to take it back, and my magic certainly agrees I should, but it's the only way to erase the look in his eyes.

His gaze softens, and for a brief second, I wonder if he realizes how hard this is for me. I look at our hands, so close yet not touching, and the electricity between us buzzes louder.

"What do I do?" he asks.

"Nothing. I'll try to send you the vision like I did the other two times. I'm not entirely sure what triggered it, but I'm hoping it won't take much time. Hands."

I set my hands, palms facing up, on my knees. He places his hands on mine, and my fingers wrap around his wrists as his do the same to mine. The contact sends a jolt through me, and for a split second, I almost pull away. But I don't. I need him to see.

My eyes flutter closed as I recall the dream from a few nights ago. Just like I'm reading someone else's memories, I flip through my own until I find it.

THE BANGING ON THE DOOR BEGINS, AND THE SMELL OF SMOKE FINDS its way into my nose. It's only then does the weight of what's about to happen press against me.

We're about to die.

I can feel it in my bones. This is the last time I'm going to see him.

Turning around to pull on my dress, I yank the sleeves up my arms. I flinch at the chill of his touch against my spine as he works his way up the laces of my corseted dress. He's careful not to tighten it too much.

His touch is gentle and reassuring, as if he doesn't feel the same impending doom that weighs on me. His calmness only makes my panic worse.

The room we're in begins to fill with smoke, and I can hear the creaking sounds of wood splintering in a fire. The sound of the flames grows louder, a cruel reminder that time is running out.

"You need to leave," I tell him, looking up into his eyes of deep blue.

His hands wrap around my forearms, and he pulls me against him. Determined eyes meet my wary ones. "I'm not leaving you. Not now, not ever."

Panic lights up my throat, or maybe that's the smoke I'm inhaling. I can feel my chest tighten as fear grips me, and the weight of his words is too much.

Doesn't he understand? He can still survive.

"They want me, not you," I whisper. "You have to run."

He's so calm about this. He's accepted his fate, while I refuse. The back of his hand strokes my cheek delicately, starkly contrasting with what lies outside the cabin.

We're drowning out the sound of the people gathered. The ones chanting "witch." The ones who have brought their pitch-forks and torches. They've followed the magical footprints straight to my door.

"I should have let them die."

I'm ashamed of myself the second it's left my mouth, but he only looks at me more lovingly. His gaze softens, filled with the kind of love that makes me want to cry. How can he still look at me that way after everything? After what I've condemned him to?

"You do not mean that," he says simply.

He's right, of course. He's always right.

I do not regret saving little Cassandra Huttons from the disease that swept our town. She gets the chance to have the future I saw when I treated her.

I do not regret saving the crops from failing this season. The townsfolk will have plenty to eat and enough to recoup last year's losses.

I...do regret saving William Johnson from drowning when we were kids. There was no doubt he was the leader of this witch-fearing mob.

"You saved them." Awe fills his tone, and his eyes shine with unshed tears.

For them, for me, or for us, I'm not sure. Maybe he's finally gotten a grip, and his sense of mortality is sinking in. My magic is praying that's the case.

"Stop looking at me like you hope I'm going to leave you here," he says.

I shake my head, pulling away from his touch. "I can't believe you'd stay here and give up your life so frivolously. You have a chance to have a normal life, and instead, you're going to waste it, dying in here with me."

He looks offended and hurt by my words. "What do you think is going to happen if I walk out of this cabin? Those people will not welcome me with open arms. I'd be running from this town for the rest of my life when I could leave this one with you. Get the chance to try again in another place and time with you, and maybe get a different ending."

The flames have made their way into the cabin, catching on the fabric curtains covering the windows and spreading across the ceiling. The heat is unbearable now, and the smoke stings my eyes. There's no escape. It will only be a few minutes before the room is engulfed, and the foundation collapses, burying us in our sanctuary from the world.

His hands wrap around my shoulders, thumbs stroking over exposed skin. "You still don't understand the extent of my feelings for you. Even now. To even call them *feelings* is a vast misrepresentation of the way my soul perfectly matches yours. I will *always* choose you. I've seen how good, how selfless, how pure you are, my love. I do not wish to exist in a world—a lifetime—without you in it."

This I understand. More than he could possibly know. His words cut deep because I know exactly what he means. I feel it too—the way our souls seem to mirror each other. But that doesn't change what's coming. Why can't he see that by asking him to run, I am doing the same thing? I am choosing his life over the comfort of him staying with me until the end.

"I know that face," he says sadly. It's almost drowned out by the snapping of the wooden beams holding this place together. Any second now. "Maybe in the next life, you will get your way, but in this one, I'm choosing to stay."

His head lowers, and his mouth catches mine like it wants to stay there for eternity. It's a soft yet demanding kiss—a perfect final one.

When he pulls his head away from mine, he wraps his arms around me and holds me against him as everything around us is incinerated, and we are nothing but ash on the wind.

THE VISION FADES SLOWLY, LIKE SMOKE DISSIPATING IN THE AIR, BUT the ache it leaves behind is fresh and raw. My fingers are still wrapped around Declan's wrists, and I can feel the tension in his body as he processes what he just saw. The silence between us is thick, almost unbearable. I can't bring myself to open my eyes just yet, not until he says something. *Anything.*

When I finally do open them, I'm met with his wide, stormy gaze. He's staring at me like he's seeing me for the first time, and the air between us feels like it's charged with a thousand unsaid words.

"You didn't tell me it was like that," he whispers, voice hoarse. His hands tighten slightly around my wrists, grounding me in the present, but I can feel his shock and heartbreak pulsing through the connection.

"I tried," I say softly, my voice sounding much smaller than I intended. My throat tightens, and I feel the weight of all the other lives pressing down on me—the ones where I lost him, the ones where he died for me.

He pulls his hands away from mine and scrubs them over his face, groaning as if he's trying to expel the emotions surging inside him. "Carolina, this...this wasn't just a dream." His voice is rough, full of disbelief. "It felt real. Too real."

I nod. "Because they were once. The memories are stored in some sort of magic mental time capsule. The ones of you in them only started in the last year or so. I didn't start seeing your face until recently. After I met you."

He stares at me, his chest rising and falling heavily. The gravity of what I've shared with him has clearly shaken him, but I don't know how else to make him see.

"And we're supposed to just accept that?" His voice breaks, the weight of all those lifetimes bearing down on him now, too. "That no matter what we do, no matter what we want, it always ends the same way?"

I bite my lip, fighting back the tears that are threatening to spill over. "It's why we can't be together, Declan. I'm trying to save you from that. I don't want to watch you die again." My heart shatters even as I say the words, but I know they're true. I can't bear the thought of losing him again, not like this.

I've already seen him almost die in this lifetime once, there was no reason to risk it again.

But you changed that. You saved him, my magic seems to remind me.

He shakes his head, disbelief etched into every line of his face. "But what if this time is different? What if—"

"It's never different," I interrupt, more harshly than I intend. "It always ends the same. We die. Over and over again, in every life, in every timeline, we die."

For a moment, the only sound in the room is the faint dripping of the shower faucet. The heaviness of the words lingers between us, each second dragging out the tension like a blade slowly being twisted.

Declan's face is a storm of emotions—anger, frustration, grief—but underneath it all, there's still that stubborn hope that refuses to die. "But what if we could change it?" His voice is softer now, more pleading. "What if we could find a way?"

I shake my head. "It's too risky, Declan. What if we just end up in the same position we always do?"

His hand reaches out, grabbing mine, his touch grounding me in the present even as everything else feels like it's spiraling. He leans forward, his face inches from mine, his voice low and fierce. "I don't care. I'd rather fight for us and lose, than not try at all."

I close my eyes, letting his words settle over me. For so long, I've been trying to protect him, to push him away for his own sake. But what if he's right? What if this time, things could be different?

It's the literal definition of insanity—doing the same thing over and over again and expecting a new outcome.

My magic flares in my chest, pulsing with indecision. It doesn't want to lose him, just like I don't. But every part of me knows the risks are too great.

I open my eyes and meet his gaze, and for a moment, I let myself imagine what it would be like to fight for us. To choose love over fear. To stand beside him, no matter what the future holds.

But then the memories crash back into me—the flames, the smoke, the feeling of his body turning to ash in my arms. The weight of those losses is too heavy, and I can't shake the fear that we're doomed to repeat them.

"I can't," I say, my voice breaking. "I can't go through that again."

Declan's face falls, the hope draining from his eyes. The

pain that flashes across his features is like a knife twisting in my chest.

"But you don't have to," he says, his voice soft and full of sorrow. "You don't have to protect me, Carolina. You don't have to carry this burden alone."

I pull my hand from his, stepping off the bed as if putting distance between us will somehow lessen the ache. But it doesn't. If anything, it only makes the pain sharper.

"I'm sorry," I whisper, my voice barely audible. My heart feels like it's breaking all over again, but I know I have to do this. I have to let him go.

Declan watches me for a long moment, his blue eyes filled with a mix of grief and understanding.

"I know," he says quietly. Then, without another word, he turns and walks out of the room, leaving me standing there, alone with the gravity of our shared history—and the future we'll never have.

As the door clicks shut, I sink onto the bed, my hands trembling with the effort it takes to hold myself together. The vision may be over, but the echoes of our past lives still linger, haunting me. And no matter how hard I try, I can't shake the feeling that this—this moment right here—was always part of the plan.

28

DECLAN

I step out of the hotel room, pulling the door shut behind me with a quiet click. The cold hallway air hits me, and I breathe deeply, trying to shake the heat that still clings to my skin from being in that room. From being near her.

Carolina.

What the hell is happening to me?

Dropping my shoes on the carpeted floor, I lean against the wall, scrubbing a hand over my face. My head is spinning, my thoughts tangled like a knot I can't seem to unravel. I've dealt with a lot of messed up things before—crime scenes, violent suspects, even the occasional cult behaviors—but this...this is different.

It's *her*.

And that vision.

God, that vision. Seeing myself *die*. I couldn't escape it, couldn't just shake it off like a bad dream. I felt it. The smoke. The fire. The crushing burden of inevitability. And Carolina, trying so damn hard to save me, knowing it was futile.

Slipping into my shoes, I push off the wall and start walking down the hallway. I don't know where I'm going. *Hell,* I don't even know what I'm trying to figure out anymore.

Maybe I just need to clear my head and get some distance before I make another mistake. Before I do something really stupid—like kiss her.

God, I wanted to kiss her. Even with everything else we were dealing with, all the danger, all the unknowns, I couldn't stop thinking about how close we came in the car. How close we were in that room just now.

Carolina wants to pretend none of this is happening between us, but I can't. Not anymore. She's all I can think about. Her magic, her visions, her damn mirror soul talk. I'm being dragged into it, whether I want to or not.

And I do want to. *God*, do I want to.

But then there's that other thing—the thing I can't shake, no matter how hard I try.

The vision of my death.

It wasn't just some fleeting nightmare or vague premonition. It was real. I could feel the heat of the flames, the smoke choking the air from my lungs. I felt the moment I realized I wasn't getting out of that cabin. The resignation in my bones, the way Carolina looked at me—knowing she couldn't save me. She kept telling me to run, but I wouldn't. I wouldn't leave her.

And I died for it.

I stop in front of a window at the end of the hall and stare out at the city skyline. It's comforting, in a weird way, to know the world is still moving out there, even while mine feels like it's spiraling out of control.

I try to focus on the other things we should be worrying about. The disappearances. The demons. Camila's stolen necklace. But instead, all I can think about is the way Carolina looked at me when I mentioned the mirror soul thing in the car and then again in the room.

That moment. That flicker of fear in her eyes.

I press my hand against the cold glass of the window, letting the chill seep into my skin.

What is it, Carolina? Why does seeing me die shake you so much?

She told me she'd seen me die in those visions, in those past lives. She's seen it happen over and over again. And I get why she's scared. I get why she's shutting me out. But the thing is, I'm not scared of dying. I've seen too much and done too much to be afraid of that. What scares me is not getting the chance to really be with her. To try, at least, to break whatever cycle we're caught in.

I rub the back of my neck and shake my head, frustration building in my chest. I'm not afraid of dying, but what the hell kind of life is this if we just keep pushing each other away?

I think about what she said earlier, how her magic made her bring me along. Like she didn't have a choice. Like it was something out of her control.

Maybe that's part of it. Maybe it's the magic that's making everything between us feel so...intense. But deep down, I know it's more than that. There's something real here, something I can't explain, and no amount of magic or visions or fate is going to change that.

I'm not going to let her push me away. Not when I know she feels the same pull I do.

With a sigh, I turn away from the window and head toward the elevator. I need air. Real air. Maybe some distance will help me figure this out. I press the button, waiting for the doors to slide open, the dim lights overhead flickering slightly. Even the hotel feels on edge, like everything's out of sync.

The elevator dings, and I step inside, leaning against the back wall as the doors close. The hum of the machinery is almost comforting; a brief moment of normal before everything gets complicated again.

I think about what she said—about her magic deciding things for her. It's strange to think that someone so powerful can be at the mercy of her own abilities. To think that someone who can see the future is just as trapped by it as the rest of us. She's strong, no doubt about it, but there's a vulnerability there she doesn't want to admit. It makes her human, despite the power humming under her skin.

The elevator doors open with a soft chime, and I step into the lobby. A few people mill about, but the place is mostly empty. I push through the glass doors, the cold autumn air hitting me like a wall. It's exactly what I need.

I've been a cop long enough to know that you can't ignore the bad stuff. It doesn't just go away because you want it to. You have to face it head-on, even when it scares the shit out of you. And right now, the thing that scares me the most isn't the demons or the disappearances—it's dying without ever getting the chance to be with her.

I stop in the middle of the sidewalk, my breath coming out in puffs. Carolina's been keeping me at arm's length since the beginning, trying to protect me from something she thinks is inevitable. But the truth is, I don't need protection from her. I never have.

What I need is for her to trust me and believe that we can fight this together, whatever *this* turns out to be.

One thing is clear: I'm not walking away from this. From her. I don't care what fate has planned or what she thinks is destined to happen.

I'm going to fight for us. For whatever this thing between us is. Because for the first time in a long time, something feels right. Even if it's wrapped in danger and magic, it feels real.

And I'm not about to let that go.

The outside chill starts to seep into my bones, my skin prickling with goosebumps as I walk down the quiet street.

Each breath I take is visible in the crisp fall air, and it clears my head just enough for me to make sense of the whirlwind of thoughts still spinning in my mind. After a few more blocks, the exhaustion from the last two days starts to settle back into my muscles.

I turn back toward the hotel, my footsteps quieter now as I make my way inside. The lobby is empty, the muted lights casting long shadows on the floor. I nod at the night clerk, who doesn't bother to look up from her book, and step into the elevator. When the doors slide open, it feels like stepping back into a different world—one where everything is heavier. My body, my mind, and everything that's waiting for me upstairs.

When I get back to the room, Carolina's already asleep. She's curled up on her side, her breathing soft and steady, her face half-hidden by a cascade of dark hair. The sight of her—so peaceful, so vulnerable—hits me in a way I wasn't expecting. It's a stark contrast to the chaos of the last few days, and for a moment, I just stand there, watching her.

I feel the weight of everything we've been through settle over me again, but this time, it's mixed with something else. Something deeper. More personal. I want to protect her from all of it—from the demons, from the dark parts of her own magic that she can't seem to control. But I can't do that if she keeps shutting me out.

I strip off my shoes and jacket and slip into the bed beside her, careful not to jostle her or get too close. The exhaustion is so thick that it pulls at me immediately, and my body aches with the need to sleep. But I can't stop my mind from wandering.

The last thing I want is to wake up and see another vision of my own death. Or worse, to find Carolina next to me, and the line between us so blurred that there's no going back. It's too much, even though every fiber of my being wants to pull her closer, to feel her warmth against me. But I don't. Not tonight.

It feels like only a few minutes pass before the sound of my phone vibrating against the nightstand pulls me out of the dark fog of sleep. There's a pressure against my chest, and I'm disoriented for a second before I realize why. Carolina's draped over me, her arm wrapped around my torso, her body pressed against my side like it belongs there.

My arm tightens around her instinctively as I reach for my phone with my free hand, my eyes still half-closed. I manage to hit the screen and mumble, "Detective O'Reilly," my voice rough and thick with sleep.

Bas's voice cuts through the haze like a hammer. "Where are you?"

I groan softly, rubbing my eyes with my thumb and forefinger, and glance at the clock on my phone screen. 6:15 a.m. Why is Bas even awake? And why is he bothering me when he should be under a mountain of paperwork?

"Did you find something?" I ask, not bothering to hide my irritation.

As I wait for his response, Carolina shifts against me, her arm tightening around my torso in her sleep. The warmth of her skin against mine sends a slow heat through my body, settling low in my stomach. It's a dangerous feeling—one I know I can't indulge. But it's hard to ignore the way my body reacts to hers, the way my heart races just being close to her. For a second, I wonder what it would be like to just hang up on Bas and stay under these blankets with her forever.

But I can't. We both know I can't.

"No," Bas finally says, his voice pulling me out of my thoughts. "The Captain hasn't seen you since the day before yesterday, and since we're in the middle of multiple active missing person cases, he sent me to track you down."

"Okay, well, you found me," I reply, glancing at the ceiling, trying to keep my voice level. "I'll be in later."

But of course, Bas doesn't stop there. "See, the thing is, O'Reilly, I'm standing in front of your hotel room, and your car's not in the lot. But guess whose is."

Shit.

Carolina stirs, lifting her head and blinking blearily at me. Her eyes widen as she realizes she's been cuddled up against me in her sleep. She pulls away slowly, sliding across the bed, and I can feel her hesitation. My body wants to follow after her, to pull her back, but my brain's still catching up to what Bas just said.

"I'm following up on a lead in New York," I say, trying to keep my voice casual, though I'm mentally cursing at how quickly things just got complicated. I rub a hand over my face, willing the pulsing in my temple to disappear. "Carolina asked to come along."

"With Carolina Castillo?" Bas's voice is full of suspicion, and I know what he's thinking. Carolina's still a person of interest in the case—at least, officially—and me being with her is going to raise more questions than I care to answer right now.

I press a hand to my forehead, staring up at the ceiling. "I came to talk to Esme Briarwood. Carolina's friends with her, and she asked to come along. I didn't see a reason she couldn't."

There's a long pause, and I can practically feel Bas piecing it together on the other end of the line. "Esme Briarwood? Why would you need to talk to her?"

"I thought she might be able to help identify the substance found at the crime scenes," I say, frowning at the pale white ceiling. "CSI couldn't figure out what it was. Might be something imported."

Another pause, longer this time. "Got it."

I let out a slow breath of relief. "You can tell the Captain I'll be back today. Anything else?"

"No, that's it. Still working on that paper trail for Owen Donovan, but I don't think we're going to find anything."

"Keep looking," I say automatically. "He was hiding something. I'm sure of it."

Bas clicks off, and I let the phone fall onto the bed with a sigh. Carolina has moved across the room, sitting stiffly in the chair by the window. She's putting as much distance between us as she can, like she needs the space to think or breathe.

"Sebastian?" she asks, her voice quiet, but there's a tension in it I can't ignore.

"Yeah," I say, sitting up in the bed and rubbing the back of my neck. My body feels stiff and sore from the past few days, and as I roll my neck to the side, I hear a series of pops that make me wince.

"What time did you get back last night?" she asks, ignoring the obvious tension between us. It's not an invitation, but it's something.

I meet her gaze, watching for any sign of what she's thinking. "I wasn't gone long. Probably a half hour after I left. Sorry about that—walking out, I mean. I just needed a second."

Her expression softens slightly. "Understandable."

That one word sends a jolt of relief through me. Maybe we're getting somewhere. Maybe things between us aren't as broken as they feel.

"It gave me some clarity on our situation, though," I say, shifting on the bed, leaning forward to rest my elbows on my knees.

"Oh?" she replies, her voice wary.

I take a deep breath, knowing this next part is a gamble,

but one I have to take. "Yeah. I decided I'm going to fight for you. For us."

Her eyes snap to mine, wide with disbelief. "What?"

"You heard me."

"I don't think I did because what I heard is absolutely impossible. No sane person would come to that decision."

I shrug, giving her a teasing smile. "I never pegged you as a coward, Carolina."

Her eyes flash with anger, and I know I've struck a nerve. "Excuse me?"

"You're so scared of a past that isn't even ours," I say, my voice soft but firm. "You're a different person in this life. You have Camila, Silas, and Luna. You've seen us together. We're inevitable."

She shakes her head, her voice tight with frustration. "The future can change. The past can't."

I lean forward, my gaze locking with hers. "And have you ever considered that this is what your magic is trying to tell you? That by showing you all the ways we end, it wants you—wants us—to find a way to survive? Or are you just too scared to let someone in that you refuse to see what's right in front of you?"

Her jaw tightens, her eyes hardening. "I'm not afraid of anything."

I stand up, crossing the room until I'm standing right in front of her, looking down into her eyes. "Then prove it."

29

CAROLINA

I shake my head at his provocation. He thinks he can get under my skin by goading me. That I'll give in to my magic if he simply says the right things.

When he walked out the door yesterday, a part of me wished I could take it all back. I wished I could let myself have this, have *him*, but I knew I couldn't. There was only so much of the future I could change before the Fates intervened.

But was that just an excuse I told myself because I was scared of losing someone else?

I couldn't be sure.

Seeing Declan die in my dreams was nothing compared to the panic I felt when I saw him get hit with Nightcrawler's energy ball.

Annabelle's words ring in my head. *You aren't alone in this lifetime. Maybe you were back then, but you have people to protect you this time. To protect Declan.*

If I wanted him in this lifetime, I'd have help—people to help me protect him and ensure a different outcome. Even so, it didn't change my parents' outcome...my grandparents'.

"You can't let a fear of a future that might not happen stop you from letting us be together, Carolina. If we're mirror souls

—if we're *fated*—no matter how much you try, we'll always have this pull, this invisible string that infinitely ties my soul to yours."

I shake my head again, a frustration growing in the pit of my stomach. "You still don't get it."

At this, anger flashes across his features. "You think *I* wasn't terrified when you went to the Underworld? I didn't sleep. I kept seeing *you* dead in my dreams. I've seen so much evil in this lifetime, Carolina. Maybe not your kind of evil, but evil just the same.

"And I may not be a warlock or ever be able to grasp what you're experiencing in your dreams completely, but your soul and mine are the *same*. We want the same things; you're just pretending that you don't."

When did he get so close?

His eyes, not his mouth, smirk at my silence. "Have you run out of excuses?"

Yes.

The moment I decided to give in, it was instantaneous. Two magnets colliding so suddenly that they may have altered space and time.

His mouth catches mine, and the stars that gather behind my eyelids are blinding. He pulls back suddenly.

"Whoa," he whispers.

I blink at him, clearing my vision. "What?"

He looks at me with an awe that I only ever get from him. "I think I can feel it. Your magic."

My brows raise, and my magic hums in confirmation, so I know he's not crazy.

"Do you want to stop?" I ask, even though I'm not entirely sure my magic will let me. It's already uncomfortably humming under my skin, prickling my fingertips.

"What's that thing you say?" he asks with a ghost of a grin. "*Cauldron*, no."

I laugh, and he captures the sound in his mouth. I groan when his teeth sink into my lower lip, and his tongue takes the opportunity to slip into my mouth. I sink into him. My body presses against the hard ridges of his like I was molded to fit into the shape of him.

"Carolina," he whispers against my lips, and I know I'm gone.

There's no escaping this, no avoiding it anymore. I'll do anything I must to keep him safe, even if it's at the expense of myself.

My fingers dig into his neck and arm, like I'm trying to fuse myself to him.

He pulls my pajama shirt over my head, leaving the top of me exposed. There's a growl that emanates from the back of Declan's throat that has my body clenching.

It's slow, his perusal of my body. His gaze shifts from left to right and back again, like he's reading me, and there's going to be a test later.

"Your turn." My voice is soft, but it jolts him like a stern command, and he strips off his shirt.

I get it now. The urge to memorize every mark and expanse of skin. I'm doing it now, too. Except he's done before me and has lost his patience.

"On the bed, Carolina." The gruffness of his voice sends a pulse to every part of my body, and there's a rush of desire that tightens my core.

This is nothing like my dreams. It's so much better. He's real and here...and maybe I'll get to keep him.

"Carolina," his tone is a warning, and if this weren't our first time together, I might try to push him and test his limits.

He turns me and walks us backward until the backs of my

thighs hit the bed, and I sit on the edge. Declan's still standing in front of me, and I look up at him from beneath my lashes.

His calloused thumb reaches up to stroke my bottom lip, pulling it down. I wrap my mouth around his finger and suck lightly, my tongue drifting over it, whirling around the tip. Declan draws his bottom lip between his teeth, and his eyes dilate, fixed on my mouth.

"God, now that I have you, I don't even know what to do with you," he says, pulling his hand from my mouth and trailing it down my body.

The whimper that comes from my mouth is a sound I've never made before. "Declan, *please*."

His brows raise at me in surprise. "I didn't take you for someone who begged."

My tongue swipes across my lips. "Guess I just want you that badly."

That spurs him forward. His hands grip the sides of my sleep shorts, and I lift my hips so he can pull them down my legs, taking my underwear with them.

His gaze is hungry when he looks down at my newly exposed body. "Lay back, Carolina. I won't ask twice this time."

I listen to his command this time as he drops to his knees, lifting my legs over his shoulders. I'm trembling in anticipation, and it worsens when his breath fans across my core.

"You like that, Carolina?"

I mumble a confirmation, my fingers gripping the sheets and twisting. He runs his tongue against my slit, and I buck forward, trying to grind myself against his mouth.

"No, this was a terrible idea. I'm sorry."

My head snaps to him, panicked that he's not going to continue. I need him like oxygen, since this room doesn't seem to have any anymore.

But my panic subsides, and my mouth waters when I see

he's pulling off his shorts, and I see his length. My core tightens, and the lust that runs through me, my magic, is almost too much to bear.

"I wish I could draw this out longer, but my body isn't my friend right now," he laughs, and it tugs at my chest.

There's all of this tension, but even still, he's him, and I'm me. I'd thought a mirror soul would consume every part of me, but it's just an extension of the two of us. A sense of completeness wraps around me.

I lean forward and reach for him, pressing my mouth against his, tasting myself on his lips. Declan's hands thread into my hair, and I grind myself against his lower abdomen, trying to get any relief from the raging inferno growing under my skin and in the pit of my core.

My magic and I grow frustrated when he pulls his hips back slightly, taking the friction off my clit. The whine that leaves my mouth makes him smile.

"I'll take care of it," he whispers as he pulls away.

He stands between my legs, the height of the bed allowing him to line up with me perfectly, and I moan at the first nudge of him inside me.

"*Fuck,*" he exhales as he notches himself further in.

He lifts my legs against his body and presses into me completely. The angle letting him hit deep inside me, causing my back to arch and my eyes to roll back in my head.

Declan drops a hand from one of my legs and expertly rubs two fingers against my clit. The pressure builds deep in my belly, and heat spreads across my chest. It feels like I'm going to explode. My hands release the sheets, and I tweak my nipples between my thumb and forefinger.

At the sight, Declan's hips begin to move faster against me, and my head tips back at the building sensation in my lower body.

"Eyes on me, Carolina. I want to see you when you come undone."

The moment my gaze meets his, and I see the veins in his neck bulge with his restraint, something unravels in me. The pressure is suddenly too much, and I spill over. Shattering into millions of tiny pieces, never to be assembled in the same way again but somehow still perfectly whole.

"*Christ,* Carolina," he bites out, his hips losing their rhythm, their pace turning punishing as I ride out my orgasm.

He's not far behind me when he stills. His hand tightens around my ankle, and he presses a kiss against it before he slowly pulls himself out of me. I wince at the loss of him.

My magic ignites at the loss of his skin against mine, and I shift uncomfortably against the sheets.

I don't have to say anything to Declan; it's like he knows how much I need him to keep his hands on me because he leans forward to gather me in his arms. My legs wrap around his waist, and my arms cross at the back of his neck while his hands grip the backs of my thighs to keep me propped against him.

Maybe he needs to feel me just as much.

"Shower?" he asks, already moving us to the bathroom as I kiss the expanse of skin that connects his neck and shoulder.

My magic grows impatient to have him again, and I feel like a hormonal teenager. I want to score lines down his back and mark him as mine. I want him to bury himself so far inside me that my magic can't tell where I end, and he begins. I want—

He hardens against me, and his skin flushes an even deeper shade of red. "Sorry, he's got a mind of his own," he says, removing one hand from my leg to turn on the shower head.

"Probably a similar one to my magic," I laugh against his chest.

"So, is this how it will be from now on?" Declan asks as I unwind my legs and slide down his body.

Holding out my hand, I summon a hair tie and pull my hair up so it won't get wet. "That would be inconvenient. We'd never get any work done."

There's a smile on his lips as he dips his head back to let the water cascade over his hair and down his body. I've never been jealous of water before, but I suppose there's a first time for everything.

"What?" he asks when he catches me staring.

I shake my head as I step into the shower in front of him. "Nothing."

"So, how does this premonition thing work?"

I raise my eyebrows. "Usually, I just touch someone, and I can see flashes of their future."

"Have you seen mine?" he asks as we swap places so I'm under the water.

I could lie to him. I could tell him no. I could keep the fact that he was supposed to die in the alley a secret.

To buy myself more time, I summon my body wash from home and pour some into my hand before passing the bottle to him.

"Are you…allowed to do that? Doesn't magic have consequences or whatever?"

I laugh. "Magic is magic. The only magic with that kind of karma is dark magic, and teleporting objects is minor magic. I don't need a spell, just a desire for something, and it appears." I demonstrate again by summoning a washcloth in my other hand.

The smile starts in his eyes and ends at his mouth as he pulls me against him. His mouth presses against mine, and I sigh in blatant satisfaction.

It feels like a fantasy. Like he can't be real. But my magic reminds me he is. It feels stronger and more complete. *I feel more complete.*

The bond we share isn't tangible. It's not something we can see or even pinpoint in our bodies. It's just an overwhelming feeling of being whole.

Declan drags the soapy washcloth across my back, and I hum contentedly.

"Stop making those sounds, or we're going to end up getting dirty all over again."

My cheeks heat, and I pull my lips together to muffle the sound that almost escapes my mouth. I'm worried it might have been a giggle.

When we're done with our shower teasing, it continues in the room with us both wrapped in towels. We're making out on the bed again, with me straddling his lap. His hands are in my hair again, like it's their favorite place to be, while mine hold onto his jaw. This time, I do giggle when he kisses me, and I feel feverish. His touch sparks flashes of heat throughout my body.

He groans when I pull away to grab my vibrating phone off the bedside table.

"Hello?" I answer, sliding off his lap.

"Hey. The crystals are about ready if you want to come by!" Esme's chipper voice rings through the haze of us.

"Okay, we'll be there soon. Thanks, Esme."

"Of course!"

I sigh when I hang up and look at Declan apologetically, "Duty calls."

He presses a kiss to my forehead and slides out of bed.

Declan's halfway to his suitcase before he turns back to me and says, "You have seen my future before. It's why you showed up at the stakeout, isn't it?"

His eyes bore into mine. He wants an honest answer.

"Yes." It's a whisper.

"Not just because you saw the demon...because you saw me die. You came to stop it. To save me."

"Yes."

He looks away, his jaw tightening. He doesn't say anything as he turns around again to get his clothes.

In the vast expanse of the empty bed, I feel the gravity of our situation press on me again.

Just like that, the spell is broken, and we're forced back into reality.

30

CAROLINA

The small brass bell above the door of *Thorn & Thistle* jingles softly as Declan and I step inside. The warm scent of dried herbs and candle wax envelops us immediately. The shop feels like stepping into another world, a haven of magic and quiet power. It settles me.

Behind the counter, rows of shelves are lined with jars and bottles, each labeled in Esme's neat handwriting. Each one is filled with ingredients that most people wouldn't look twice at, but to witches, each one is a tool—each one has a purpose.

Esme's leaning over the counter as she carefully arranges a set of black tourmaline crystals into a small wooden box. The soft glow of candlelight flickers across the room, casting long shadows that dance against the dark green walls. It's peaceful here, almost too peaceful considering everything that's happening in Grove Meadow. But that's Esme's magic, I suppose. She creates calm where there should be chaos.

"Esme," I call out softly as we approach, not wanting to startle her.

She straightens, her face breaking into a warm smile when she sees us. "Carolina, Detective O'Reilly. You're right on time. The crystals are ready."

She slides the box across the counter as we approach, her movements steady and sure, like someone who's been practicing magic for centuries instead of just a few decades. I can sense the charge from the crystals even before I touch them—a soft hum of energy that pulses just beneath the surface, strong and ready. They've been specially enchanted, their power drawn from the earth and charged with protection spells that should be enough to ward off whatever dark magic is swirling through Grove Meadow. At least for the time being.

Declan, ever the skeptic, stands beside me, his gaze shifting from Esme to the crystals with that familiar mix of curiosity and wariness.

"These will help?" he asks, his voice low but firm. There's an edge to his tone, a need for assurance that what we're doing isn't just grasping at straws. That they'll actually help keep us safe.

Esme nods, her expression soft but serious. "Yes. The crystals are charged with protection charms, powerful ones. They'll help create a barrier around wherever you place them, keep out any unwanted energy." Her eyes flick to me for a moment, something unsaid lingering in the air between us.

She knows we're up against something bigger than just a few missing people. Something darker. But we don't say it out loud.

Declan's eyes narrow slightly, his sharp instincts clearly picking up on something as he leans closer. "What's that smell?"

I hadn't noticed it at first, but now that he's pointed it out, I catch the faint scent of sulfur hanging in the air, acrid and sharp, mixing with the usual earthy smell of the shop. It's subtle, but it's there, like something clinging to the edges of the room.

Esme, ever composed, doesn't flinch. "Sulfur is part of the

process," she says easily, her hands wrapping the crystals in a small velvet pouch. "It's used in the charm for grounding. Helps bind the magic to the crystals, ensuring they hold their charge."

Declan doesn't look entirely convinced, but he nods, letting it go. I'm not sure if he trusts Esme or magic generally, but I trust her, and that's enough.

I step forward and take the pouch from Esme's hands, feeling the weight of it in my palm. The crystals hum softly against my skin, their power vibrating through me, and for a brief moment, I feel that same stillness I had earlier, that sense of quiet satisfaction that comes when something is finally right. But it's fleeting. There's too much to worry about, too much at stake for me to hold onto that peace for long.

"Thank you," I say, meeting Esme's gaze. She knows I'm not just thanking her for the crystals. I'm thanking her for the work she's done for us and for being one of the few people we can rely on.

"Stay safe, Carolina," she says softly, her eyes lingering on me for a moment. "Both of you."

Declan gives her a small nod before turning toward the door, and I follow him out into the cool autumn air.

I call Camila to tell her we're on our way back, and we agree to spend the rest of the day working out the new prophecy. She says that Silas hasn't heard from Sam yet, so we've got no other information to go on.

Declan unlocks the car, and I slide into the passenger seat, cradling the pouch of crystals in my lap as if they could anchor me to something solid. I glance at him as he settles into the driver's seat, one hand gripping the steering wheel and the other one on my thigh.

The quiet stretches on as we pull out of the parking lot, the soft purr of the engine the only sound filling the car. I can feel the questions swirling inside him, the things he wants to ask but isn't sure how to. And I know I should say something—anything—but I can't find the right words.

My magic, for once, feels satisfied, almost content, like it's found something it's been searching for. But the feeling is edged in fear for what could happen and what almost happened to Declan.

I can't bring myself to regret telling him the truth when he asked about the stakeout. He deserved to know, but the presence of the truth is heavy between us.

Maybe he would have chosen differently if he'd known that he'd already almost died in this lifetime.

Declan glances at me out of the corner of his eye, and for a moment, I wonder if he's going to break the silence. But he doesn't. Instead, he shifts his focus back to the road, his jaw clenched in that way I've realized happens when he's deep in thought.

The road back to Grove Meadow is dark and winding, the trees lining the edges casting long shadows that seem to stretch out toward us as we pass. The day is gloomy, and a fog starts to roll in as we get close to town. I shiver, but it's not from the cold. There's something in the air, something I can't quite place, but it's there, lurking just beyond the edge of my senses.

We're almost to *Cup & Cauldron* when Declan finally speaks. His voice is quiet, almost hesitant, as if he's unsure whether to say the words or let them hang in the silence between us. "Carolina...about this morning."

I stiffen slightly, my grip tightening on the pouch in my lap. I knew this was coming, but now that it's here, I'm not sure how to respond. My magic stirs beneath my skin, a soft, restless hum, like it's waiting for me to say something. But I can't. Not yet. Not when everything is still so raw, so uncertain.

"I should have—" I start, but the words catch in my throat. I don't know what to say. I don't know how to explain what happened, how to make sense of the way my magic reacted to him, the way it felt so…complete.

Declan shakes his head, his gaze still fixed on the road ahead. "I know why you didn't," he says softly, almost as if he understands what I'm struggling to say. "Thank you…for saving me."

I give him a tight-lipped smile when he looks at me. Eventually, we'd need to discuss things. Perhaps after we dealt with whatever this *joined power* was, we'd be able to…try. Try being mirror souls. Try being together.

Yes, if we survived this. We could try.

Declan pulls into a space in front of the shop, and the unease that's been building inside me all evening sharpens into something more tangible. The lights in the shop are off, the windows dark, and there's no sign of Camila. I frown, stepping out of the car as a chill runs down my spine. Something's wrong.

"Camila?" I call out as I push open the door, the familiar jingle of the bell above it doing little to calm the knot tightening in my chest. The shop feels…off. The air is thick with something I can't quite name, something dark and heavy.

Declan steps in behind me, his hand instinctively going to the small of my back as we move further inside. "Where is she?" he asks, his voice low, steady.

"I don't know," I whisper, my eyes scanning the empty space.

I move behind the counter, and that's when I see it—a note hastily scrawled in Camila's handwriting. My heart sinks as I read the words.

Bas called me down to the station to answer some questions. Be back soon. Don't worry.

Don't worry. As if it's that simple. As if I'm capable of not worrying when everything about this feels wrong. My fingers tighten around the note, crumpling it slightly in my hand.

"Bas called her down to the station," I say, showing it to Declan. His frown deepens as he reads it, his worry echoing mine.

"That's strange," he murmurs, his brow furrowing. "Bas didn't mention anything about needing to interview her. I gave him enough paperwork to last weeks. Maybe he found something and thought Camila had information. I'll call him."

I look around the shop, and something still feels off, but I can't place it.

"No answer," Declan says, sliding his phone in his pocket. "He's probably in the middle of interrogating her."

Shaking my head and wrapping my arms around myself, I ask, "But why wouldn't she just text me?"

Declan lifts a shoulder. "Maybe she tried, and we were in a dead spot on the drive, so it didn't go through?"

I feel the familiar tingle of anxiety creep up my spine. "Let's go to the magic room. We need to figure out this prophecy from Annabelle. I'm sure we'll hear from Camila soon."

Declan nods, following me toward the back of the shop. The magic room feels safer and more contained, but even the familiar scent of herbs and old spellbooks can't settle the unease gnawing at me. I pull out my notebook, flipping through the pages where I've been scribbling down everything I can about the prophecy, but my thoughts are scattered. I can't focus.

Declan hovers beside me as I try and organize my thoughts, his presence equal parts grounding and distracting.

"Show it to me again," he says. I turn the notebook toward him, the page with the updated prophecy open. His brows furrow, and his jaw clenches.

"'Spirits are drawn into the void.' This has to refer to the disappearances. You said that the demon had taken over Elijah's body, right? Maybe their souls are going to the void."

I nod slowly, processing. My thoughts are becoming clearer. "'When men fall, a darkness will return.' They're using the souls to summon a wielder of dark magic."

Declan looks at me. "But *who*? Who's summoning it?"

This was the question. Nightcrawler said it wasn't demons.

"And what's this 'joined power?'" Declan asks, tapping the notebook paper. "We've been thinking that it must be two individuals working together to summon whatever it is, but is it possible that it's what stops it?"

"What do you mean?"

"I mean, what if it's fate that this thing is summoned? 'The threads of fate intertwine, heralding either ruin or redemption' and 'a darkness will return, and a joined power will rule the worlds of might and magic.' Maybe this is a prophecy not about the ruin of the Mortal World, but its salvation."

"Even if that's true, we still don't know who either of those things are about," I tell him, turning the notebook back toward me to study it again.

"Maybe Luna and Silas know something about other prophecies and this 'joined power.' Looking at it from a different perspective could yield something new."

He could be right. If the 'joined power' was meant to save us from whatever dark power was being summoned, then—

Declan's phone rings in his pocket.

"It's the captain," he says, his brow furrowing as he answers. "O'Reilly."

I watch him carefully, the tension in his body telling me something's wrong. My heart thuds in my chest, and I have to remind myself to breathe as I wait for him to speak.

"What do you mean, 'where am I?'" Declan's voice is tight, sharper than usual. "I thought Bas was interviewing Camila at the station."

I freeze, my heart skipping a beat.

"He hasn't been there since yesterday?" Declan's expression hardens, and my stomach drops. "No. No, I didn't know. We've been... Look, I'll figure it out."

When he hangs up, the look on his face is enough to send a wave of panic through me.

"Bas isn't at the station," Declan says, his voice grim. "He hasn't been there since yesterday, and the captain is pissed. He thought we were both off the radar together."

If Bas isn't at the station with Camila, then where is he? And where the *hell* is Camila?

The panic I've been trying to keep at bay surges forward, threatening to overwhelm me. I push past Declan and head back out into the shop, my heart racing.

"Luna—Luna?" I call out aloud and through our bond, reaching for the familiar thread that's always there, always connecting us. But there's nothing. No response.

A cold chill grips my chest. "I can't feel Luna," I whisper, my voice trembling. "Something's wrong. Something's really, really wrong."

Declan's hand is on my shoulder, trying to pull me to the surface, but it's not enough. I feel like I'm spiraling. "What do you mean you can't feel her?"

I don't answer him because that's when I see it—the painting on the wall. *Charmingly Familiar*. The one that always changes with the seasons, the one that always feels alive. But something's different.

I move toward the painting on the far wall. My heart skips a beat as I draw closer, the hairs on the back of my neck standing on end.

Silas and Luna, normally so present, so full of life, are still. Too still. Trapped within the painting, their forms frozen as if they've been bound by something—or someone.

"They're trapped," I murmur, my voice barely audible as the realization crashes over me.

"What?" Declan's voice is sharp, and I can feel his eyes on me, searching for an explanation.

"The familiars," I say, pointing at the painting. "It feels different. They should be able to come and go from that painting. It's been spelled. Something's trapped them in there."

Declan steps up beside me, his hand brushing against mine, sending a jolt of warmth through my skin. "Who could have done this?"

I shake my head, my heart pounding in my chest. "I don't know," I say, the words barely escaping my lips. Panic tightens my chest, and I feel like I'm drowning. "If they're trapped, then Camila..."

I can't finish the sentence. The weight of it, the fear, it's too much. I swallow hard, trying to push down the rising dread, but it's no use.

"We need to find her," I say, my voice shaky. "Now."

31

CAROLINA

Standing frozen in front of the painting, my heart races as my magic thrums beneath my skin, pushing against me, urging me to act. Silas and Luna are trapped, their forms motionless, eyes wide and pleading from within the canvas. My hands hover over the painting, hesitant for a second.

Familiars are guides for witches and warlocks. Sometimes, they come into their post as a punishment, like Silas, but most others choose this path, like Luna. Without their familiars, witches become vulnerable—familiars are a source of magic for us and an invaluable wealth of knowledge. For those reasons, trapping familiars in such a way—it's not just dark magic. It's personal. Whoever did this wanted to send a message.

"I can fix this," I whisper to myself, though my voice trembles. I don't know if I'm trying to reassure Declan or myself.

Declan moves beside me, his gaze darting from the painting to me, his concern palpable. "What do you need me to do?"

"Just...stay close." My voice sounds stronger than I feel, but I don't have time to doubt myself.

I take a deep breath, drawing on the energy in the room, focusing on the threads of magic that pulse through the shop. Whoever cast this spell wasn't expecting me to unravel it. At least, I hope they weren't.

Placing my hands flat against the surface of the painting, my fingers tingle as my magic meets the barrier trapping Silas and Luna. It's a strong spell, but I can feel the cracks in it, the places where it's weak. My connection to Luna thrums when it senses her inside the painting, guiding me to the points of pressure, the knots that hold the spell together.

I recall the reverse entrapment spell from one of *abuela's* spell books and murmur the incantation under my breath, focusing on the bond between me and Luna.

> By the stars and by the sea,
> I call upon the power in me.
> Break the chains, shatter the key,
> What was trapped shall now be free.
> As I will it, so mote it be.

My magic responds instantly, surging forward, searching for the source of familiar energy of my familiar. The painting shudders beneath my hands, the surface rippling like water, and for a moment, I think it might work. The barrier starts to give, the edges fraying under the force of my spell, and then, with a sharp crack, the magic shatters.

Declan pulls me back at the sound of my gasp, my back colliding with his front. Silas and Luna tumble out of the painting, landing in a heap on the floor, disoriented but free. I drop to my knees beside them, relief flooding my body as Luna slithers into my lap, her long, smooth form coiling around me protectively.

Silas, ever the troublemaker, shakes himself off with a haughty flick of his tail. "About time," he mutters, his voice rough from being trapped. But there's an edge of fear in his tone that he can't quite hide.

Declan crouches beside me, his hand resting lightly on my shoulder before running his fingers over Luna's scales. "What happened?"

Silas glares up at me, then at Declan. "Esme," he says, his voice dripping with disdain. "She came here hours ago. Used some kind of charm to teleport herself straight into the shop."

My heart skips a beat. That can't be right. "Esme? That's impossible."

Silas levels me again with his glare.

It's true, Luna says softly through our regained bond. My magic welcomes her in my mind like a lost friend.

"She doesn't have teleportation magic," I say, shaking my head. "She's an inactive witch. She can't even cast. She's strong, but even that's a lot of magic for a charm."

"That's what I thought," Silas snaps, pacing in front of us, tail lashing in agitation. "But there she was, plain as day, standing in the middle of the shop, talking about how she came to warn you both about something. Annabelle was involved in the disappearances, she said. But Camila—"

Luna tightens her coils around me, her voice cool and steady. "Camila didn't trust her. She didn't believe Esme, not after what you told her last night and earlier today."

I nod slowly, the pieces clicking together in my mind. I had told Camila about my concerns, about how something felt off with Esme, especially after the sulfur smell in her shop. We both knew sulfur wasn't usually used for grounding crystals. It was tied to darker things, things witches didn't mess with unless they were desperate—or hiding something. But it was Esme. We wanted to trust her.

"What happened?" I ask quietly, dread curling in my stomach as I glance between the familiars.

Luna hisses softly, her head resting on my arm. "Esme panicked. She realized she'd made a mistake—Camila's suspicion caught her off guard. She tried to backpedal, but before Camila could act, Esme used something—dark magic."

I stiffen, my hands balling into fists. Dark magic? Esme has always been cautious. Dark magic requires more than just a charm or a potion; it needs a caster. As an inactive, Esme couldn't...

God, what has she done?

Silas growls, pacing again. "She used it to trap us in the painting. I tried to warn Camila, but I couldn't break free. By the time she realized what was happening, it was too late. Esme used some kind of binding spell on her and took her..."

"Where?" My voice is barely a whisper, fear tightening in my chest.

"The Underworld," Silas says darkly, stopping in front of me, his green eyes blazing with frustration and anger. "She took her to the Underworld."

The words hit me like a blow, knocking the air from my lungs. My mind reels, trying to make sense of it.

The Underworld. Esme took Camila to the Underworld. Why? For what purpose? My thoughts race, but all I can think of is getting her back.

Declan places a hand on my shoulder again, his voice level. "We'll get her back, Carolina. Whatever it takes."

I swallow hard, looking up at him. His face is set in determination, and something inside me steadies. He's not running from this. He's not turning away, despite everything he's seen. He's staying, and that means more than I can put into words.

But I can't think about that right now. Camila needs me.

She's trapped in the Underworld, and I can't just stand here and do nothing.

"I have to go after her," I say, my voice firmer than I feel. I push to my feet, Luna sliding off my lap and coiling at my feet. "I'll need a portal, something strong enough to get me there and bring me back."

Declan's grip tightens slightly. "Are you sure about this?"

"I don't have a choice," I say, my heart heavy but resolute. "I have to go. *Alone*," I tell him so he doesn't get any ideas about coming with me. "It's not safe for you to come. The Underworld—it's not meant for humans. You wouldn't survive it. Remember how it felt when you saw my vision? It will be so much worse down there. It even wore on Camila and I."

Declan opens his mouth to protest, but he stops himself, his jaw clenching in frustration. I can see the battle waging in his eyes—the need to protect me, to fight alongside me, but he knows I'm right. If he comes with me, the Underworld will tear him apart.

"Then I'll help from here," he says, his voice low but determined. "I'll do whatever I can on this side. But you bring her back, Carolina. You both come back."

I nod, swallowing the lump in my throat. "I will."

I turn back to Silas and Luna, my mind already racing through everything I'll need. Opening a portal to the Underworld requires power—more power than I usually tap into. It was easier to do it with Camila beside me because there were two power sources to conjure it.

Luna slithers onto the counter, her eyes gleaming with ancient wisdom. "You know what you need, Carolina. The portal spell is deep magic. You'll need a tether to Camila, something that connects you both. Otherwise, you'll never find her."

"Here," Declan says, reaching into his pocket and

producing Camila's necklace. "I wanted to return it to her. I grabbed it from the station after you two went to the Underworld."

"Thank you," I say, taking it from him. "This will help."

Silas, still pacing, flicks his tail impatiently. "You don't have much time. The Underworld...it distorts things. Time moves differently down there. Every minute she's trapped could be hours, days even."

"I know," I say, my voice grim. "But I'm going to find her."

I grab the necessary items, my mind laser-focused on the task ahead. I'm a Castillo witch. I've been to the Underworld before, and I survived. I'll do it again.

Declan watches me, his face tight with worry. "I'll be waiting for you. Don't take too long down there, Carolina. Don't get lost."

I give him a small nod, unable to speak past the knot in my throat. This is it. I'm going back to the Underworld, and I don't know what I'll find. But one thing is certain—I'm not leaving without my sister.

32

DECLAN

The air in the magic room is thick with tension, silence settling over me like a suffocating blanket. I've sequestered myself in here, needing the space—needing to think, to breathe—but it's useless. My mind is consumed by one thought: Carolina is in the Underworld.

She's in the *Underworld*.

Carolina is *alone* in the Underworld.

The very idea gnaws at me, ripping through every shred of calm I can muster. I want to be with her. Hell, I *need* to be with her, but I know I can't.

The Underworld—it's not meant for humans. You wouldn't survive it. Carolina's voice rings in my head, but it doesn't stop the gnawing ache, the helplessness clawing at my insides, knowing that while she's facing God knows what while I'm stuck here, useless.

I glance down at Luna, coiled on the floor beside me, her dark eyes watching me with an intensity that only a familiar can have. Silas is somewhere in the corner, pacing again, muttering something under his breath about how this is all a bad idea. I don't disagree. But what choice do we have?

Carolina had to go. And me? I had to let her.

My fists clench involuntarily, the frustration boiling up inside of me again. It feels like the walls are closing in, like I'm trapped here when I should be doing something—anything—to help her. My mirror soul. My soulmate. I know that now.

Carolina Castillo, the witch who upended my life, is more than just a woman I care about. She's *it* for me. And she's facing an entire realm of danger while I'm stuck here, helpless.

I pace across the small room; the familiar scent of herbs and incense that normally feels grounding now feels stifling. I don't even notice the sound of the shop's door opening until I hear footsteps approaching, too heavy to be anyone who should be here.

I turn in time to see Sebastian step into the room, his face twisted with something dark, something I've never seen on him before.

"What the hell are you doing here, Bas?" I ask, my tone sharp.

Sebastian doesn't respond right away, his gaze scanning the room, then landing on me with an intensity that sends a chill down my spine. Something's wrong. *Very* wrong.

I glance down at Luna, who has slithered off to hide somewhere. At least, I hoped. In the corner, Silas has stopped his pacing to stare wide-eyed at my partner.

"I should be asking you the same thing, O'Reilly," he says, his voice low, almost too calm. "But I already know the answer."

I narrow my eyes, taking a step forward. "What the hell are you talking about?"

He takes a step toward me, something dangerous in his eyes. "You're siding with them, aren't you? The Castillo sisters. The witches."

My heart hammers in my chest, my instincts screaming at me that this isn't the Sebastian I know. He's always been cautious, sure, but this? This is different. "What are you talking about?"

He shakes his head, a bitter smile twisting his lips. "You don't get it, do you? This is all for the good of the town. They've poisoned this place, corrupted it. Esme and I...we've been working to get rid of them. To *cleanse* Grove Meadow."

My blood runs cold, and I feel like I've fallen through the floor beneath me. "You've been working with Esme?"

"Of course," he says, his eyes wild. "She knows what needs to be done. The disappearances—they're not permanent. Esme told me that once the witches are gone, the people will come back. No one gets hurt."

Rage boils up inside me, my fists clenching. "You've been *working* with her? You're responsible for this? You've been sending people to perform summoning spells?"

Sebastian doesn't flinch, his expression unwavering. "It's for the good of the town, Declan. You know what they are. You've seen it. They don't belong here. Once they're gone, everything will be back to normal. I wouldn't risk my job if I didn't think they were truly evil."

My stomach twists, and I take a step toward him, fury bubbling over. "You're an idiot if you believe Esme. She lied to you, Bas. She's using them to summon some kind of dark magic."

He shakes his head, his jaw tightening. "You don't know what you're talking about. Esme's been trying to protect us. She's been—"

"She's been *using* you!" I snap, my voice rising with anger. "She's manipulating you, just like she's been manipulating the town. She doesn't care about bringing anyone back, Sebastian. She's trying to summon a darker power, and she's using those people as sacrifices."

Sebastian's eyes flash with fury, and before I can react, he lunges at me.

I barely have time to move as he swings at me, his fist grazing my jaw as I duck. My heart races as I realize this isn't just an argument. Sebastian is *attacking* me.

"Are you out of your damn mind?" I shout, dodging another swing. "Esme's using dark magic, Bas. You're not thinking straight!"

"She told me the truth!" he yells, his eyes wild, his movements frantic. "You've been brainwashed by them. By the witches."

He lunges again, and this time, I don't hesitate. I block his punch and counter with a hard right hook that sends him stumbling back. But he's quick to recover, and the two of us collide again, fists flying, each of us landing blows.

I feel the sharp pain of his knuckles connecting with my ribs, but I grit my teeth, pushing through it. My mind is racing, every instinct screaming at me that this is wrong. Sebastian isn't just some guy off the street. He's my partner, my friend. Or at least, he *was*.

But now? Now, he's an enemy. He's been corrupted by Esme, twisted by whatever dark magic she's been using.

I grab him by the collar and slam him into the wall, my breath coming in hard gasps as I pin him there. "You're wrong, Bas. Esme's lying to you. She's not saving anyone. She's *using* them for dark magic."

Sebastian struggles against me, but I hold him firm, my grip tightening. His eyes are wild, unfocused, like he's lost in some delusion. "You don't understand," he hisses, his voice low and dangerous. "You're protecting the enemy."

I grit my teeth, my rage barely contained. "No, Bas. *You* are."

With one final push, I slam him into the wall, his body going limp as he slumps to the floor, unconscious.

I stand there, breathing hard, my fists still clenched, the adrenaline still pumping through my veins. The room is quiet again, save for my ragged breathing and the low hum of magic in the air.

I turn to Luna, who had been watching silently from her usual spot beneath the couch, her dark eyes focused on me. "What now?" I ask, my voice rough.

Luna slithers forward, her eyes narrowing. "Something's wrong."

I frown, still catching my breath. "What do you mean?"

Luna's head rises slightly, her gaze flicking toward the far corner of the room. "I can't feel Carolina's magic anymore."

A cold wave of dread washes over me, my heart skipping a beat. "What do you mean you can't feel her?"

Luna's eyes meet mine, and for the first time, I see fear in them. "I think something terrible has happened. I can sense our link, but her magic isn't responding."

My blood runs cold as her words sink in. *Carolina. Something's happened to her.*

I feel my heart pounding in my chest, my thoughts spinning out of control. I can't lose her. Not now. Not when she's everything.

My legs twitch, every instinct screaming at me to run and find her. But I can't just go charging into the Underworld. It's not like I know how to even get there—*hell*, I'm not even sure how the whole thing works. I glance down at Sebastian's unconscious body, my hands still trembling with adrenaline, and then I turn back to the familiars.

Luna's words are still hanging in the air, sharp and cold: *Something terrible has happened.* My throat feels dry, my chest tight. I crouch down to Luna's level, locking eyes with her, needing some kind of direction, some kind of plan. Anything.

"What do we do?" I ask, my voice coming out rough, like gravel in my throat.

Luna coils tighter, her eyes shifting from me to Silas, who looks agitated, his fur bristling, tail flicking back and forth in rapid, angry swipes. I can see the gears turning in his head, the familiar intensity of a plan forming, but he's not saying anything yet.

"*What do we do?*" I repeat, my patience thinning. Every second feels like a lifetime, and the pressure of helplessness is starting to choke me. I can't just stand here.

Silas finally speaks, his voice rough but measured. "There's a way," he says, stopping mid-pace. "With Luna's power, we can open a portal that will lead you to Carolina. But..."

"But what?" I snap, my heart racing.

Silas shoots me a look. "It's dangerous, and there's no guarantee you'll be able to find her. You're not someone with magic, Declan. Down there, it's not just about knowing where you're going—it's about feeling it, being able to connect with her magic, or the Underworld will swallow you whole. You'll be lost."

I swallow hard, my gut twisting at his words. He's right, of course. I don't have magic. I don't know the first thing about navigating whatever hellscape the Underworld is. But I can't sit here. I can't just let Carolina face that alone, not if there's even a chance I can help.

"I don't care," I say, my voice steady despite the turmoil inside. "I want to try. Just open the damn portal."

Silas snorts, clearly not impressed with my stubbornness. "You don't understand, O'Reilly. You're talking about diving headfirst into a place that will eat you alive. *Literally.*"

I stand up, squaring my shoulders. "I don't care about the risks. If there's even a chance I can get to her, I'm taking it."

Luna flicks her tongue, her eyes narrowing slightly as she considers my words. "There's more than just finding her, Declan," she says, her voice calm but pointed. "If something has happened to her—something that severed her magic—you might not be able to bring her back. You could lose her. *Permanently.* And if you get lost…we may not be able to pull you out either."

Her words hit me hard, and for a second, the room feels too small, like the walls are closing in. I can't even imagine what that would feel like, losing her for good. But the alternative? Sitting here, waiting, doing nothing? That's not an option. I can't just let her disappear into the void of that place without even trying to help.

I look between Luna and Silas, my hands trembling but my voice firm. "You don't understand. I can't lose her. Not like this. If there's even the slightest chance I can get to her, I'm going."

Silas lets out a frustrated growl, pacing again. "You're an idiot," he mutters. "A reckless, stubborn idiot."

"Tell me something I don't know," I say, my voice sharper than I intended. "Are you going to help me or not?"

Luna slithers forward, her dark eyes narrowing in thought. "We can open the portal," she says slowly, as if weighing every word carefully. "But once you're down there…you'll be on your own. We can't guide you through the Underworld. We'll use a spell that will find a familiar's lost witch, but you'll need to rely on your mirror soul bond with her to be able to sense her connection to me. It will be tricky…bonds connected by bonds aren't the best way to do this, but…"

"It's all we've got right now." I nod, already set on my decision. "I'll find her."

Silas stops pacing and looks up at me, his green eyes

flashing with a mixture of irritation and grudging respect. "You're going to get yourself killed, you know that?"

"I'll take my chances," I respond, my voice steady despite the fear crawling up my spine.

The room is quiet for a moment, the weight of my decision settling over us like a heavy fog. Then, without another word, Silas and Luna move into action.

"Move this rug," Silas orders, pawing at one of the heavy orange and red Persian rugs behind the couch.

Once I've rolled it out of the way, Luna slithers toward the center of where it had been, positioning herself in a drawn-out circle I hadn't even noticed was etched into the floor.

"Declan, there's an amethyst candle on the potion table. Light it and bring it to the circle. You'll stand next to me. We're going to open a portal using the familiar's lost witch spell. If I'm strong enough and Carolina is still alive somewhere in the Underworld, it should open a portal like the one she opened. It will only close once you've returned *with* her. You must work as fast as you can down there."

I nod, lighting the candle and placing it in the circle.

Luna begins an incantation, and the air around us starts to shift. The magic in the room becomes palpable, like the very walls are vibrating with energy.

By the bond we share, pure and true,
I call to you, as you call to me.
Across all realms, no force can break,
This tether of ours that none can shake.

Through flame and water, air and stone,
I seek your path, I am not alone.
Your light guides me, your essence near,

I follow the pull, I feel you here.

Wherever you are, you'll come to me,
Wherever you are, you are with me.

I can feel it in my bones, the heft of the magic pressing down on me, thick and heavy. My heart races as I watch her work, my stomach twisting in knots. This is it. There's no turning back.

The air around us seems to shimmer, like reality itself is starting to bend. It seems to twist in unnatural ways until it tears in two right down the middle. Like the two other portals before, there's a swirling array of colors that calls to me, begging me to step into it.

My heart is pounding in my chest as the urge to step forward, into the portal, grows. The magic in the air growing thicker, almost oppressive.

I look to Luna, who nods at me slowly. Encouraging. "I'll bring her back."

Luna's eyes look torn between hopeful and sad, like Carolina's not the only one she's worried about returning after all this is over.

"We'll all come back," I tell her with more confidence than I feel.

I look back at the portal and step inside. My breath catches in my throat as the room starts to shift, the edges blurring, the world around me warping and twisting. My head swims, and for a moment, I feel like I'm falling—like the ground has been ripped out from under me.

And then, suddenly, there's nothing.

No sound. No light. Just darkness.

The Underworld is colder than I remember. The air is damp, heavy, clinging to my skin like a second layer of something suffocating. Shadows twist and shift at the edges of my vision, dark forms that I can't quite make out but feel pressing closer. It's like walking through a nightmare, one where the walls bend and stretch, making the space seem both endless and claustrophobic at the same time. Every step I take echoes in the eerie silence, reminding me that I'm not supposed to be here.

The maze-like caverns feel alive, their twisted stone walls pulsing with some dark, unnatural energy that thrums beneath my feet. The light—or what little of it there is— flickers faintly from cracks in the stone, casting everything in a sickly, pale glow. I cling to the shadows, keeping low, moving silently. I know better than to let myself be seen here.

My heart pounds in my chest, but I force myself to focus. I need to find her. I need to find Camila. I'm clutching her necklace so tightly that I know her name will be engraved on my palm permanently.

The path twists and turns, each passageway narrowing, then opening into cavernous expanses. I glance around at each turn, checking for movement, for anything lurking in the darkness. The back of my neck prickles as I can't shake the feeling that something—someone—is watching me.

The Underworld is full of things that shouldn't exist—things that would tear me apart if they knew I was here. But none of them matter. All that matters is finding Camila and getting us both out of here.

A faint noise catches my ear—like the clink of metal, distant and hollow. My pulse quickens. I follow the sound, my steps quick but careful. The ground beneath my feet is rough and uneven, like the jagged, broken bones of the earth. The sound grows louder the further I go, until it leads me to an open cavern, a vast and empty space where the ceiling disappears into shadows far above.

And there, in the center of the room, is Camila.

She's trapped in a freestanding iron cage. Collapsed on the ground, her head leans against the bars, and her hands grip them tightly. Camila's head is ducked, and her wild hair cascades over her face, blocking it from my view.

My heart clenches at the sight of her, and for a moment, I can't breathe. She must sense me because she looks up, her eyes locking onto mine, wide with shock and relief. I can see her face now, streaked with dried tears, and her cheeks have dirt on them.

"Carolina," she breathes, her voice hoarse, as if she's been screaming.

I rush forward, my heart racing. "Camila! Are you okay?"

"I'm okay. I'm not hurt," she says, but there's a tremor in her voice that betrays the fear she's trying to hide. "But you shouldn't be here. Esme—"

"I know," I cut her off, my voice hard. "I already know about Esme."

My hands grab the cold iron bars, and I pull, but the cage

doesn't budge. My magic flickers beneath my skin, reacting to the dark energy surrounding the cage. There's something else here, something more than just iron holding her in. I can feel it —the dark magic woven into the bars, a protective spell designed to keep her trapped.

"The lock," Camila says, her voice trembling and weak. "It's enchanted. I've tried everything."

I grit my teeth, frustration boiling inside me. I can feel the magic pulsing from the lock, twisted and wrong, like something crawling under my skin. Like with the painting, I search for cracks in the spell, weak points that I can break through, but it's strong—too strong for me to break without knowing exactly what spell was used. And if I force it...

Before I can say anything, the air around us shifts, and I feel a presence behind me. My blood runs cold as I turn to see two figures emerging from one of the cavernous structures. Esme... and someone else.

The figure beside her is cloaked in a long, dark robe, his face hidden beneath a hood that casts deep shadows over his features. But even through the darkness, I can feel the power radiating from him. It's suffocating, pressing down on me like a weight I can't escape.

Esme's face is pale, her eyes empty, like the life has been drained from her. But it's her presence here, in this place, that hits me the hardest. The betrayal is like a knife twisting in my chest, sharp and unforgiving.

Esme. The woman who grew up with us. The girl who danced in our kitchen with our mom and created recipes with *abuela.* The witch we've always treated like a sister...now standing there, working with this *thing.*

I feel sick, my stomach churning with disbelief. This is what it's come to? All her talk about helping us figure out who was behind the disappearances, about keeping the darkness at bay, and now she's standing next to it. Helping it steal the souls of people she'd grown up with.

The cloaked figure steps forward, and I'm hit with a wave of cold, raw power. The shadows around him seem to cling to him, shifting and swirling like they're alive. Slowly, he lifts his hand, pulling back his hood.

My breath catches in my throat, and my hand wraps around one of Camila's. My magic balks at the sight of him, but I can't let it show, even if my skin is peppered with goosebumps.

The figure beneath the hood is impossibly handsome—devilishly so, with sharp, chiseled features and eyes that glow faintly, like embers. But there's something off about him. His face isn't quite solid, more translucent, like he's only halfway here. Not fully summoned. Not yet.

Esme hasn't completed it.

"This is who you've been trying to free," I whisper, my voice shaking with rage. The weight of betrayal crushes me, but I don't let that show either. I can't. "This *thing* is what you were working for?"

Esme doesn't respond, but her eyes flicker with something —regret, maybe. Or guilt. It doesn't matter. Not now.

The figure, the being Esme has been trying to summon, turns his gaze on me, his eyes gleaming with a dangerous, predatory light.

"Ah, Carolina Castillo," he says, his voice smooth, silky, with a darkness lurking just beneath the surface. "I've been expecting you."

My heart skips a beat, and I step closer to the bars, instinctively shielding Camila from his gaze. He knows who I am. Of course, he does.

"And your sister," he continues, his voice dripping with amusement. "Esme has done quite well in bringing me this far, but we've run into a little...*complication*." He says the last word with a cruel, wicked smile that makes my stomach churn.

His eyes flicker to Camila in the cage, then back to me, the smile still twisting his lips. "You see, we're not quite finished. Your dear friend Esme hasn't completed the summoning yet. And that's where you come in."

I can feel the blood drain from my face, but I stand my ground. "What are you talking about?"

He takes a step closer, and I can feel his power pressing against me, cold and overwhelming. "It's quite simple, really. Esme was sick of watching active witches treat her like she was nothing. The same as a mortal even." His lip curls in disgust at the thought.

I look at Esme, hoping to see something in her face that will convince me he's lying to us. That she would *never* stoop so low for power. Except her face shows me nothing but regret and sorrow. A piece of me dies in that moment.

"So she came to me for help, but there's not much I can do in this form. I needed some...help returning to my corporeal form. You see, the summoning requires a sacrifice. A soul, to be specific. And Esme...well, she's been very helpful in providing those."

My stomach turns, bile rising in my throat as I realize what he's saying. The missing people. She's been *feeding* him their souls so he can return to full power.

"But *why*?" I hadn't meant for it to slip out, but now that it has, he's looking at me like I've disappointed him.

"Carolina, I thought you were the smarter one. That's what Esme says. Unless you mean, why me? Why now? In which case, I'll let Esme explain," he says, turning to look at her expectantly.

Her face pales even more so than before. Everything about

her seems frail. She won't look at me; her gaze is glued to the ground between us.

"I...I just wanted to be like you. To feel powerful. I found a spell...to summon power. I didn't think it would work. My spells never do—"

He clicks his tongue. "Didn't the girls teach you, Esme? You must be so careful with spells, especially ones that summon dark magic...you never know who might be listening." His lips pull over his sharp teeth.

My skin crawls at the sight. Something about him seems familiar, and I try to place him in my memory, but I can't.

"He answered in my dreams. Told me that he could help me get active magic if I helped him. I thought he was just trapped in the spirit world..."

"And then what, Esme? Tell them what I gave you." She turns her head away from us. "Fine. I knew Esme couldn't help me without at least some active magic, so I gave her a little of mine."

Esme had dark magic. Why hadn't I been able to sense it? Maybe it was just a kernel. Something not even my magic could detect. But whatever it was, it was enough to compel the town to sacrifice themselves and teleport into the shop to take Camila.

"But why would you do this to us, Esme? We're your family."

It's the first time Camila had said something to her. Her voice is rough and empty. She's accepted that Esme has done this but doesn't understand why.

I think back to my first spell. The one that gave Susie acne. I remember the traces of the dark magic, but I also remember how powerful I felt. The idea that my magic could bend to fulfill any desire I had. I couldn't imagine how alluring that must have felt to an inactive witch. Someone who only feels the surface of magic.

"I'm sorry," Esme says, hanging her head.

"She's not, but," he says, his voice softening to a mocking whisper, "there's one more soul I need after you stopped her from bringing me the last one using the proper ritual. Now, I need one much stronger...The soul of someone very special to you. Someone...connected to you. Someone who's beaten death in this lifetime."

At this, Esme's head whips up, and shock coats her features. She starts to shake her head. "That wasn't the deal. You said you wanted them here so they'd be out of your way. So you could complete the summoning."

I freeze, my blood turning to ice as his words sink in. He's not talking about Camila. He's talking about—

"Your mirror soul," he says, ignoring Esme, a wicked grin spreading across his face. "Declan O'Reilly. I can feel him. I know he'll come for you. I've already muted your connection with your familiar. She'll send him here to find you, and when he opens the portal...we'll take him. We'll use his soul to complete the summoning, and you'll both get to watch."

My heart stutters in my chest, terror and fury coursing through me. I can feel my magic stirring, thrumming beneath my skin, but I can't let it loose. Not yet. Not while he's standing there, so sure of himself.

I can't let him take Declan.

"Over my dead body," I hiss, my voice shaking with rage.

The figure laughs, the sound cold and hollow, echoing through the cavern. "Oh, Carolina," he says, stepping closer. "That can be arranged."

34

DECLAN

The Underworld is hell—literally.

The second I step through the portal, everything about my body rebels. My skin tingles, my chest tightens like I'm breathing through a straw, and every step I take feels like walking through quicksand. The air is thick, suffocating, and wrong in a way I can't even put into words. It's like being underwater for too long—my body just knows I don't belong here, and it's doing everything it can to make me feel it.

I push forward, ignoring the pain gnawing at my lungs, trying to keep my head clear. But the place doesn't make it easy. The caverns twist and stretch, like the walls themselves are alive. I glance around, trying to get my bearings, but every turn looks the same. Dim light seeps out of cracks in the stone, casting long, eerie shadows that flicker and shift, making everything seem like it's moving just out of the corner of my eye.

My heart pounds in my chest, every instinct screaming at me to get out of here. But I can't. I won't. Carolina is somewhere in this godforsaken place, and I'll be damned if I leave her here. I just have to find her.

I don't have to go far before the air in front of me ripples—like the shadows themselves are bending—and then, suddenly, two figures shimmer into existence, right in front of me.

What the hell?

Before I can even react, the figures—tall, gaunt, and definitely not human—grab me by the arms. They don't say anything. They don't need to. Their grip is iron, and no amount of struggling is going to break me free.

I try to fight them off, but it's like hitting a brick wall. They don't even flinch. My head's spinning from the stifling air and the weight of whatever power holds me in place. They drag me through the twisting caverns, deeper and deeper into the Underworld, and I have no idea where they're taking me, but every step feels like it's pulling me further away from the world I know.

The chamber they take me to is massive; there doesn't seem to be a ceiling— only a sea of darkness. The way it moves as if it's alive almost distracts me from the two iron cages in the room.

I see Camila first, who looks petrified at my kneeling on the ground between the two demonic lackeys sent to retrieve me.

Carolina, on the other side of me, doesn't look petrified; she looks destroyed and defeated, slumped against the bars, head tilted up at the top of the cage.

"Carolina!" I shout, my voice hoarse.

She looks over at me, her face filling with anguish. "Why did you come?" Her voice is a broken, hollow sound that fills me with my own sense of anguish.

"Luna said she couldn't feel you anymore. That something terrible must have happened to you," I tell her, my eyes darting across her face, looking for any sign of injury.

"Not yet," a voice from further into the chamber says, but I can't see where it came from until someone else steps forward from the darkness.

He's tall—unnaturally tall—with a translucent face that seems almost too perfect, like he's carved from marble. But his eyes...there's nothing human in them. Shadows swirl around him, twisting and coiling like they're part of him, extensions of his body.

"Ah," he says smoothly, his voice like cold silk. "The mirror soul. I was wondering when you'd arrive."

I yank against the two figures holding me, glaring at the shadowy figure. "Who the hell are you?" I demand, my voice rough, my body aching under the strain of this place.

He smiles, a cruel, mocking grin that makes my skin crawl. "I go by many names," he says, his voice dripping with amusement. "The Dark One. The Shadow Lord. The Devourer of Souls. But you may call me...Mal."

My gut twists. The power radiating off him, the way the shadows move around him—it's enough to tell me that this guy is bad news.

"Let her go," I say, my voice shaking with fury.

Mal laughs, low and chilling. "Oh, but where's the fun in that?"

Before I can react, one of the shadows around him lashes out, wrapping around my neck. It's cold—unnaturally cold—and it tightens in an instant, cutting off my air. I gasp, clawing at the dark tendrils, but my hands pass through them like smoke. I fall to my knees, choking, my vision going dark around the edges.

"You've made this far too easy, Detective," Mal says, his voice calm, almost bored. "I knew muting Carolina's familiar bond would get you down here. Mortals are *so* predictable. You just walked right in. How convenient."

I struggle against the shadow wrapped around my throat,

but it's no use. It squeezes tighter, and I can feel myself slipping. I'm losing air fast. I can barely hear Carolina's frantic voice from the cage. My chest burns, my mind racing. I can't die here. Not like this. Not when she needs me.

"I'll...do it," I manage to choke out, my voice barely audible. "Whatever you want, whatever you brought me down here for. Just...let her go."

Carolina's shout echoes through the chamber. "No! Declan, don't!"

Mal's cold eyes shift to her, and his smile widens. "So noble, aren't you?" His gaze flicks back to me. "You'll complete the summoning then? You'll give yourself up for her?"

I nod, or at least I try to. The shadow around my neck loosens just enough for me to breathe, but I can feel its icy grip still pressing against my skin, reminding me just how little control I have here.

"Only if you let her go," I repeat, my voice firmer this time.

"No!" Carolina shouts, her voice raw. "Take me instead. I'll offer my soul in exchange for Declan's. You don't need him."

My heart slams against my ribs.

What the hell is she doing? She and Camila are the only chance at stopping him. She needs to stay alive.

"Carolina, no!" I yell, struggling again, but the shadow tightens around me once more, silencing me.

Mal tilts his head, considering her offer. "Your soul?" he murmurs, his voice full of intrigue. "Now that is tempting."

"No!" I manage to shout, my throat burning from the strain. "Don't listen to her. Take me."

Mal seems to be enjoying this, his eyes gleaming with dark satisfaction. "Hmm," he muses, his shadows swirling around him. "Perhaps...a compromise."

Before I can react, the shadow around my neck releases me, and I collapse to the ground, gasping for air. But then, before I can even get to my feet, the shadows shift again. They move with lightning speed, wrapping around Carolina's throat and lifting her from the cage.

For a moment, she becomes a literal shadow as her body seems to pass through the iron bars.

I scramble to my feet, panic surging through me as I watch her struggle, her face pale, her hands clawing at the dark tendrils wrapped around her neck.

"No!" I scream, but before I can do anything, Mal flicks his hand, and I'm suddenly yanked back—thrown into the same cage that Carolina had just occupied. The iron bars are shut, trapping me inside.

I grab the bars, shaking them violently, but they don't budge. My heart is pounding in my chest, fear clawing at my insides as I watch Mal lift Carolina higher, his shadows holding her like a puppet.

"Let her go!" I shout, my voice cracking. "Take me! I'll do whatever you want. Just let her go!"

Mal laughs, the sound echoing through the chamber. This whole exchange entertains him, like Carolina and I are just pieces on a chessboard he can move around however he wants.

Carolina's eyes lock onto mine, wide with fear and desperation. But behind that fear, I see something else—something fierce. She's not giving up. She's fighting.

And so will I.

"Don't touch her," I growl, my voice low and dangerous.

Mal's cold smile widens. "Oh, I plan on doing much more than that."

35

CAROLINA

he Dark One. The Shadow Lord. The Devourer of Souls.

A story that parents tell their witchlings to get them to eat their vegetables, practice their spells, and, above all, never use dark magic. Our version of the boogeyman. He was real, and Esme had helped him.

If you believed the lore, he was made up of the pieces of good witches that dark magic stole. He was the ultimate evil, seeking to enslave the Mortal World and release the demons from the Underworld.

Long ago, a coven of witches had banished him to an in-between form, too strong to destroy permanently.

As the nightmare fuel goes, he lies in wait in the plane between life and death for someone to be foolish enough, desperate enough, to summon him. Or if you're a witchling, if you did enough bad things, you could be the one to summon him accidentally.

Between the realms of flesh and phantom, the threads of fate intertwine, heralding either ruin or redemption. That was what the prophecy said.

Declan had been right. The souls were going to that in-between...to Mal, the Devourer of Souls.

The shadows tighten around my neck, cold as ice and suffocating, cutting off the air in my lungs. They're nothing like the ones my magic creates. These are empty and deadly.

I claw at the tendrils of darkness, but it's useless—Mal has me in his grip, and there's no escape. I can feel the power surging through him, dark and ancient, a force far beyond anything I've ever encountered. And for the first time, I realize how close I am to losing everything.

I try to turn my head to look at Declan, but the shadows keep my head locked in place. All I can see is Mal and Esme.

Esme, who seems to shrink by the second as the weight of her actions seems to seep into her truly, still won't look at me.

"I know we just met, but you've already been a thorn in my side for too long, Carolina," Mal says, his voice smooth and dangerous, like a predator playing with its prey. His shadowy limbs tighten around me, lifting me higher off the ground. "It's time to end this."

I can't breathe. Panic surges through me, but before I can even begin to process what's happening, Esme's voice cuts through the chamber, sharp and desperate.

"Mal, wait!" Her voice is shaky, her face devoid of any color. She's moving toward him, her hands raised in a pleading gesture. "You don't want to do this. Carolina's power—her premonitions—they're valuable to you. You could use her, harness her ability to see the future. She's worth more to you alive than dead."

Mal pauses, his eyes narrowing slightly as he turns his gaze toward her. The shadows around my throat loosen just enough for me to suck in a shallow breath. But the fear in Esme's voice —it catches me off guard.

"Her premonitions?" Mal muses, his voice filled with amusement. "You think I need her little visions of the future to further my goals? I already know how this ends."

Esme's expression falters, her desperation growing. "But—"

Mal waves a hand, cutting her off as the shadows ripple with his movement. "I tire of your interference, Esme."

One of the shadows snaps out toward her, lashing through the air, stopping just short of her face. Esme flinches, the fear in her eyes unmistakable, but she doesn't back down.

"Please," she whispers, her voice trembling. "You said you wanted power, control over this realm and the next. Carolina can give that to you."

I can feel the disgust boiling inside me. Esme is trying to save me, not out of any real concern for my life, but because she still thinks she can use me. She still believes she has some control over this situation, over me. But she doesn't. Not anymore.

Mal turns his attention back to me, his shadowy tendrils still coiled tightly around my body. For a moment, his cold, calculating gaze flickers with interest, as if he's considering Esme's offer. He tilts his head slightly, studying me like I'm some kind of puzzle.

But then, that cruel smile spreads across his face again. "No," he says, his voice soft and mocking. "I don't need her powers of premonition. She's not useful to me in that way."

My heart skips a beat. This is it. This is how it ends. He's going to take my soul, but at least Declan might be spared. I have to hope Camila's been working on a way to get out of her cage and will be able to get Declan home.

Mal's grip tightens once more, and I feel the icy shadows sinking deeper into my skin, wrapping around me like a noose. My vision begins to blur, darkness creeping in at the edges, and I know I don't have much time.

But then, Mal's voice softens, almost thoughtful. "No," he

continues, as if reconsidering. "Killing her is too simple. Too quick." He pauses, his smile widening. "I want to break her."

I freeze, my body trembling in his grip. *What?*

Mal's eyes gleam with wicked amusement as he looks down at me, then back at Esme. "You want to see her suffer, don't you, Esme? To see her brought to her knees, her power broken, her spirit shattered. That's the dark magic in you. It wants more vengeance for being trapped down here by witches like *them*." His voice is full of dark, sick satisfaction, and I can feel the weight of his words pressing down on me like a physical force.

Esme's mouth opens, but she doesn't respond. Her fear has grown to terror, a realization that she won't be able to gain control of this situation. Mal is playing a game far beyond her understanding.

Mal's attention shifts back to me, his shadows tightening around my body. "And you want to live, don't you, Carolina?" he murmurs, his voice dripping with mockery. "I'll give you a choice then. A choice between your sister...and your mirror soul. You choose which soul I get."

The breath I've barely managed to reclaim escapes me all at once. *No. No, no, no.*

I can't speak. The sob that's been building in my chest finally breaks free, loud and raw, and my hands claw uselessly at the shadows around my neck again. "No. I won't choose between them," I rasp, my voice a broken plea.

Mal's grin widens, dark satisfaction gleaming in his eyes. "Oh, but you will," he says softly, his shadows snaking tighter. "Or they're both dead, and your soul is mine."

My heart feels like it's tearing in two, my mind spinning with the impossible choice he's putting before me. The pain is unbearable, not just from the physical grip of the shadows but from the severity of what he's asking of me.

"Lina." Camila's voice comes from the cage where she's still trapped, weak and trembling. I know she's been watching this whole time, and the guilt I feel for bringing her into this horror is more than I can bear. Even if I could, I wouldn't look at her—I know if I did, I'd shatter completely.

"Carolina." Declan's voice is softer, weaker than Camila's, but somehow it cuts through the haze of panic clouding my mind. I choke back another sob, forcing myself to listen.

"Carolina," he repeats, his voice breaking with the effort. "You have to save Camila. It has to be her."

I try to shake my head, but the shadows hold me fast, my body frozen in Mal's grip. "I can't," I whisper, my voice barely more than a broken sound. "I can't lose you again. Not again."

"This is the price, Carolina." Declan's voice is pleading, full of so much pain that it makes my chest ache. "This is the price of the time we had, and we'll pay it to save them. All of them."

The shadows loosen for a second, and I gasp for air, trying to process his words. He's talking about the mortals, the people of Grove Meadow. The ones who have never cared about us, who have only ever feared or hated us. Why should we sacrifice for them?

What have they ever done to deserve our sacrifice?

Declan's voice pulls me back, his words raw with desperation. "Maybe in the next life, we'll get more time. You have to believe that, Carolina. There's a world...a time...where we can be together, but not now."

My heart breaks. Because he's right. It's always like this with us—always a world where we're torn apart, always a time where we have to lose each other. But what kind of life would it be without him?

I don't know where I end and where Declan begins. He's more than just a part of me—he *is* me. My mirror soul. My twin flame. The magic between us is deeper than anything I've ever known.

This isn't a choice between Declan and Camila. Mal *knows* that if he kills Declan, he's signing my death sentence, too. Because every time he dies, a piece of me dies with him. I'd still live, but I'd be empty. A shell of a witch. I might as well be mortal.

"No," I whisper, shaking my head, my voice raw and full of anguish. "No, I won't lose you again."

Mal makes a sound of impatience, his shadows tightening slightly. "As heartwarming as this all is, Carolina, you must pick now. You're wearing on the last strand of my tolerance, and it is considerably less amusing with every passing second."

I swallow hard, my mind racing. *Camila could bring him back.*

Couldn't she?

Camila's strong, stronger than anyone gives her credit for. But could she pull him back if I chose her? Could she undo this? My heart is pounding, and the shadows feel like they're sinking deeper into my skin, drawing out every ounce of strength I have left.

And then Mal says it, cold and final. "Choose. Now. Your sister or your mirror soul. One lives, and one dies."

The words cut through me, and I feel them pressing down, crushing me. My sister. My mirror soul. The two people I love most in this world, and Mal is making me choose which one I have to lose. Forever.

I don't want to do this. I can't. The sob I've been holding back breaks free, ripping from my chest like a physical wound. This isn't fair. This is cruelty beyond anything I've ever known.

"Carolina," Declan's voice is gentle now, soft and pleading. "Choose her. Save her. She'll need you to stop him. You can't let her die."

"No…" I whimper, my voice is raw and broken. "No…"

My heart is in my throat, every breath like a knife. I close my eyes for a moment, trying to gather myself, but nothing makes sense.

The memories rush through me, fast and furious. Declan, holding me through every lifetime, his eyes filled with love. Camila, my sister, everything we've lived through together. How can I choose between them?

My fingers curl into the shadows again, my body shaking with sobs. I know what I have to do, but it doesn't make it any easier. It doesn't make the pain any less unbearable.

I'm trembling, caught between the two people I love most in this world, torn apart by the impossible choice Mal is forcing me to make. Camila or Declan. My sister or my mirror soul.

But then, through the haze of pain and heartbreak, one clear thought pierces through.

If I lose Declan, I'll lose myself. But if I lose Camila, I'll lose everything.

A joined power will rule the worlds of might and magic. What if it's about the two of us?

I lift my head, tears streaming down my face, and look Mal in the eyes. "I choose Camila," I whisper, my voice barely audible.

After everything I've done to avoid it, I was the one sentencing him to death in this lifetime. The Fates were cruel.

Mal's smile stretches wider, his eyes gleaming with cruel satisfaction. "Very well."

And then, in an instant, the world shifts. Mal's shadows release me, and my knees hit the ground. Before I can even register what's happening, they wrap around Declan, lifting him into the air within the iron cage.

"No!" I scream, rushing forward, but it's too late.

Before I can reach him, Mal's shadows coil around my

throat again, dragging me back, tightening until I can't breathe.

"You made your choice, Carolina," Mal says, his voice soft and mocking. "Now you get to watch him die."

The shadows around my throat pulse, tightening with Mal's command, squeezing the air from my lungs as my heart pounds in my chest.

I can feel myself breaking, unraveling at the seams, my body fighting against the force of Mal's grip and the devastating reality of this decision.

"Stop!" Esme's voice is louder than I've ever heard it, cracking through the tension in the air. She raises her hands, her eyes wild with determination.

Mal's eyes narrow, a flicker of surprise crossing his face as Esme starts chanting. The words are sharp, foreign, and filled with a power I've never heard her use before. She's an inactive witch—this shouldn't be possible, but Mal had given her powers to help him.

"What are you doing?" Mal snarls, the shadows around me pulsing as if they're reacting to his anger.

But Esme doesn't stop. Her hands glow faintly as she continues to speak the incantation in the foreign tongue, the words spilling from her lips faster and faster. I feel the air around us shift, like something is being pulled—drawn toward her.

Mal growls, his shadows flickering, but he's too late to stop her.

"No!" he bellows, but Esme's spell is already in motion.

The chamber trembles, and the shadows that had once been Mal's weapons begin to recoil, writhing as if they're being pulled back into the darkness. I feel the grip around my neck loosen, then fall away completely. I collapse to the ground, gasping for air, my chest heaving.

"Esme..." I whisper, but my voice is lost in the chaos. I watch as the shadows swirl around her, consuming her. They're dragging Mal with them, pulling him into the abyss, but they're taking her, too.

"No!" I scream, forcing myself to my feet, but I'm too weak, too broken to stop it.

Esme turns to me, her face strained. "This...is the cost," she says, her voice trembling but resolute. "To send him back to the in-between...I have to go, too."

Her words hang in the air, and before I can respond, the shadows surge, enveloping both Mal and Esme in a swirling mass of darkness. I reach out, but there's nothing I can do.

And then, with a deafening roar, the shadows collapse inward, disappearing into the ground.

They're gone.

The cavern is suddenly still—too still. The only sound is the echo of my own ragged breathing and the soft clink of Camila's cage as it swings slightly. I rush to her, my hands trembling as I pull the iron bars open, the magic that once held them in place gone.

"Camila..." I whisper, helping her out of the cage. She's weak, barely able to stand, her body trembling against mine. But she's alive.

"I'm okay," she murmurs, her voice shaky but determined. "Carolina...Declan..."

My heart seizes in my chest as I turn to where Declan had been trapped. The cage door is open now, the magic gone, and I rush to him. But when I reach him, I realize something's wrong.

He's collapsed on the ground, his face pale and his breathing shallow. His body looks frail, like the life is being drained out of him.

"Declan!" I scream, falling to my knees beside him, my

hands gripping his shoulders, shaking him. "No, no, no. Declan, stay with me."

But he doesn't respond.

Camila stumbles over, collapsing beside me. Her eyes are filled with panic as she presses her hands against Declan's chest, trying to summon her magic. But I can see it—she's too weak. The time we've spent in the Underworld has taken too much from her. Her magic is flickering, faint and unsteady, and Declan...he's slipping away.

"Carolina, I can't," Camila says, her voice trembling with exhaustion. "I don't have enough..."

Panic grips me, squeezing my chest. Declan's skin is cold under my hands, his breathing shallow, barely there. I can feel him slipping further and further away with every passing second.

"No," I whisper, tears streaming down my face. "We're not losing him. I won't lose him. Not after everything."

Camila looks at me, desperation in her eyes. "What do we do?"

I close my eyes, forcing myself to focus. There's only one answer. Camila doesn't have enough power to heal him on her own—but together, maybe we can. Our magic is linked—two sides of the same coin.

A joined power.

We've never tried anything like this before, but we don't have a choice.

"Try it with me," I say, my voice shaking with fear and determination. "We have to try to combine our magic. It's the only way."

Camila hesitates for a second, her exhaustion clear in her eyes, but she nods. "Okay," she whispers.

We kneel on either side of Declan, our hands hovering over

his chest. I can feel the faint spark of his soul slipping further and further away, but it's still there. He's still there.

"Ready?" I ask, my voice barely a whisper.

Camila nods, and together, we begin.

I reach deep inside myself, summoning every ounce of magic I have left. I feel Camila doing the same beside me, her energy flickering and joining mine. The air around us hums with power, our magic intertwining and growing stronger.

We've never combined our power like this, but it feels right. Like we were always meant to do this together.

I focus on Declan, on the bond between us, the magic that's connected us across lifetimes. *My mirror soul.* I can feel him slipping further, and I push harder, pouring everything I have into him.

"Come back," I whisper, tears streaming down my face. "Please, Declan, come back."

The magic swells, filling the room with light, and I feel a surge of power flow through me—through us—into Declan.

For a moment, nothing happens.

And then, slowly, his chest rises. His breathing deepens. Color returns to his face.

"Declan…" I whisper, my hands shaking as I lean over him.

His eyes flutter open, and for a second, I can't breathe. He looks up at me, confused but alive.

"Carolina…" His voice is weak, but it's there. He's *there.*

I collapse against him, sobbing with relief, my hands gripping his shirt as I press my forehead to his chest.

He's alive.

We saved him.

The warm scent of coffee and burning sage fills the air of *Cup & Cauldron*, a stark contrast to the cold, uninviting atmosphere of the Underworld. The comforting hum of familiar magic pulses through the walls, grounding us in the here and now. Camila and I are back, safe, with Declan sitting beside me, his hand still wrapped loosely around mine. But even with that comfort, the weight of what we've been through hasn't left me. I doubt it ever will.

Silas is curled up on the counter, his eyes narrowed in thought as he listens to us recount everything that happened. Luna slithers across the floor, her dark scales catching the soft candlelight, her gaze sharp and focused.

"So," Silas says, his tail flicking lazily. "Esme's gone, then? For good?"

"Gone," Camila confirms, her voice tired but certain. She's sitting on the floor next to me, resting against the counter, her head tilted back, staring at the ceiling as if she's still processing everything that happened. "She used some ancient spell—one I've never heard of. It cost her her life."

"And Mal?" Luna hisses, her eyes narrowing as she coils next to me. "He's not coming back?"

I shake my head. "No. Esme's spell dragged him back into the shadows. He's...gone for now. His magic must have caved in on itself when Esme used it against him."

For a moment, there's silence. The familiars exchange a glance, and I know they're both thinking the same thing—this fight, this nightmare we've been living through, is finally over. Or at least, that's what we want to believe.

Silas flicks his tail again, a thoughtful expression on his face. "So, what about Bas?"

Camila stiffens slightly at the mention of his name, her fingers fidgeting with the edge of her shirt. Bas—the man who'd worked with Esme, who had unknowingly played a part in her dark plans. I know she doesn't want to talk about him, but we have to. He's still passed out in the magic room.

"We'll wipe his memory," I say firmly. "Of Esme, of the summonings, of everything he did with her. He's not a threat if he doesn't remember. It'll be like none of this ever happened to him."

Camila nods slowly, her eyes tired but grateful. "It's better this way. He didn't know what he was getting into. He thought he was protecting the town."

"Then it's settled," Silas says with a yawn. "Bas will forget everything, and you two can finally get some rest."

Before I can respond, Declan's phone buzzes on the table. He pulls it out, frowning as he reads the caller ID.

"It's the police captain," he mutters, swiping to answer the call. "O'Reilly."

I watch him as he listens to whatever the captain is saying, his eyes widening slightly in surprise, then softening with relief. "You're sure?" he asks, his voice quieter now. "All of them?"

I sit up straighter, a knot of tension forming in my chest.

When Declan finally hangs up, he turns to us, a strange expression on his face—part relief, part disbelief.

"They've returned," he says slowly. "All of the missing townspeople...except Elijah. They've been found, safe, back in their homes."

I blink, trying to process the news. "They're back?"

Declan nods. "They don't remember anything. No memory of where they were or what happened to them. It's like they were never gone."

The relief that floods through me is overwhelming. For weeks, we've been living under the weight of those disappearances, the town's fear and suspicion hanging over us like a cloud. And now...it's over. Well, almost. There's still Elijah, who will always be missing even though we know he's gone, but at least the others are safe.

Camila leans her head against my shoulder. "Their souls must have been freed when Esme cast that spell. Good. That's good. One less thing to worry about."

We sit in silence for a while after that, the weight of everything slowly beginning to lift. There's still so much we need to process, so much that needs to be dealt with. But for now, I'm just grateful that we're safe, that the people we fought for are back, and that the nightmare we've been living through is finally over.

Declan excuses himself to check in at the station while we deal with Bas.

He's still slumped on the ground where Declan left him, and I summon my magic to flip through his memory.

I see images of Esme running into him in town months ago. Then there's an emptiness about him. A spell Esme cast to get him to do her bidding in town so that we couldn't sense her. I see him at meetings at Hazel's Inn with everyone who had gone missing. I see him in Camila's room, taking her neck-lace. I see it all…and then I erase it.

> *From the threads of time, I sever the strands,*
> *What's known to thee, now slips from thy hands.*
> *Memories once clear, now drift away,*
> *As mist in morning, they fade with day.*
> *By night's dark grace, I let thee be,*
> *What's forgotten shall no longer see.*
> *What was known is no more, let it be free.*

Camila watches from beside me, arms wrapped around herself.

"Esme spelled him. He really didn't know what he was doing," I tell her, touching her arm in comfort.

"That's good, I suppose. That he isn't evil, I mean."

I let out a laugh that surprises us both, and it's only a moment before we're both hysterical. The laughs morph into tears, and we're wrapped in a hug that feels endless.

"I'm sorry," I whisper when we pull away.

"Why are you sorry?" she asks, wiping under her eyes.

"I'm sorry I didn't pick you right away. I just…I couldn't…"

There are no words for my betrayal of our sisterhood, but I hope she can forgive me one day.

"Don't be sorry, Caro. I can't imagine how hard that deci-sion was. I can only hope to be as strong as you. If I had to choose between you and my mirror soul…I'm not sure I would have made the same decision." She looks guilty at the admission.

"I appreciate you saying that. We should probably get him back home, yeah?" I ask, inclining my head at Bas.

"Yeah, I'll take him. I could use some normal, mortal air. Hey, where did that joined power idea come from? Something you thought of in the moment?"

I shake my head. "Declan, actually. The prophecy mentions a joined power. He suggested that instead of it being about who we were looking for, it was about a power to unite to save the Mortal World."

Her face grows puzzled. "But a joint power didn't stop Mal. Esme did. Do you think that means it was about them, and we stopped the prophecy?"

Cauldron, I'd love to believe that, but the Fates never let us off easy.

"Let's worry about that another day. For now, I want to think we've reached some semblance of normal."

She gives me a small smile before using her magic to levitate and cloak Bas in invisibility like we had Declan and Nightcrawler just a few days ago. Though it had felt like centuries.

Later that night, there's a knock on the door of the apartment. I'm not surprised to see it's Declan, but I am surprised to see his suitcase beside him.

"That's a little presumptuous, don't you think?" I ask, moving aside for him to pass me.

He raises his eyebrows at me. "Is it? I figure it's the least you could do for almost having me killed."

I scoff as we climb the stairs to my room. "That's not funny."

"No," he agrees, "but we should talk about it."

A sinking feeling grows in my stomach. The guilt I felt about not picking Camila right away is nothing compared to the feeling of devastation that filled me, knowing that I risked Declan's life on a theory that Camila and I could save him.

I shut the door as he drops his stuff at the foot of my bed.

"C'mere," he says, sitting on the edge of the mattress.

I stand between his legs, and he does me the favor of starting this conversation.

"You did the right thing, Carolina," he tells me, bringing my hands to his neck before his hands go to my waist to pull me closer against him.

"It doesn't feel like that. It feels like I gave in to everything I was trying so hard to avoid."

His eyes are soft as he looks at me. "You did exactly what you had to do to keep Mal from doing what he planned. I know that was hard for you, but we're here now. You've saved me again, and now we get to be together. In this lifetime."

I wanted to see it that way so badly. I wanted to believe that was the only time we'd be in a situation like that, but there was no guarantee. We were right back where we started.

"I know that face," he frowns, reaching up to smooth the crease between my eyebrows. "How about this? We don't think about the future." I laugh, and it makes him smile. "Okay, maybe just not the distant future. Let's think about...5 minutes from now."

His smile is infectious. "5 minutes from now?" I ask, amusement filling my voice.

"Yeah, read my future, Carolina. What do you see in the next five minutes." He presses my palm against his cheek, and I lower the barrier I usually place my premonitions behind.

My body stills, and Declan's future fills my head. I see him pressed against me. His hands are in my hair. His mouth is on my skin. I'm a voyeur to our own escapades, and when I pull away, my body is tight with anticipation.

I'm tugging off his shirt. He laughs but complies, lifting his arms for me. "Someone's in a rush."

"We're on a time limit," I remind him. "Wouldn't want to piss off the Fates...again."

"*Cauldron*, no. We wouldn't want that," he agrees, stripping off my jeans as I pull my shirt over my head.

Our mouths find each other in a frenzy of touching and pulling off articles of clothing. His lips are rough against mine.

"*Gods*, I love you." Once again, words are flowing out of me before I have time to filter them, but any concern I have about saying them disappears when he responds.

"I love you, too," he says, smiling against my mouth. "It's good we got that out of the way, Caro, because with what I'm about to do to you, you're going to think I hate you."

I preen at the use of my nickname coming from his mouth. It's distracting enough that I don't question what he means by the latter part of his statement. It becomes abundantly clear a minute later.

"Declan, I swear to—"

"No, no. I didn't get to take my time with you last time, Caro," he says, lifting his head from between my legs. "And if recent events have taught you anything, it's that we need to savor these things."

"*Oh fuck that*," I groan, my magic flaring.

Declan lets out a surprised, but thoroughly aroused sound, when he finds himself underneath me. I lower myself onto him, tipping my head back at the feeling of him stretching me.

"*Jesus*, Carolina," he moans, shifting so his chest is pressed against mine.

His teeth nip against my neck, and my fingernails dig into his shoulders when he hits a spot deep inside me.

"*Fuck*," he says when I rock against him.

He flips me beneath him again and dips his head to take a nipple in his mouth, biting down just slightly as he pumps into me again.

I think he hates me when he pulls out slowly before rocking into me again. He's making me work for it, and I'm growing impatient.

"*Declan*," I whine when his pace becomes torturously slow.

"You want something, Carolina?" He looks at me challengingly. "Then take it."

My magic flares again, pinning him back underneath me. We're wrapped in my shadows, and Declan's eyes widen at the sudden change in scenery.

"They won't hurt you," I tell him quickly, worried he might be afraid of them after Mal.

He blinks at me, confused. "Of course they won't. They belong to you, just like I do."

The gentleness of his voice and words spurs me forward. A heat gathers between my legs, and his lips part at the feeling of me tightening around him.

"I take it back. You might kill me like this," he says, gripping my hips and moving me against him at a pace that has him groaning and me seeing stars.

I'm climbing impossibly higher. I roll my hips so my clit rubs against him every time he thrusts forward.

"Declan," I mumble as I start to come undone.

Once again, I find myself underneath him, and I fall in love with this fight for dominance over each other's pleasure. I let him win this time as he continues his unforgiving pace, and my body continues to tighten around his.

"Fall, Carolina," he whispers against my breast. "I've got you. Always."

And I do. The pressure bubbles over, and the sounds that come from my mouth are unlike any I've ever made. They're raw and sated and happy.

I love him.

Just when I think it's over, it starts all over again. Like I'm falling through every lifetime where we didn't end up together, and I'm painting a new ending.

Declan's face is flushed, and sweat dots his temples as he continues to find his own release. His red waves of hair fall forward as he looks down at where we're connected, at where he's sliding into me.

Reaching down, I slide my thumb and index finger around the base of him, adding pressure that has him bucking wildly.

"*God,* you're so good, Carolina. So fucking tight. So perfect."

He's murmuring praises as he continues to watch us slide together. The sight is so erotic that it has me building again. I can feel it.

His head lifts to look at me. "Again?"

Declan's face is haughty, like he wants me to praise him for getting me there again.

"Don't be cocky," I whisper, my voice hoarse.

"Never," he says, kissing my lips. I slip my tongue into his mouth and stroke against his at the same pace he's thrusting into me.

The heel of my palm digs against my clit, and I go off. He stills on top of me, and I know he's right there with me.

His breathing is still ragged as he rolls off me and lays beside me. We're quiet, and I let the shadows slowly fade away.

"So," Declan begins after a few minutes, breaking the silence, "if someone were to order a 'medicine ball' not knowing what it was, would you give it to them?"

I break out into laughter. "After all that...that's what you want to ask me?"

He props himself onto his elbow. "It's *killing* me, Carolina. I must know."

I slap his chest and laugh again. "The dying jokes are not

funny, but we'd just give them an actual tea. Usually with honey and lemon. You know other coffee shops have 'medicine balls' too. I hope you're interrogating them just as much."

"I'll be the one asking the questions here, Miss Castillo."

I can't stop the fit of giggles that erupt this time, and I let myself enjoy it.

I let myself savor *us*.

After I shower, I fall into bed beside Declan, his arm wrapping around me as I close my eyes, my body sore with fatigue. Camila is getting ready for bed in the bathroom next to my room, and I can hear the faint sound of her moving around before the quiet settles over the shop like a blanket. Safe. For now, we're safe.

But the peace doesn't last.

At exactly 3:03 a.m., a scream rips through the house, shattering the quiet.

I jolt upright, my heart pounding as I throw off the covers. "Camila!"

Declan is already on his feet, his face pale. Together, we race down the hallway toward Camila's room. I fling the door open, and there she is—standing in the center of the room, her face white with fear, her eyes locked on the figure standing in the corner.

Sam.

I freeze, my breath catching in my throat. Sam, not in the Underworld, but here, in *our* home.

"What the hell are you doing here?" I demand, my voice sharp and filled with alarm. My magic hums beneath my skin, ready to strike if I need to.

Sam raises his hands, a gesture of peace, but his expression is anything but calm. "I didn't come here to fight," he says quickly, his eyes flicking between me, Declan, and Camila. "I came here to warn you."

"Warn us about what?" Camila snaps, her voice shaking with a mix of fear and anger.

Sam's expression darkens. "The portal Luna opened to let Declan into the Underworld only closed once you got back. It let...things out while it was open."

I feel my stomach drop. "What do you mean?"

"I mean demons," Sam says, his voice grim. "Creatures that should have stayed in the Underworld. They've escaped. And now they're loose in the Mortal World. If you don't send them back—if you don't destroy them—they'll wreak havoc on the humans."

The room feels like it's spinning, the weight of his words sinking in. We thought we'd ended this, that Mal and Esme were the end of the nightmare, but we were wrong. The Underworld was leaked into the Mortal World, and now we have a whole new problem on our hands.

I meet Camila's wide, fearful eyes, and I know we don't have a choice.

We have to stop this. *Again.*

ACKNOWLEDGMENTS

Thank you for reading *Something's Witchy* and taking a chance on my first attempt at something that isn't exactly a contemporary romance. This book has taken me so long, but it has been such an exciting and different experience than all my other books.

I grew up watching *Charmed* and *Sabrina, the Teenage Witch* every day after school. I wanted to be Piper and Zelda for as long as I can remember. Every fall, *Practical Magic* (and *Rudy?*) was on repeat in my house. I'm pretty sure I dyed my hair red in middle school because I wanted to be Gilly Owens, but my wardrobe, even now, was strictly Sally-inspired.

Over a year ago, I decided to write a witchy romance book with a cozy mystery as the plot, and I'm so excited I did. Like my other books, I fell in love with these characters and their stories. From Carolina's fear of falling in love to Luna's fear of... well, everything, all of these characters are so unique and special to me. I hope you loved them, too.

Also, like all my other books, I couldn't have done it without the support of my favorite people:

Parker, thanks for being my biggest support and my favorite person. Our love story will *always* be my favorite. Thank you for also designing this cover. I'm as obsessed with it as I am with you.

Lauren...what *is* an acknowledgment? Just kidding, we won't get meta here. This one was a doozy for us, wasn't it?

Thanks for listening to me ramble about circular plotlines and reminding me that writing is supposed to be more fun than work. You'll always be the Stella to my Harper, but I hope you see yourself in these characters, too.

Isa, Sam, and Tessa, I'm not lying when I say this book would not have been written without our writing groups. Thank you for being a sounding board, making me laugh every week, and always being there to commiserate about anything and everything. You are all the epitome of girls' girls.

Jasmin, Kayla, and Shiba, thanks for always checking in on me, even when I swear I'm not having a meltdown (I usually am), and always supporting my writing. I hope you love this one, too!

Finally, thank *you*, dear reader. Thanks for taking a chance on this genre shift. You make this writing journey so much more fun! Your support means the world to me.

Sierra Spencer

ABOUT THE AUTHOR

 Combining all the feet-kicking and giggling of a happily ever after with the dichotomy of flawed and complex characters, Sierra writes stories that demand to be felt. When Sierra isn't composing heartfelt and cozy love stories, she writes about developmental science as a graduate student. She lives in Southern California with her friend-to-enemy-to-lover spouse and their dog. She enjoys cooking, game nights, and a good data visualization.

Get updates on sierraspencer.com or scan/tap the QR code below to subscribe to the Sierra Spencer Newsletter!

instagram.com/sierraspencerbooks

tiktok.com/@literarilysierra

amazon.com/stores/author/B0BR9PZCHS

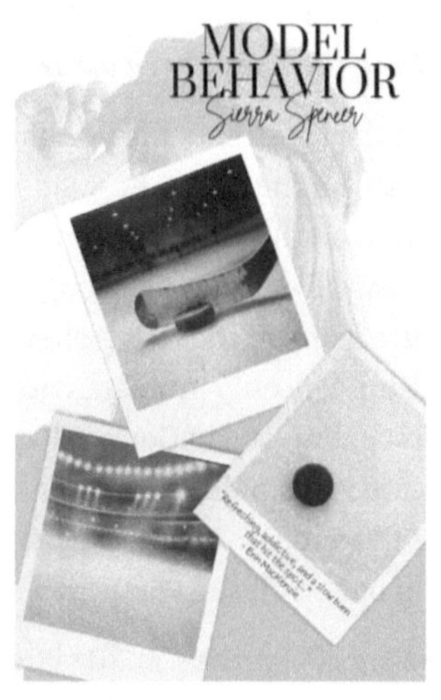

Serena MacPherson's mind races faster than the camera shutters as her photo gets taken. Flashing lights and magazine spreads are her life. Liam Richter has smoother skills on the ice than off it, and he'd rather avoid the limelight at all costs. When Liam gets talked into doing a photoshoot to announce his new residency as hockey captain, he leans into Serena's help on set —literally. Their on-camera chemistry has rumors flying about them. Surely, there has to be something real about it.

Model Behavior is for the readers who know finding someone doesn't necessarily mean finding yourself, but it's nice to have company...

In this steamy small-town romance, all bets are off. Olivia and Whit are two beautifully broken characters who learn that trying to be what other people want them to be is a one-way route to unhappiness. Good thing they have each other...

Olivia met the love of her life in a bar off 2nd Ave. on the Upper East Side. She lost him on the same street nine blocks down. Olivia thinks she might find some closure in the town where he grew up. The only problem with that is that no one in Connor Bay wants anything to do with her. The standard in a small New England town is much different than in New York, and Olivia finds herself struggling with what version of herself she wants to be.

An accident sent Olivia's life veering off course. Can her late husband's hometown set it right again? Maybe with a little help from his best friend.